E

Imprudent Lady

Imprudent Lady

Joan Smith

WALKER AND COMPANY
New York

First published in the United States of America
in 1978 by the Walker Publishing Company, Inc.

Published simultaneously in Canada by Beaverbooks,
Limited, Pickering, Ontario

ISBN: 0-8027-0589-8

Library of Congress Catalog Card Number: 77-90132

Printed in the United States of America

10 9 8 7 6 5 4 3 2 1

Chapter One

It was a joke often repeated in the Mallow household that Prudence had been well-named. "You are a prudent little thing," her papa would say, when she returned from shopping with a bolt of wool to make herself up a snug shirt for winter. "Oh my dear, we chose aright in naming you Prudence," her mama would laugh, when she declined going on a picnic only because the sky was heavy with clouds. "And this is my prudent little Prudence," was Papa's favourite manner of introducing her to company. With these playful sallies it was well established that Prudence was the wittiest name in the language, and the most appropriate for Miss Mallow.

It was, alas, a virtue not shared by her parents. Papa, with little money and no management, ran his estate into mortgage and Mama, with a lamentable lack of foresight, had failed to produce a male heir to secure what remained upon his demise. It was entailed on a male relative, and the improvident widow found at forty-four that she had an unmarried daughter and herself to maintain on two hundred pounds a year, which was all that remained of her own jointure. It was inevitable that she would dip into her capital if forced to live on such a pittance.

1

Prudence knew it if Mama did not, and when Mr. Elmtree, Mrs. Mallow's widowed brother, offered them a roof over their heads, they accepted.

Mama foresaw many hardships, every one of which came to fruition. Clarence was a fool, a bore and a skint, she said, and so he proved to be. He gave them room and board and in return expected that they be housekeepers, hostesses, seamstresses, walking witnesses of his charity, and worst of all, admirers. Clarence was an artist, not a good one, but very prolific. He painted portraits of those on the fringes of society, and each spring he painted three scenes of Richmond Park. He accepted no pay for his work, being a gentleman, nor indeed was any offered, but he took his work seriously. A dozen times a day Miss Mallow or her mother was forced to admire his pastel blobs, reading into them character, beauty, sentiment, and all else they lacked.

The Mallow ladies were also required to be chaperones when Mr. Elmtree was painting a lady. He harboured the dread that traps were being laid for him and his two thousand pounds a year. If his sitter were a female between seven and seventy, he insisted that either his sister or his niece be in the studio. One could not but wonder if it was the reason for his inviting them to Grosvenor Square. They had also to keep up a constant barrage of compliments on his skill, but he too was very helpful in this latter sphere. "I am adding a little dab of ochre here to give a shadow under the nose," he would say. "Have you ever seen this done before?"

As neither lady was intimate with the painting profession, they must confess they had not.

"I fancy it is my own invention. I haven't heard of Lawrence or the others doing it. Certainly Romney did not. He makes the whole face pink. No expression to it. No expression at all. See how I am shading in the corner of the eye here? I learned this one from Leonardo. I cannot claim it for my own. The *Mona Lisa* has such eyes as this."

2

Prudence stared in astonishment at the two agates reposing in the flat pink face on the canvas and said weakly, "How very nice. Yes, quite like the *Mona Lisa*."

"Not *quite* like," he contradicted, giving hope that he had some sense of aesthetic discernment after all. But no, he went on to say: "I think I have gone da Vinci a step better. He left off the eyelashes, you see. When you take a look at the *Mona Lisa*—I have a good engraving of it in my study—you will see he forgot the eyelashes. I don't know how he came to do it, for I read somewhere he was three years painting La Gioconda, but he certainly forgot the eyelashes. I will put a nice long lash on Mrs. Hering, and I shan't spend three years to do it either. Three days it takes me to complete a portrait. If I worked five days a week, which I don't, I could produce eighty-seven of these portraits a year. I don't see Lawrence producing eighty-seven pictures like this a year."

"No, certainly not like this," Prudence insisted in a choked voice. She received a smiling nod from her uncle for her acumen.

"No, I think Lawrence could pick up a trick or two from me, but he is quite spoilt with attention. That exhibition of his at Somerset House—lamentable. I blushed for him, poor fellow, to see everyone praising such likenesses. He had a *wart* on Lady Cassel's nose. You'd think anyone who calls himself an artist would have painted it out. But his sensitivity is entirely lacking. He can only paint a pretty picture if he has a pretty subject."

No one had ever accused Mr. Elmtree of painting a wart—or a wrinkle or a grey hair for that matter. He flattered his sitters, in his own way. No matter what faded, spotted or hag-ridden face sat before him, it emerged smooth and pink in his reproduction. If too thin it was rounded, if too long, shortened, and if at sixty or so his model's hair had the poor taste to turn grey, it was revealed in his picture in a modish blue or purple shade. He had also a talent for reforming a nose or

3

enlarging an eye, and was better than a dentist for re-
juvenating teeth on those rare occasions when he allowed a
subject to smile. Usually he insisted on the pose of Mona Lisa
and the expression.

After many such sessions with him, Prudence became bored
with her chore and began to take a book to read surreptitiously
while he painted. "Ho, I see you are as prudent as your name,"
he rallied when he discovered what mischief she was up to.
"Never wasting a minute, hey? But I suppose you are burning
your eyes out on a trashy novel. Young ladies read too many
novels nowadays. I never read. There is nothing in books. They
are a waste of time. You'd do better to come here and see how
I am adding a little yellow to the crimson to give it an orange
tone for Mrs. Hering's coquelicot ribbons. I fancy that is how
Titian got his pretty orange tones. Da Vinci, now, had no
notion of an orange colour. He was well enough at an old blue
or grey, but he had no notion of orange."

Reading proved difficult with the number of interruptions
necessary for praising his progress, and Prudence tried writing
letters instead. She hoped this might inhibit his chatter, to see
her actively engaged, but it only led him to remark that if she
was so fond of scribbling, she shouldn't waste her time and
eyesight writing letters, but should get some reward for her
labours. The reward of an answer from a friend was nothing to
him.

"If you like writing so much, I'll speak to a friend of mine in
the writing line, Mr. Halcombe. He is a fine fellow, writing up a
history of Sussex—nobody will read it. He was saying he
wanted someone to make a fair copy for him. You will enjoy
having something worthwhile to write, and will make a little pin
money on the side. A girl in your position with no money
should be thinking of that. You won't always have an uncle to
take care of you."

The job sounded onerous, but the pin money attractive, and
Prudence agreed to do it. As it turned out Mr. Halcombe had

written only three chapters of ten pages each, and those were copied in two days. But the idea caught on with her, and Mr. Halcombe promised to speak to his publisher to see if other writers might require her services. Soon she was regularly employed in making fair copies of others' work, and rather enjoying it, especially the novels. She found herself wondering what would happen to the heroine, trapped in some seemingly hopeless situation, and would read and continue copying to discover her fate.

Soon Prudence began fashioning her own heroine in her spare time, and toying with her predicament. One day she finished her copying early, and to fool her uncle sat pretending to work for gain—which was not only permitted but encouraged—but actually writing a story of her own. She finished eight pages, and when she ran out of legitimate work would press on with her own story.

Forty portraits later it was done, then copied in her best copperplate and delivered to Mr. Murray for his perusal. Prudence had met the publisher several times when delivering or picking up work, and he had formed a good opinion of her judgment, so when she shyly handed him her manuscript, he read it with a kind eye. It was not the style in vogue at the moment, with Mr. Scott's romantic novels sweeping the nation. Here were no tribal chieftains, no wars or warriors, nor even much in the way of a love story, but a keen ear had been at work to hear conversation, and a sharp intelligence to sort it out and render it into story form. He decided on a short run, a small advertisement, and a hope for profit over the long haul.

Mr. Murray had no vision of a vast and immediate audience such as Miss Burney and Scott enjoyed; certainly nothing in the nature of his top writer, Lord Dammler, and he was not out in his judgment. Miss Mallow's book sold slowly at first, but continued to sell fairly regularly. When the second came out a year later, it sold better and he reissued her first. On her twenty-fourth birthday her third was published, and she felt her position was secure. Prudence had found her niche in the world. Under Clarence's roof, unfortunately. The monetary rewards for her work did not permit her to set up a creditable establishment for herself and her mama, but if her social life was restricted and her private life tedious, her work was a compensation. She felt she could be content with her lot, and Clarence was kinder to a promising writer than to a penniless niece.

If some doubts assailed her as she lay alone in her four-poster nights, they were reasoned away. She was not young, not rich, not very pretty, and not married. She was and would likely always be a spinster. So be it. She would make do with it. The hopes that had come to London with her of meeting and eventually marrying some eligible gentleman had been slow in dying, but after four years they had died at last, or so she thought. The morning after her birthday, she bound back her dark curls and set, for the first time in her life, a cap upon them. It was a pretty cap with blue ribbons to match her eyes, but it was a cap nevertheless—an announcement to society that she had consigned herself to the anteroom of life forever as a spinster.

"Oh Prue," her mother wailed when she saw what her daughter had done, "you are too young! Clarence, tell her this is nonsense."

He was much inclined to, as she had not consulted him on the matter, but his innate selfishness held sway. He liked very much to have an authoress sharing his house. Then, too, with his wife gone, the women made the place more comfortable. For one thing, there was always someone there to paint or to watch him paint, to ask him if anything interesting had happened when he returned from a walk, or to admire his new jackets and move the buttons if they had to be moved, and his sister, Wilma, was an excellent housekeeper, even if she did spend too much money on food. "No such a thing," he answered jovially. "Prudence knows what she is about. She is not called Prudence for nothing. She is better off single. Why should she marry some stupid fellow to have to wait on hand and foot?" Why indeed, Prudence silently agreed. I have *you*.

"And he would think to take charge of her earnings, too. No indeed, she is wise to set on her caps. Dashed pretty it looks, too, my dear. Dashed pretty. I have Miss Sedgemire coming in for a sitting today, Prue, at eleven o'clock. Will you bring your work to the studio and stay with us? She is single, you know, and on the catch for a husband, poor soul. She would like to move her luggage in here well enough. Has been dropping hints these two months that she would welcome an offer. I never pretend to understand what she is up to. It is the best way with her sort. But I shall enjoy to paint her. She has nice hands. I'll have her fold them like Mona Lisa."

"But she is only twenty-four," Mrs. Mallow insisted.

"Nonsense. Thirty if she's a day. She colours her hair. It is grey at the roots."

"I mean Prudence."

"Oh Prudence, yes, she is twenty-four. Getting right on. There is nothing so vulgar as an older lady chasing after the men, making laughing stocks of themselves. She is wise to put on her caps and put herself out of it all. Very *prudent* of her." He looked about him for some appreciation of his wit. Wilma and Prudence smiled dutifully, and attacked their poached eggs.

Chapter Two

The only difference putting on her cap made to Miss Mallow was that she thought rather more than she used to about marriage. Her noble resolve to forego nabbing a husband did not inhibit her daydreaming about it, but they became wild, improbable dreams now, untethered to reality. She let her vivid imagination soar, and was pursued in her mind by princes and nabobs, by foreign generals and handsome wastrels, by scholars and sportsmen. One particularly dreary day, with rain sliding down the windows of the studio and the smell of Clarence's paints in her nostrils, she even imagined she was the object of Lord Dammler's devotion. He combined the attributes of many of her dream lovers in one person. He was a lord—a marquis to be precise—he was an intellectual and a poet, he was a rake, a sportsman, and the handsomest man in England.

He had risen to prominence a year before with the publication of his *Cantos from Abroad*. Upon coming into his title and dignities two and a half years before that, his first act had not been to take over the reins of Longbourne Abbey, his late uncle's estate, or take his seat in the house, or even take a wife, but to take the first ship leaving England's shore and spend the next three years circling the globe. He had travelled those parts of the world known to few westerners—Greece, Turkey, Egypt, across vast Russia into China, from China by schooner to the Pacific Isles. He had returned via the Americas, North and South according to his poems, and finally across the Atlantic home to England. He had left an unknown young nobleman, and returned a legend. His first set of poems preceded him by six months in the hands of a friend, and by the time he landed the *ton* was on tiptoe to meet him.

His *Cantos from Abroad* were tales in verse loosely based on his voyage. The hero was named Andrew Marvelman, which was soon discovered to bear a strong resemblance to his own—Allan Merriman. The circumstances too were remarkably similar—a young gentleman with wealth and duties thrust suddenly on to his shoulders. A mystery and point of deep interest was the reason for his precipitous flight at the very point in his career when it was most probable he would remain at home. The reason was widely held—though not explicitly stated—to involve a liaison with a lady. Certainly ladies and females of all sorts and degrees featured prominently throughout the cantos, as did villains, intrigues and dangers of all kinds. There were harem girls who were in turn replaced by czarinas and Indian princesses as he jaunted recklessly from country to country, being shipwrecked, shot at, mauled by tigers, Musselmen, Cossaks and Indian chiefs. But a bigger and more dangerous event yet awaited Dammler when he was presented to panting Society. It was said by one wit that every man in England was jealous of him, and every woman in love with him. Dammler modestly retorted that the case had been overstated; only those ladies and gentlemen who could *read* had fallen into a passion of one sort or another over him.

His exquisite person, allied to his high rank and wealth, would have been enough to set him up as a marital prize, even without the glamour of his travel and poems, but it was the poetry and the plethora of rumours preceding his landing that lent him that certain extra charm—the magic that surrounded his name. On that first evening when his name was announced and he stepped into Princess Lieven's ball to shake hands with his hostess, there hadn't been a sound in the room. Every eye was turned on him; even breath was suspended at the climax of the moment. There was total silence. "I never heard the likes of it since Beau Brummell's famous question to Alvanley about the Prince Regent—'Who's your fat friend?'," the Princess Lieven stated later.

Dammler was tall and supple, his body lean from the rigours of travel, his shoulders wide and straight. His amorous and aggressive exploits left a residue of weariness on his face, and this, combined with the tan he had picked up, saved him from being *too* handsome. One shock the *ton* had not been prepared for was the black eye patch over his left eye, but this was in no way a distraction from his charms. Quite the contrary, it was the *coup de grace*. His coats, his interesting drawl, his habit of hunching his shoulders and throwing up his hands could be and were studiously followed by his imitators, but they none of them were ready to go to the laughable length of either sticking a patch on a good eye, or removing one and giving themselves just cause to wear the patch. In this he was unique. Before he was in the room a minute the Princess had asked the reason for the patch.

"I was hit by a Cherokee's arrow as I fled downstream in my canoe, ma'am," he answered smiling. "I lost the maiden I was trying to rescue, unfortunately, but I saved the eye. My patch can come off in a few months."

"Don't be in a hurry," she answered promptly. "Let us get used to *one* such dangerous eye before we are challenged with two."

"You are too kind, but only think, Princess, if I had the use of both, I could see you twice as well." He ran an admiring glance over the gaunt lady as he spoke.

"Oh you are naughty, milord," she tittered, enchanted with him.

"I am you know, but don't tell anyone, or you will frighten away the ladies," he laughed, and within seconds he was surrounded by them.

No polite party had seen such an unseemly scramble since the Prince of Wales entertained King Louis of France at Carlton House. A "squeeze," of course, was all the go, but a stampede was what Princess Lieven's ball was rapidly disintegrating into. She had to hustle the guest of honour into a private parlour and bolt the door to save him from having the hair pulled from his head, and the black jacket ripped from his back.

"I had thought I was returning to civilisation," he told her, and she later told waiting Society. "It seems I am back among the savages. You ought really to have warned me, Princess, and I'd have brought my pistols."

"What you need is a bodyguard," she told him, and before long it was necessary for him to acquire not one but two. When he sauntered down Bond Street or rode in the park, he was accompanied by two men, each six-and-a-half feet tall and as broad as doors, to stave off the mobs. One was a jet black Nubian picked up on his peregrinations, the other a dour Scotsman with red hair and freckles. These persons accompanied him everywhere, but Society soon learned that Dammler did not like being pulled about and disappeared if physically handled. The colourful trio was a windfall for the cartoonists. The escorts were dubbed Dammler's "Guardian Angels," and were represented by Gilray with wings and halos in the pictures that decorated the store windows.

The question uppermost in the mind of Society was, naturally, which fortunate female would attract Lord Dammler. His behaviour was maddeningly provocative. He would partner some dashing heiress for one or two days—appear with her at the opera and the balls—then two nights later she would be replaced by another. Rumours were rampant as to his having a wild but secret affair with this married lady or that widow, but they were not credited by the knowing. No lady would remain silent if she had indeed made a conquest of such magnitude. She would shout it from the rooftops. Several did lay claim to having entrapped him, and he was too polite to deny their lies outright, but only smiled and said, "Possibly, I don't seem to recall the name of the lady I was with last night."

It soon became obvious that his affection centered on no *lady*, but a young female of quite a different sort. He was frequently seen in company with a lady of pleasure of exquisite beauty, whose outstanding attraction was her hair. By some alchemy it had achieved a shade somewhere between silver and gold. She appeared in the park in a phaeton pulled by a matched pair of horses from the royal stud at Hanover, of much the same colour as her hair. She also appeared in an enviable collection of gowns and jewels.

Cantos from Abroad was in every hand and on every lip, in every book shop window and on every polite table top, and Lord Dammler's fame rose higher, till it seemed he must be giddy from such heights. He was amazed and amused, tolerant and good-humoured, but eventually bored with it all, and began retiring from the gay social round. He dispensed with his "Guardian Angels," and to escape for a spell, he accepted an invitation to a house party at Finefields, the estate of Lord Malvern and his pretty young wife Constance. No daring friend ever inferred to the Countess of Malvern that she had been well-named. Her affairs were infamous throughout the land. It was generally assumed that she had added Dammler to her long list of admirers. Certainly the lady did nothing to deny the rumour.

Stories sped back to London of orgies and affairs of unprecedented decadence, of a duel between Dammler and Malvern over the Countess's honour. "Dammler mustn't have taken to her," Princess Lieven quipped. "Malvern is very piqued if his friends don't make love to Constance." The poet was more discussed in his absence than in his presence, and when he returned to town, there was a fresh arrow in his quiver. He brought with him another installment of his *Cantos from Abroad*—those stanzas completed during the last six months of his tour, now polished and ready for publication. They involved the last lap of his journey home, with a detour into South America and the sea voyage aboard a ship which contained an improbable school of nuns and a licentious crew. The cantos were an immediate success. Miss Mallow, like everyone else with a guinea to spare, dashed out and bought a copy to delight her idle hours.

Perusing them, she wondered that anyone could bother to read her own dull stuff, with characters no more interesting than her Uncle Clarence, whom she had converted into a lady who wrote bad music which she constantly compared to Bach, with that gentleman on the short end.

Prudence and the poet lived and wrote in the same city, worked for the same publisher and public; their lives travelled in parallel lines, never touching. Lord Dammler occupied a large part of Miss Mallow's mind, but he did not know of her existence. She was, in fact, once drawn to his attention by their mutual editor, Mr. Murray.

"Have you had a look at this novel, Dammler?" Murray asked one day when Prudence's latest work was on his desk.

"I don't read novels, except for Scott's," Dammler drawled, without ever glancing at the three volumes, nicely bound in blue with gold lettering.

"Oh, well if you care for Scott, I daresay you wouldn't like this. Tame stuff—domestic, but good. Scott likes it. While you're here, I mean to give your arm a little twist. There's a dinner in honour of Mr. Wordsworth next week at Pulteney's Hotel. I'm enjoining my more illustrious writers to attend and pay him homage. Will you come?"

"No."

Murray sighed. "Just for the dinner—put in an appearance, Dammler. Your absence will be remarked upon."

"I am already promised to my aunt, Lady Melvine, that evening."

"She'll understand."

"I trust Mr. Wordsworth also is capable of understanding—though one might be forgiven for doubting it from what he writes. Do give him my regards."

"Come after dinner for the speeches."

Dammler stared, the brilliance from his one visible eye conveying worlds of astonishment. "What—*purposely* commit myself to sit for hours on a hard chair to listen to undeserved praise being heaped on Mr. Wordsworth. You are run mad, John. Mad as a hatter."

"Well after the speeches then. Come in about ten o'clock, just to meet Wordsworth and say how do you do."

"Oh, very well, if I happen to be in the vicinity. Pulteney's you say?"

"Yes," Murray smiled, taking this, as indeed it was meant to be taken, as a promise.

An invitation to the same party was extended by letter to Miss Mallow as a special treat. Murray had a good notion of the dull existence the poor girl led and wished to do her a favour. She was thrown into transports of delight, and for five days was in a fever of happy activity having a new gown made up, and dreaming of the famous people she would meet. This was her first foray into public literary life, and she looked forward to at last meeting other authors. Murray told her Fanny Burney would be there and had expressed a particular desire to meet her. Miss Burney was the most famous female writer of the period. Prudence felt she had reached the pinnacle of fame. It never occurred to her Lord Dammler might attend.

He might as well not have for all the effect her presence had on him. Murray introduced them just as Dammler was about to slip out the door fifteen minutes after his arrival. Neither Murray nor Wordsworth regretted his hasty departure. Once he had ambled in attention had been pretty well diverted from the guest of honour. It had taken a team of six strong men to get Wordsworth through the crowd surrounding the young poet. They shook hands and exchanged compliments unheard due to the general noise.

"Oh, Dammler, here is someone you ought to know," Murray said as Dammler headed for the door. Prudence had managed to sidle up to get a better look at him without being discovered. "Miss Prudence Mallow, one of my rising writers."

"Charmed, Miss Mallow," the poet said in his drawling voice, with a formal bow from the waist and a smile that kept Prudence from work for two days.

She nearly forgot to curtsy, but stood staring at Dammler with an awestruck expression, taking in every detail of his face and form. She hadn't known such perfection existed on earth. In fact, she had to step up her idea of heaven upon seeing him.

Familiar with this reaction on the part of young ladies, Dammler shouldered the burden of conversation and asked, "What is it you write, Miss Mallow, novels or poetry?"

"Poetry," she answered, with no intention of deceiving him, but not aware of what she said.

"I shall look forward to reading it," he told her, and bowed himself away.

Prudence's daydreaming rose to a higher pitch as a result of this encounter. The hero she had envisioned from the prints and cartoons in magazines and shop windows was filled out, improved, born anew upon a vision of the real man. Around three o'clock that morning as she lay wide awake reliving the evening, she recalled that she had not offered a word of praise to the poet on his work, nor offered to give him a copy of hers, which was surely hinted at by saying he looked forward to reading it. She arose from her bed, lit her taper, and inscribed her own copy to him that instant. The top corner of the first volume was a little dented from having been dropped, but the damage was not very noticeable. She pondered over what message to inscribe, and decided on the formal "Best wishes to Lord Dammler from Miss Mallow." This book handled by herself would soon rest in *his* hands. Words and ideas culled from *her* brain would be transmitted through his eye to his brain. It was an intimacy never looked for. She fell asleep wondering what he would think of her book, and awoke with a headache to send it off to Mr. Murray to deliver to Lord Dammler.

Next morning when Dammler stepped into Murray's office for a business meeting, the publisher gave him the three volumes of Miss Mallow's first book.

"How extremely kind of her," he said with a sort of sneering smile. "I am now expected to call in person and thank her, I collect."

"A note will suffice."

"I shan't encourage her advances. *You* will kindly thank her on my behalf, John."

John smiled, used to Dammler's offhand ways. A half hour later Dammler was sitting in Lady Melvine's saloon being scolded for leaving early the evening before.

"I have brought you a gift to make it up," he said, giving her the volumes from Miss Mallow. "By a new writer Murray is encouraging. Very good he tells me."

"Miss Mallow," Lady Melvine read the name. "I am not familiar with her writing. Is she pretty?"

"No."

"What is she like?"

"I have no recollection, but she cannot have been pretty or I would have. I seem to recall she wore a cap."

"Ah, an older lady."

He nodded, and began to quiz his aunt about some foolishness or other.

Chapter Three

"You are looking pulled today, Prudence," Clarence said in a jolly mood as a result of her glorious evening just past. How Sir Alfred, currently posing for his portrait, would stare when he mentioned casually that his niece had met Dammler, and thought him a pretty good sort of a fellow. Prudence was his niece when she was good, and Wilma's daughter when she was not. "It is a result of gallivanting with all the smarts and swells. So you saw Lord Dammler, eh? I daresay you will be taking off your caps and legging it after him, like all the other girls."

Prudence smiled wanly but said nothing.

"Prudence is too prudent for that," her mother countered gaily with the stale old joke.

"I have been thinking, Prue," Clarence continued, "now that you are famous and hobnobbing with all the elite, you will want your portrait taken."

"No indeed, there is no need for another. You have done three or four of me already, Uncle," Prue reminded him.

"Don't be shy. I would like to do it. Sitting three-quarters profile, like Mona Lisa, with a pen in your hand or a book in your lap to show your calling." Here was a daring departure from the usual pose. A pen in the hand would be a new challenge for Uncle Clarence, and as to adding a book, this use of symbols was a whole new career for him. "I shall have Sir Alfred stick a flower in his lapel," he added, beaming with anticipation as the full possibilities of this ploy washed over him. "He is a horticulturalist, you see. Raises flowers in that little box he calls a conservatory. Well, well. I don't see Sir Thomas Lawrence using this idea. I daresay he will snap it up when he hears what I am up to. Don't mention it if you happen to be talking to Lawrence," he warned Prudence, apparently under the misapprehension that henceforth her days would be spent gadding about from one gathering of celebrities to another.

She did not bother to mention it to Sir Thomas Lawrence or anyone else, though Clarence certainly imparted his secret to everyone he met. Mrs. Hering was to return her portrait to have a feather painted into her hand, symbolic of her passion for her "wee feathered friends," as she called them. Clarence was desirous of adding a symbol to the three-quarters profile of Mr. Arnprior, still drying against the studio wall, but did not like to put a fish into his hand, although fishing was his sole enjoyment. The day was saved by remembering Prue's book. He would paint a copy of Walton's *Compleat Angler* and hang it cunningly in mid-air beside the sitter, there being no table or other object in the picture to hold it. Clarence's backgrounds were filled in with a wide brush in one solid colour, blue if the model was a blond, pink for a brunette, and yellow for those aged persons with blue or purple hair.

Prudence was not required to chaperone Sir Alfred's sitting, so she was free to pursue her own interests for the next three days. She was pleasantly surprised and highly gratified to receive a visit from Miss Burney a day after the dinner party, and elated to be invited the next day to ride out in her carriage. It seemed the walls of social London were at last beginning to tumble down and let her enter. During the ride, Miss Burney took her to call on "a dear friend," Lady Melvine, one of the leading hostesses of society.

Imagine Prue's joy to discover, when she entered Lady Melvine's saloon, a copy of her novel lying on the side table. Lady Melvine was a tall, handsome woman in her middle years, with a sharp tongue and a ready wit. She liked to discover new personalities and to be the first to have them at a party. Prudence found her interesting, but not particularly likable.

"So *you* are Miss Mallow," she said, examining Prudence closely. Not at all fashionable, she observed. "I thought you'd be older. There's a good deal of discernment in your books, my dear. You've a sharp tongue. I like that. Too mealy-mouthed, most of our female writers. Oh, not *you*, Fanny. Don't poker up on me. And certainly not Madame de Staël—*au contraire* in *her* case. I have been reading *The Composition* all afternoon—a strange title you have chosen, Miss Mallow. Not very catching, if you will pardon my saying so."

"*The Composition* assumes more interest as the story progresses," Prudence pointed out. "I believe you must still be on Volume One." This volume lay open, face down, on the table.

"So I am. I am a slow reader, but I like it immensely." She picked the book up and pointed out to Prudence how far she had got. "I'm just here where the niece is being driven mad by her aunt's eternal playing of the pianoforte."

With the book in her hands now, Prudence noticed a little indentation in the upper corner, exactly where the copy she had given Dammler had been marred. Curious, she opened the cover and examined the fly leaf. Her surprise was great to see it was the same copy, with her own words inscribed. Lady Melvine noticed her expression and explained, "Dammler gave it to me yesterday. He particularly recommended it to me."

"Did he indeed?" Prudence asked. "He enjoyed it then?" He

hadn't read a word—she only sent it to Murray yesterday. It was a slap in the face.

"I'm sure he did."

"That's odd. He must be a remarkably fast reader, ma'am. He hadn't read it Monday evening, and I sent it to Murray Tuesday, the same day he passed it to you."

"Well, there now, we are found out!" Lady Melvine laughed. "It never does to lie, does it? The fact is, Miss Mallow, Dammler seldom reads a novel. He likes philosophy and history and that serious sort of thing. Novels are for us ladies."

"His poetry would not indicate a taste for philosophy or history or anything so serious," Prudence was goaded by her hurt into saying. "In fact his *Cantos from Abroad* are nothing but a totally incredible novel in rhyme. Mine is at least believable."

Lady Melvine was delighted to hear this. She had been looking for a needle to annoy Dammler and hoped she had found one. "You *dislike* the book then?"

The fact was that Prudence adored the cantos, so swashbuckling and splendidly told, but it was the hero, and the knowledge of his alter ego that made them so enjoyable. She equivocated, "I liked it well enough—something different you know."

"Damning with faint praise!" Lady Melvine encouraged her. "What did you find particularly incredible?"

"It was a strain to credit that he had single-handedly rescued three Indian maidens while being pursued by a band of marauding scalp-hunters, and on the very same evening got out of the wilderness in time to attend a ball in some large city or other, and be seduced by the governor's wife."

"Oh, but the matter of being chased by Indians is true—it is how he injured his eye," Lady Melvine assured her.

"I'm sure it is true he attended a ball as well, and even made love to the governor's lady, but it is unlikely so much excitement occurred in one day."

20

Fanny Burney, with her usual tact, refused to criticize a popular writer. "It is a matter of pacing, Miss Mallow. The events naturally did not occur one on top of the other, but for the sake of maintaining excitement, Dammler plunges us on from one adventure to another without describing the duller portions of the trip. And what are *you* planning to write next? My next is to be set in Rome."

"Since Dammler is taking the *world* for his background, ma'am, I mean to send my next heroine into the cosmos, and confront her with planetary creatures to give a little excitement, which seems to be what is craved today. She will fly up from Plymouth in a balloon in the morning, land on the moon for a quick battle with twenty thousand or so strange creatures, free a prison full of hostages before lunch, be initiated into the secret of longevity, and bounce back to London for tea with the Prince of Wales. I don't want the thing to drag."

Lady Melvine chuckled in glee, but Fanny Burney said, "How droll you are, Miss Mallow," and determined to drop the quaint creature before she became an embarrassment. The two ladies later took their leave, and Miss Mallow realized from the manner of her new friend that she had displeased. There was no mention made of their going out together again. That evening Prudence reread *Cantos from Abroad* and found an inconsistency in every line. The story was ridiculous, the happenings so far-fetched as to be absurd. The whole could hardly have been compressed into a lifetime, let alone a couple of years. As she read, a smile lingered on her face at the charm of the account.

The next day she set to work on a new book of her own and pushed her daydreams aside. Uncle Clarence would not be put off; yet another likeness of her had to be taken, and during the three days she sat with a book in her lap and an enigmatic smile on her face, like Mona Lisa; no writing was possible, but her time was well spent in planning her plot and characters. Between bouts of agreeing with her uncle that he had indeed outdone them all to paint a book into the picture—and her own book, too, with the title perfectly legible—she dreamed up her new heroine and named her Patience.

"Da Vinci now," Clarence informed her, "would never have made the title clear enough to read. Couldn't even remember an eyelash. I have used Gothic script, too, just like *your* book."

The portrait done, it was lined up to dry with Mrs. Hering and her feather and Sir Alfred and his flower. There was no difficulty in telling which was hers. She wore a cap.

Uncle Clarence's next victim was to be a young boy of eight years, so again Prudence was released from playing chaperone. Her mama requested her company to go to Bond Street to shop, but her creative juices were flowing and she elected to stay home and write. Uncle Clarence was having a small dinner party that evening to show her off to his friends and let them feast their eyes on a girl who had actually met Lord Dammler, and so her evening would be wasted. She sat in the study which had been given over to her on the day her first book was published. Uncle Clarence was a great appreciator of success. Since her meeting with Dammler there was talk of installing a row of shelves in the study to hold her books. The room's sole claim to its title at the moment was its holding a desk and a set of pens.

Great was her surprise when a servant came to the door and told Prudence she had callers. "Mr. Murray and another gentleman," Rose said with importance. "He's wearing a black thing on his eye, miss. Handsome as can be. Would it be the poet?"

The description sounded very much like it, and Miss Mallow felt overcome. He had come in person to thank her for the book!

His coming (it was indeed Dammler), was not so flattering as it appeared. He had bumped into Murray downtown, wanted to talk to him, and when the latter said he had to stop at Miss Mallow's for a moment, Dammler had perforce come with him.

The lady's name had not even registered till Murray reminded him who she was. But he was well-bred, and when Prudence went with shaking knees to the saloon, he claimed joy at another chance of talking to her, and thanked her for sending him the book. She was overwhelmed anew at his grandeur. No hint of a sharp insinuation as to what he had done with the book was made. She said so little that she was afraid she was appearing stupid.

Mr. Murray gave her some papers to sign, and she wrote her name blindly without looking to see what she was putting her signature to.

"Miss Mallow is a trusting person, John," Dammler chided upon seeing this, and Murray made a joking reply which went unheard, and consequently unanswered, by Miss Mallow.

One thought was uppermost in her mind. She had not complimented Dammler, and that she was determined to do. "I have read all your poems," she said in a stricken voice. "I liked them very much."

"Thank you, ma'am," he replied. As she said nothing further, he went on in the interest of civility to add mendaciously, "and I read the book you so kindly sent me, and liked it very much indeed. We writers must stick together and praise each other, must we not?"

"Yes," she said, and thought to herself—he's lying. How well he lies. She could see that the visit, an unparalleled chance for making a favourable impression on Dammler, was going poorly. Not a word could she think of to say. But the meeting soon took a turn for the worse. Uncle Clarence, alerted by a servant as to who had come to call, came dashing into the saloon, a white rag in his hands with which he wiped paint from his fingers.

"Lord Dammler, indeed this is an honour," he said in a sonorous voice, without waiting for an introduction. "My niece has been telling me all about you." He grabbed Dammler's hand and pumped furiously.

"This is my uncle, Mr. Elmtree," Prudence said helplessly, and from that one speech on, she couldn't have got a word in if she had wanted to. Dammler's works, which Clarence had never read, were praised to the skies. Shakespeare, Milton—all those fellows were nothing to him. From Lord Dammler he turned to his niece's works. There was no danger of her being Wilma's daughter today. They too were admired, unread, as being the only thing in the English language capable of comparison to Dammler's cantos. "I don't give praise lightly," he added in a judicial manner. "I have no opinion of books in general—go a year at a time without opening a book—but serious literature of the sort you two write is always a pleasure to read. Yes, I will certainly read *Cantos from Abroad*. Read them *again*," he amended, as Lord Dammler's mouth fell open at this conclusion to his long encomium.

The poet indicated by a slight jerk of his head to Murray that he would like to leave. Appalled at the meeting, Prudence did nothing to detain them.

"Oh, a glass of wine. Surely you will do me the honour to take a glass of wine before you leave," Clarence said. He gave no chance for refusal, but pulled a cord and summoned a servant to fetch it at once.

The delay gave Clarence a chance to mount his own hobby horse. "Are you interested in art at all, your grace?" he asked the guest.

"Yes, indeed. I saw some very fine pieces in Greece," Dammler answered, thinking to get over the next quarter of an hour with a good discussion of art. The poor fellow was a fool on the subject of literature, but might know something of art, as he had raised the subject.

"Oh, Greece, there is nothing there but rubble," Clarence informed him, dismissing at a word the entire classical heritage. Dammler stared, and a smile slowly formed on his face.

"Indeed?" he said in his most drawling, affected voice.

"Smashed to bits, all of it. You've seen those pitiful broken bits and pieces Elgin had carted home. A scandal. The man is senile, not a doubt of it. No, when I saw *art* I refer to painting."

"Ah, yes, painting. Well, I spent some time in Italy. Rome is worth seeing, and Florence of course . . ."

No mere tourist was to take the floor. "I daresay you are familiar with the *Mona Lisa?*"

"Yes," Dammler answered, slow to give up hope, and thinking still to hear some esoteric bit of history or lore connected with the famous painting.

"It's by da Vinci," Clarence told him in a knowing way.

Dammler's smile reappeared, accompanied now by a wicked twinkle in his one visible eye. "So I hear," he agreed in an encouraging tone.

"I believe our guests are in a hurry, Uncle," Prudence mentioned.

"Not at all," Dammler contradicted.

"Hurry? Nonsense, we are discussing art. Ah, here is the wine. How pleasant it is to sit chatting with cultured gentlemen who are interested in something other than politics and the price of corn."

"You were saying something about the *Mona Lisa,*" his guest reminded him. Murray frowned an apology at Prudence, and accepted a glass of wine.

"Yes, so I was. It is a wonderful painting, the *Mona Lisa. La Gioconda* the dagos call it." Miss Mallow's heart sank to her shoes, but there was to be no escape. "Clever the way da Vinci set up the model so he wouldn't have to paint her 'head on.' That is the most difficult pose to paint because of foreshortening. The whole thing has to be foreshortened from that angle—dashed tricky business. And he cut her off just below the waist, too, to eliminate the problem of proportion. When you get into a full length portrait you have proportion to contend with. He avoided all that by posing her cleverly and cutting her off at the waist. I sometimes use that pose myself when I am in a hurry."

"You do some painting yourself, do you, Mr. Elmtree?" Dammler asked with a show of interest.

"I dabble a little. Not professional, you know, but the way you dabble in rhyming. Just for my own enjoyment."

"Just so," the premier poet of England agreed.

"Yes, I did a likeness of my niece a while ago. Something on the lines of the *Mona Lisa*. But I gave Prudence an eyelash, of course . . ." He rambled on with his stunt of using a symbol, and Lawrence's jealousy of him, the incredible speed of eighty-seven portraits a year. Each of his follies was dragged out before Murray finally pulled Dammler away, protesting that the visit was too short.

"A man like that is better than a week at a spa," Dammler said as they walked to the carriage. "I had some fear the English eccentric was a dead species, but I am happy to see he is alive and well and living in Grosvenor Square."

Back in the house, Clarence turned to his niece and said, "Well, well, he seemed a pretty nice fellow, your new beau."

"He is not a beau, Uncle," Prudence replied, defeat in every line of her body.

"Ho, you are a sly puss. Nabbing a marquis under our very noses. Not a beau, indeed. Wait till I tell Mrs. Hering and Sir Alfred."

"I wish you would not . . ."

"Nonsense, I am not ashamed to know him. He is a capital fellow. Knows all about art. I shall drop him a note and ask him if he would like to pose for me."

"Oh, Uncle, indeed you must not!"

"I can slip him in between the Purdy twins and Mrs. Mulgrove—a week Monday I can start. Monday to Wednesday—three days. He will be no work at all. It will take very little fixing up to make him look well on canvas. He has a fine eyelash—pity about the patch, but I will paint that out, of course."

Mr. Elmtree could not understand why his niece went into a

fit of desperate giggles, but charitably assumed it was due to her great luck in nabbing Lord Dammler for a beau. He was dismayed he had forgotten to get the fellow's address to drop him a line for his appointment. Prudence did not mention the efficacy of Mr. Murray as an intermediary, and the subject dropped.

Chapter Four

The following week was a calm one for Miss Mallow, allowing her to catch her breath after her spate of public life. She sat home working most days and went with Uncle Clarence and her mama to one very dull dinner party and with an aged female friend of her uncle to a concert of antique music. Lord Dammler was feted at Carleton House by the Prince Regent, found that an unknown young female had smuggled herself into his apartment during his absence one evening and was waiting for him in his bedroom, was requested to write a comedy for presentation at Drury Lane, won a thousand pounds at faro, enjoyed a flirtation with Lady Margaret Halston, and was presented with a paternity suit for a child conceived while he was still in America, by a girl who knew his reputation but not his itinerary. It was a calm week for him, too.

On Friday evening he stopped at Lady Melvine's to take her to a rout he would prefer to have missed. He found her dressed and ready, a hideous purple turban on her head and an excess of diamonds sparkling about her person.

"Setting up as a shop window, Het?" he quizzed her.

"Don't I look horrid? But I haven't a stitch to wear, and the diamonds detract attention from this old gown, don't you think?"

"They certainly detract from your elegance. Nothing is so vulgar as too many diamonds. You don't need both the necklace and that awful cluster of brooches, do you?"

"No matter, when I walk in with *you* I will be the envy of them all."

"You forget I have a reputation to maintain, Auntie."

"The reason I am so ill prepared is that I have spent the whole afternoon reading another book by that Miss Mallow you recommended."

"Oh, has she written more than one?"

"Three—all delightful. *The Cat in the Garden* is the one I have just put down."

"Sounds monstrously exciting," he drawled, then yawned behind long fingers. "Is it about animals then?"

"No, it is a two-legged cat referred to in the title. An old tabby like me who lurks about her garden seeing things she shouldn't, and telling."

"Which she also shouldn't. I'm surprised at such dissipation coming from Miss Mallow's pen."

"You cannot know her well!" Hettie laughed.

"Hardly at all. Don't tell me *you* have her acquaintance."

"I've met her. Fanny Burney brought her to call on me last week, and sat with her lips pursed the whole visit at her protegée's impertinence."

"I think we must be speaking of two different ladies. My Miss Mallow could not by the broadest interpretation be called impertinent."

"Not to your face maybe. She does a fine job of ripping you up behind your back."

"Indeed!" He looked stunned. "May I ask what she said? We are virtual strangers. It is odd she should speak to my discredit."

"It is rather your works she dislikes than yourself."

"I seem to recall she complimented me on the cantos."

"Ask her sometime for her true opinion."

"I am asking *you*, Hettie. What did she say?"

"My, how your head has become swollen! A fellow writer may not find a single fault in your work without your mounting your high horse. Well, it was nothing so very bad after all. She only took exception to your being chased by Indians and rescuing three women and emerging unscathed to attend a ball and dally with the governor's wife the same night. I must say, it seemed a point well taken."

He shrugged. "I am not a novelist who counts up the hours in a day, but a poet. Was there anything else?"

"She was not happy at your hogging the whole world for your setting. She is to launch her next heroine off into the cosmos and out-do you in wonders."

"She is welcome to try her hand at it. I make no claim to having visited the stars. Is that the sort of thing she writes?"

A peal of laughter escaped Lady Melvine. "Good God, no! She was funning. Very down to earth indeed. She couldn't be more so. Well, I have her three books here. See for yourself."

"I don't read novels."

"Suit yourself. You're missing a good bet."

He picked up *The Composition* and glanced at it. "Very well, I'll try it. It will lull me to sleep one night, I expect."

"Indian giver!" Hettie charged. "Oh, by the way, if you chance to be speaking to her again, she knows you gave me the book—and the very day you received it, too, so don't put your foot in it."

With a tapered finger, he reached up and adjusted his black patch. "Now I wonder if *that* is what got her hackles up? I've already told her how much I enjoyed it."

"Oh, when did you see her again?" Lady Melvine naturally had no hope of making a romantic conquest of her nephew, but she took a proprietary interest in his affairs.

"Last week. I found her a dead bore—not a word to say for herself, but she has an uncle whose acquaintance I could come to cherish."

Hettie teased him to say more, knowing by his smile there was some joke in the matter, but he refused to satisfy her vulgar curiosity. The rout was a squeeze, at least until Lord Dammler took his leave, when several others left as well. He went to a club and lost half the money he had won the week before. As he was about to step out of his carriage before his apartment, his hand brushed Miss Mallow's book, and with a shrug he carried the three slim volumes into the building. It was not yet late. Taking a glass of ale, he opened Volume One, skimming a line here and there. He smiled at a telling phrase or a description, and before long was reading in earnest. Unlike his aunt, he was a fast reader. Before he went to bed, rather late, he had finished the second volume, and before he had his breakfast in the morning, he finished the third and was converted to Miss Mallow's growing list of supporters.

Had he been informed beforehand that the novel was about a youngish spinster and her boring aunt, living alone in a quiet neighbourhood with only a country person for romantic interest, he wouldn't have opened the cover. But though nothing much happened, he kept turning the pages, eager to peer into the minds and hearts of these normal people. It had an air of reality about it—that, he fancied, was the trick. No preposterous doings of the sort he wrote about—no, to face the dreadful truth, here was *literature*, and what he wrote was claptrap. He sat musing for some time on the matter, and the more he compared the prim little lady's work with his own tales, the more dissatisfied he became. He went out and bought copies of the other two novels, and spent an afternoon reading *The Cat in the Garden*. Having already met her uncle, he recognized him as the musical lady in *The Composition*. He marvelled at her nerve in serving up such a parody—she, who looked as though butter wouldn't melt in her mouth. She knew, of course, that the old boy didn't read. But who was she writing about in this other one? He was convinced it was a real person, and one he was curious to meet. Tired with reading, he went out to a dinner party that evening and found himself seated beside "Silence" Jersey, the most renowned chatterbox in London. He smiled to think what Miss Mallow would make of her. The fact that she was never silent removed nine-tenths of the burden of conversation from him, and he thought again of Miss Mallow. On an impulse he decided he would call on her again—take her out for a drive to get her away from the babbling uncle, and see what she had to say for herself. He figured he could draw out a shy young lady without too much trouble. How the *ton* would goggle to see him driving in the park with an unknown little spinster! This too amused him.

Next day he stuck to his resolution, and prepared himself in the morning to pay her a visit. He was amazed to find himself a little nervous. Not in a missish quake, of course. He had supped with princes and dined with princesses, flirted with duchesses and countesses without a qualm, but he did feel a qualm at calling on this little lady no one had ever heard of. The thought had taken hold that she would be judging him, as she so obviously had judged her uncle, and found him wanting. What would she write of himself if she decided to slip him into one of her books? "A gentleman who brought Society to its knees with the aid of an eye patch and a piece of doggerel . . ." No, she would cut closer to the bone than that.

But when he was later confronted with the live novelist, the qualm seemed to have transferred itself from his bones to hers. She looked quite thunderstruck to see him in her saloon, but not so surprised that she failed to warn the butler there was no need to disturb Mr. Elmtree. No more than he did she want that tongue ruining their visit. Her mother, a sensible but not remarkable woman, sat with them for ten minutes, at the end of which time Dammler repeated the mention of a drive. "I will take good care of your daughter, ma'am" he assured Mrs. Mallow.

"Prudence is pretty well able to take care of herself " she replied.

"She is well named," he smiled.

Prudence looked at him closely. At that instant she realized he was mere flesh and blood. The most pleasing combination of flesh and blood ever seen, perhaps, but a mere mortal after all. Her awe of him fled like a small cloud before a howling wind.

"I wonder how many times you have had to listen to that platitude," he said as they went out the door.

"More times than I care to remember."

"And it isn't true either," he said, giving her a hand into the carriage. It was far and away the grandest carriage Miss Mallow had ever been in. Papa had kept a little gig, and Uncle Clarence had a lumbering old coach that had been in the family twenty years. Dammler's was a spanking new one, shiny with a crest on the side. Silver mountings gleamed everywhere, and in the interior the seats and squabs were covered in real tigerskin.

"Oh, how *savage!*" she laughed.

The carriage seemed suddenly to be in very poor taste. "I am not prudent either, to have put my pelts to such a base use. I'm sorry I didn't keep them for rugs."

"Surely walking on them is no more noble than sitting on them?" she remarked.

It was a mere nothing—a thoughtless comment to fill time till they should be moving, but again it made him feel foolish.

"Why did you call me imprudent?" she asked, trying not to show in too obvious a manner her interest in this magnificent carriage. There were little doors and silver pulls mounted on the side, which raised her curiosity.

"To have treated your uncle Elmtree so was a shabby trick, Miss Mallow."

She looked at him in amazement. Could it be he considered meeting himself such a treat he felt her uncle to have been deprived because she told the servant not to call him? Certainly Clarence would think so, but for Dammler to suggest it himself was a piece of pride she could scarcely swallow without chewing it a bit.

"What *have* I said to make you hate me already, ma'am?" he asked. "I intended to be on my best behaviour. You must own you gave him a fine raking in *The Composition*."

"Oh, you mean you *read* it?" she asked.

"Indeed I did, as soon as I could tear it out of Hettie's hands. I lent it to her," he added, not considering it a real lie, as he had no notion of returning the gift.

"Oh, but he never guessed, nor would he if he ever got round to reading it. How did you figure it out? My changing him to a woman fooled everyone else. Not even Mama suspected."

"I saw what you were up to at once. Bach's fugues are the *Mona Lisa*, and the baroque counterpoint is her foreshortening. I don't think you worked in an analogy to the eyelashes, did you?"

It was horrid to laugh at Uncle Clarence, but so very nice to have someone who understood and did not disapprove, that she could not suppress a smile. "No, nor the symbols either—they are a recent innovation."

"Lawrence will snap it up in no time," he warned her with a quirk of his black wing of eyebrow, and a conspiratorial smile.

"And claim it for his own—that is another of his tricks to be watched out for. He took to putting on a bit of impasto to highlight the nose as soon as ever Uncle Clarence invented it."

"Plagiarist! He'll be posing them in three-quarters profile with their hands folded if we don't keep a sharp eye on him. I adored your books. You are a *real* artist with words."

She flushed with pleasure, but demurred, "It is yourself who is the acknowledged artist."

"Humbug—don't try to gammon me. They're claptrap, Miss Mallow, and you know it."

"Oh, indeed they are not! They are stunning tales. I like them excessively."

"That is not what I hear," he wagged a finger at her. "Now that you are famous you must watch your tongue. And it will take some watching, too, I'll wager. I have it on good authority Miss Burney was chagrined at your impudence, and Lord Dammler is certainly offended at your criticism of him. Especially as it was so very much to the point."

"Oh, but I didn't . . ."

"Didn't claim you must send your heroine off to the moon, since *I* had grabbed the world for my playground? Of course you did. Hettie's tongue runs like a river, but she doesn't lie."

"I—I was only funning, you know."

"I know, now that I have met you. Come to know you a little I mean." He was anxious to know her better. She was different from anyone he had met since returning to England. "I wish you will tell me all about *The Cat in the Garden*. Who is she?"

"She, as you might guess now that you are on to my trick, is a man—a horrid old nosey Parker who lived near us in Kent. He was a bachelor of a certain age—funny how they haven't the reputation for malice and spite we spinsters have, but they are just as bad. He was always peeking over the hedge when I had company."

"So *you* are Emily. I didn't suspect that."

Emily was a lively young lady with much of Prudence in her. "No, I made her up," she said, remembering she had been something of a beauty. "I just used the circumstance of a nosey person making mischief and fabricated from there."

"I don't think I could do that."

"Surely you made up at least half of the adventures you wrote about. They could not *all* have happened to you."

"They all happened to somebody. Some of them I had

second hand, but I didn't make any of them up out of whole cloth. That is the leap of imagination that defies me."

Prudence looked skeptical. "I didn't think, from reading your works you would stick at anything."

"I have been taken for Marvelman because of the name I chose. He was not meant to be me. The cantos were just scribblings to wile away time when I was bored of an evening. It can be boring far away from company, or in the thick of it, for that matter."

As they entered the park, a sensation was caused by the appearance of Dammler's carriage. It was recognized and every second vehicle they passed wanted to stop for the occupant to have a word with him. There was no guessing from his smiling face and joking conversation that he was bored. Certainly Prudence was not. She hadn't had such a day before in her whole life. Dammler introduced her to a few notables, but usually he just said a few words and drove on.

"How do you find life in a fish bowl?" he asked with a disparaging smile during a brief interlude when he was let alone.

"Very exciting, but I don't know how you stand the pace if it's always like this."

"It is frequently worse," he said tersely. "This was a poor idea coming here. We can't talk. I should have known how it would be. We'll head for the outskirts."

The excitement died down as they entered the Chelsea Road, and conversation was again possible. They drove and talked for a long time—about their work, his travels, but very little about Prudence herself. As he left her at the door he said, "Next time we'll talk about *you*, Miss Mallow. I have been running off at the mouth about myself, which is a poor way of getting to know you. Tomorrow?"

She nodded and entered the house in a dreamlike state to be rallied by her uncle about her new beau. "Knew all along he was sweet on you. I could tell by his eyes—eye. I'll have to remember to paint that patch out. He is a good-looking fellow but for that one little blemish. What had he to say for himself?"

"He spoke highly of your work, Uncle."

"Did he indeed? Odd as he has never seen it, but I daresay they are whispering about me at Court. Sir Alfred, you know, would slip them the word about my symbols. He is often at Court. So he is anxious to see my work, is he? Well, I shan't mind to show him about my studio as he is practically one of the family. When does he come again?"

"Soon I expect," Prudence answered prudently.

"If he happens to drop by while I am in the studio, don't hesitate to send for me. I am only doing the twins. I shan't mind stopping for a minute. Or bring him in. Let him see how to pose." This about a gentleman whose likeness had been taken by the greatest artists across the whole of Europe, and who knew the Mona Lisa's pose as well as she knew it herself. Prudence bit her lip. Her uncle's nonsense, which had long since become nearly unbearable, was funny again, for in her mind she shared it with Dammler.

"We must not make too much of it Clarence," Mrs. Mallow warned. "It is just courtesy on his part because they are both writers."

"Pooh, he is in love with her. I have already told Mrs. Hering. She was green with envy. She would like you to take him to call one day, Prue, when you and Dammler have nothing better to do."

"Uncle, you mustn't say such things. What if he should hear? I'd be mortified."

"You are too shy, my dear. Such a fellow as Dammler wants a little encouragement. He is bound to be backward, being handicapped as he is."

"What do you mean? How is he handicapped?"

"Why, his eye, to be sure. But don't let it put you off. I'll take care of that, and posterity will never know the difference. What symbol would he like?"

"It is not settled you are to paint him, Uncle."

"I have agreed to it. There is no problem. The only question is a symbol. Mention it to him the next time he comes "sparking" you."

"He is not "sparking" me."

"What a girl. She won't say a thing till she has his ring on her finger."

The matter was settled in his mind, and any objections were only coyness. He had already told Mrs. Hering, and would tell everyone else he met in the next two days.

Chapter Five

Dammler called the next afternoon as promised, and by standing with her pelisse ready to fling on, Prudence escaped without subjecting him to teasing jokes from her uncle. They avoided the park this time, and drove north towards Harrow. It was his intention to draw out Miss Mallow about herself that day, but she felt her monotonous life could not be of much interest to him. While he was under sail over stormy oceans, she had sat in her backyard reading, or in her study writing. His talks with foreign kings and chiefs and emperors must be more entertaining than her visits to a sick friend with a bowl of restorative pork jelly, or cutting out an underskirt; and in the end he did most of the talking, and she most of the listening.

It was only their second outing, but they seemed already like old friends, and Prudence ventured to ask, "What was it that caused you to take your trip around the world? It is hinted at in the cantos, but not explained."

"There was a good reason for leaving it vague. It wasn't fit to print."

"Yet another liaison in your crimson past?" she asked leadingly. She had already heard of a few.

"Mmm. It does me no credit, and the lady in the case even less. Why did *you* leave Kent?"

She told him in a few words. It seemed always thus. His questions could be answered in a second, whereas the answers to hers, she was sure, held an interesting story. She wished strongly to hear it. "Was she an English lady?" she asked to urge him along. He had already told of intrigues with a Russian and an Indian.

"Yes, a married lady, a neighbour of my uncle's." He then tried again to revert to her life. "And how did you come to take up writing novels?"

The tale of her copying experience was equally dull and explained in two sentences. "What was she like, the married lady?" Prue pressed a little harder.

"*Now* I wouldn't think her anything out of the ordinary. A ripe lady—thirtyish—still very attractive, in a mature way that appealed to my youth. I was just down from Cambridge at the time, you remember. Not up to snuff at all."

"She took care of the matter for you, I collect?"

"You are quite determined to hear the whole salacious tale, I see. So be it, but don't say I didn't warn you. She was my uncle's mistress. He was a widower, and she also was widowed. She lived in one of his houses, and the relationship between them was known by everyone except my green self. When he lay dying, she came every day to sit and talk to him, and stayed around in the evening to talk to me."

He stopped, and Prudence said, "That's not so bad."

He looked at her askance. "The evenings were not *entirely* devoted to talk. You know how these things progress—or perhaps you don't. But they *do* progress, believe me. Under the guidance of an expert, as my uncle's friend most assuredly was, they progress far and fast. I fell in love with her in about two days, or minutes. The day after my uncle died, I asked her to marry me and was cut to the quick when she laughed in my face."

"You offered *marriage* to such a woman?"

"I was young, and so stupid I can hardly believe it myself. *I* knew nothing, but she had more sense. She didn't want to be saddled with a jealous young hothead of a husband. No, indeed, my offer scared her out of her wits. She fled to the local innkeeper for solace, and I, my heart in tatters, couldn't get far enough away." A nostalgic smile at his foolish past made him look as if he almost regretted her refusal still. "Well, of course I really had an itch to travel anyway, or I shouldn't have gone so far, or stayed so long. I never told anyone else that story, Miss Mallow. You worm everything out of me, and you are the very one I oughtn't to tell such bawdy tales to, a proper little lady like you. And you tell me nothing of yourself, oyster. Tell me all about your suitors. I'll wager you had a string of them in your salad days."

Miss Mallow didn't feel she was quite wilted yet, but she had the impression Dammler thought her older than she was. She tried to think of a romance from her youth. There was only Mr. Springer, whom she had idolized without ever a hope of return. He was the prize catch of her neighbourhood; all the girls were after him. She had known his mama fairly well, and she fashioned a piece of fiction around him, leaving it very vague, but not so one-sided as it had been.

"Why didn't you have him?" Dammler asked when she finished.

"I don't know," she answered, smiling to think how quickly she would have had him, had he ever asked.

"Have you ever regretted not marrying?" Obviously he considered marriage at her advanced years out of the question. The cap, of course . . .

"No. Oh, no, I have my work, and I enjoy it."

"And so do we all! I am happy you showed Mr. Springer the door. I know him you see, and always found him a bumptious fellow."

"You know him!" she gasped, then remembered too late that

41

Ronald Springer had gone to Cambridge, had been there, apparently, at the same time as Dammler.

"Yes, he was at college with me. Not the same department, but I remember him very well. A pompous ass, always getting straight A's. He can't be very old. I thought he was around my age."

"Whereas *I*, of course, am seventy-five!" she retorted.

"Oh, ho, I've done it again. Pushed the foot right into the big mouth." He put his face into his hands and grimaced. "Forgive me?" he asked, looking at her with playful fear. She laughed, but still some slight resentment lingered, and he set about talking it away. "It seems to me you managed to learn more of life in your backyard and study than *I* did in all my travels. There's more sense in your books than in a tome of philosophy."

She was forced to object to this flattery, but was overruled in his finest manner till she was restored to spirits. As well as thinking her older than she was, or perhaps because of it, he also assumed her to be worldlier. He spoke of things that shocked her, but she was determined not to show it. She had no desire to appear like an insular little country bumpkin, but occasionally she was found out, and he would laugh and say he was debauching her.

To Clarence's and Miss Mallow's delight, Lord Dammler called again a third day to drive her out. Prudence was bothered once again to have to put on her same plain round bonnet and navy pelisse, so very *spinsterish*—no wonder he took her for an old, unmarriageable lady. She was bothered even more that Clarence was on hand to tease them.

"So you two are off again," he beamed, rubbing his hands in pleasure. "You are cutting all her other beaux out," he added. Prudence hadn't a beau to her name, and Clarence of all people must know it.

"I am making myself a host of enemies, no doubt," Dammler returned pleasantly.

"Ho, they are all jealous as can be. This will make them look lively."

"What nonsense you talk, Uncle," Prudence said, tying up her bonnet springs as fast as her fingers could move.

"I guess I know a suitor when I see one," he laughed merrily. "She is as sly as can hold together," he added aside to Dammler. "She never tells us a thing. You will be having the banns read before she admits it. What a girl."

Dammler looked more surprised than pleased at this, and took Prudence to task about it the minute they were in his carriage.

"Is it possible your uncle takes us for lovers?" he asked in a choked voice.

Prudence would gladly have put a noose around her uncle's neck and pulled it tight, but she had to make it seem a joke. "You must know you cannot dance such attendance on me without having fallen under my spell. All my callers are suspected of concealing a ring in their pockets which they try at every opportunity to put on my finger. But you know what a sly creature I am. I keep both hands in my pockets. Mr. Murray was highly guilty, till he mentioned his four children. It is all that saved him from the altar."

As he already had categorized Clarence as a fool, Dammler accepted this answer in good part. Eager to kill the subject, Prudence said immediately, "I ought really to be shopping today. I am in need of a new bonnet."

"Don't let me deter you," he answered with the greatest alacrity.

"Oh dear, is it that bad?" she laughed. Strange how she could already accept anything from him without embarrassment. Really he was the easiest person to get on with.

He darted a look at her, hesitantly, but soon laughed. "You look a quiz in that round bonnet, Miss Mallow. It is for protection from your legions of suitors I know, but I have been wanting to suggest a new one since the first day we drove out together. Let me take you to Mlle. Fancot, in Conduit Street. All the go. I take all my—ah—friends there."

"I don't think I want *that* sort of bonnet," she returned.

"Afraid you'll be taken for a lightskirt? You won't. But I would like you to look less like a maiden aunt as I mean to be a good deal in your company, and preferably *not* under your uncle's roof."

With such an enticement as this held out to her, he could have demanded a whole new wardrobe and got it. "Mlle. Fancot it is."

A neat turn was executed in the middle of the road, and they proceeded to Conduit Street. "Oh, I haven't much money with me," she remembered.

"Put it on tick. Everyone does. I'll vouch for your credit. I daren't suggest paying for it."

"You had better not. They'll mistake me for one of your—ah, *friends*."

"No they won't!" he laughed, so hard that she could not like it. Was she *that* old looking?

Miss Mallow was in the habit of purchasing her bonnets, and most of her other necessities (she rarely bought a luxury), at the sale counter at the Pantheon Bazaar. Though she had lived in London for some years, she had never been in the elegant small shops, had no notion such grandeur existed in mere commercial buildings. There was glowing mahogany and velvet drapery everywhere, and the saleswoman looked like a very fashionable young lady.

"Good day, Fannie," Dammler said, as they stepped in.

"*Bonjour*, Lord Dammler," Fannie replied. She smiled a smile Prudence could only describe as lascivious—looking up at him through her lashes with a parting of the lips.

"My—cousin wants a new bonnet. Something dashing."

Fannie's bold gaze flicked over Prudence with very little interest. "*Bien entendu*. This way, mam'selle."

"No, no, don't shove her off in a closet, Fannie. I want to see what she's buying. Bring the bonnets out here."

Fannie smiled and swayed across the store in such a provocative way that Prudence felt quite ashamed to be of the same sex. She looked out the window to avoid looking at Dammler, who was completely absorbed in Fannie's departing figure. Fannie reappeared a moment later with an armful of bonnets surely designed in heaven. They were not hats at all—they were miniature gardens, with slips of satin roses nestled in beds of soft green, bound up with narrow bands of ribbon.

"How about this one?" Dammler asked, lifting out a buff coloured chip straw with a band of buds around the joining of the rim and poke. "Try this one, Miss Mallow."

She tried it, and it was so beautiful she decided to have it, even if it cost two or three guineas. Fannie mumbled a few words that sounded strangely like *five* guineas, but she surely could not have heard her aright.

"Do you just want the one?" Dammler asked.

Was it possible a lady ever bought *two* bonnets at one time? Even as he spoke he lifted another delight from Fannie's hands. It was a glazed navy straw, with a daring tilt to the brim, and one blood red rose dripping over the tilt. It looked positively wicked, and totally irresistible. She tried it on. "That's more the thing, don't you think, Fannie?" Dammler asked.

"Very nice. Charming," Fannie said to Prudence. "You like it, mam'selle?"

Prudence was too overcome to agree. She looked like the woman she had recently been longing to be. Sophisticated, a little naughty, almost beautiful.

"I'll take it," she said, without even thinking about the price.

"Wear it," Dammler said. "Throw the old round bonnet in a bag, Fannie—or do you want to bother taking it, Miss Mallow?"

Prudence was not utterly lost to thrift. She decided to keep it, but with a recklessness new to her, she took the chip straw and the navy glazed, and said airily to send the bill to Grosvenor Square.

"That's more like it," Dammler congratulated her. "Where shall we go to show off the new bonnet? Dare we risk the park?"

Prudence was strongly inclined to risk it, but it seemed Dammler had only been joking. They drove through Bond Street—and didn't risk getting out and walking—to show it off. Prudence felt that just perhaps the *male* heads turned to view them took a look at her as well as her escort. The females, she knew, had their eyes turned on Dammler alone.

"This will put your suitors at each others' throats," he quizzed her. "Clarence will have to bar the door."

On their next trip out—the trips were becoming a regular thing—she wore the chip straw. The bill that arrived the next day had been staggering but was worth it. She had the money saved from her parsimonious shopping in the past, so there was no worry of running into debt.

Dammler set his head on one side and declared, "Very chic. People will be saying you're my new flirt if you keep this up." This promising speech was followed by a chuckle to show how well they two understood the unlikelihood of such a thing. Prudence laughed a little harder than he, and waltzed gaily out the door with a heart slightly cracked.

Some subtle changes took place in their relationship as it progressed. Dammler's attitude could not have been described as reverential or anything like it even at the beginning. He admired and respected Miss Mallow's books and brains initially, then he began to like her dry wit, her understatement, her way of not pretending to be impressed with his past (and present) affairs, which he coloured bright, to shock her. When she wore her new bonnets, he thought she was rather sweet looking, in an old-fashioned way. They talked and laughed together for hours. If anyone had told him they were well suited, he would have been shocked.

More than one friend did enquire of Dammler the name of his new friend, and he was at pains to make clear she was a *professional* friend. "The new lady novelist Murray is all excited about," he would explain. Murray had, in fact, taken more interest in her since Dammler had taken her up. "You must have read her marvelous books—very clever. I adore them." Both the books and the author gained more from such speeches as these than from a hundred less exalted persons liking them. They were put on the reserved list at the lending libraries so that several ladies had to purchase a copy for themselves.

One day Dammler met an acquaintance as he came out of Hettie's house. It was a Mr. Seville, a nabob with whom Hettie had become friends. She wasn't overly particular, Dammler noticed. "Oh, Dammler, how have you been?" Seville asked.

"Splendid, what's the news?"

"Little to tell. Say, who's the pretty new chit I see you driving with these days?"

"You mean Miss Mallow, I believe. Not a chit, by the way, but a lady. A professional friend—a novelist. Very clever woman."

"That so? Not your *chère amie* then?"

"Good Lord, no! You must have seen me with Cybele. Well, you were at the opera last night." Dammler spent many afternoons with Miss Mallow, but his evenings were still given over to his customary pursuits.

"Yes, I did see you, but since when do you limit yourself to one?"

"When the *one* is Cybele, who can afford two?"

"No, she didn't come cheap, I'll swear. Lovely gel, though. And this Miss Mallow is a writer you say."

"Yes . . .", Dammler went on to mention her books. "A very superior person. The best female novelist we have today I think."

"I'd like to make her acquaintance some time."

"I'll try to arrange it," he said, and thought to himself, in a pig's eye.

Chapter Six

The day finally came when Prudence received her first invitation to a *ton* party. It was Lady Melvine, eager to attach a new talent and always inviting twice as many people as her rooms would hold to ensure a squeeze, who sent her her first card. Prudence was greatly thrilled, yet there were problems, too. The card had only her name on it; her mama and uncle were not known to Lady Melvine. She was not a little girl, yet to go all alone to her first fine social occasion could not but be intimidating. Suppose she got there and didn't know a soul except the hostess? And even she might very well not recognize her to see her again. She really wondered that her name had been recalled, imagining Dammler to have been instrumental in the invitation. A further difficulty loomed in that both her mother and Uncle Clarence assumed she was going with Dammler. She disliked to disabuse them of the assumption lest they should think she ought to stay home, or worse, that Clarence would start to be happy to escort her.

Dammler, she knew, had begun his play for Drury Lane and was not calling as often as formerly. The day of the ball arrived and though she had sent in an acceptance and had a new gown ready, she was by no means sure she wouldn't develop a migraine when the hour for leaving rolled around. It was three o'clock. Writing proved impossible with such a decision before her and she sat in her study, now not only shelved but with several portraits of literary giants decorating the walls. Uncle Clarence had been busy while she gallivanted. There were Shakespeare and Milton on the east wall, and Aristotle between the windows, all regarding her with enigmatic smiles between closed lips, and all with their hands folded, a pen or a book to indicate their calling. With startling ingenuity, Shakespeare held a candle, which in some obscure manner represented his particular field to be drama. It was at the candle that Prudence was looking when a servant came to the door and announced Dammler. The marquis was not a foot behind her, for he never paid much heed to formality.

"Thank you," he said over his shoulder to Rose and stepped in. "Do I disturb the genius at work? You should keep a dish of apples to throw at inconsiderate scoundrels like myself who barge in uninvited when you are busy. Shall I leave? I can come back later—just tell me when you will be free."

"No, do come in. I am particularly stupid today. I can't get a word down on paper."

"That was exactly my problem, so I came to you."

"What, are you run into difficulties with the play? You said it was going well."

"So it was, till this hussy of a heroine I've saddled myself with started cutting up on me. She is supposed to be a concubine of a Mogul but she has taken the notion into her head she's real, and I can't keep her in line."

"But that is marvelous! When that happens, I know I am on the right foot. Give her her head. She will know what to do better than you."

"But I have a plot of whose exigencies she is unaware, you see." He sat down and threw one leg over the other. As usual, he was dressed in the height of fashion, and Prudence was aware of her own plain bombazine gown. "Her name is Shilla. She was sold to the Mogul at the tender age of eight—they snare 'em young in the East. She is now a virgin of sixteen, having by a series of ingenious ruses saved herself from his advances, but he is quite determined to have her."

"Will they put such a thing on the stage, milord? I hadn't realized it was so risqué a story you were engaged in."

"You should have!" He threw back his head and laughed. "Really, Miss Mallow, the name is Prudence, not *prude*. It is a comedy, but in the best classic tradition, anything of interest will occur offstage. You didn't think I planned to show the seduction?" Prudence was shocked but hid it as best she could, for like any lady of strict upbringing she was anxious to be thought more worldly than she was.

"The thing is," he went on, "she is supposed to pretend she is sick to stave him off a little longer—waiting for God only knows what—*I* have no plan to rescue her. But the silly chit is falling in love with him. Now, what shall I do with her?"

"What is she telling you she wants to do?"

"I blush to confess it, but she plans to run away in the dead of night in the melodramatic manner of popular fiction. She must have been dipping into Mrs. Radcliffe's Gothic novels when my back was turned. She hopes for him to come after her and make her number one wife, I imagine."

"It sounds an excellent plan. The ladies will adore it, whatever the gentlemen may think. They would prefer him to use brute force or some vile scheme to have his way with her, I suppose, but if Shilla has decided she will bolt, bolt it is."

"You don't think it too hackneyed?"

"No, you will wrap it up in your fine silver phrases and the world will take it for a new thing."

"It would never happen in the East," he shook his head dubiously.

"Who will know that except yourself?"

"Only *you*. Can I count on your discretion?"

"You may be sure I won't mention it to a soul."

"I'll let her bolt then. Now, you have helped me. What is your stumbling block? If you have a refractory hero on your hands I will be happy to trim him into line for you."

"No, it's not that. I'm not in the mood, that's all."

He looked around the room, and for the first time spotted Uncle Clarence's pictures. "Good God! No wonder you've run dry with such a gallery to watch you. The work of Mr. Elmtree, no doubt. I recognize the pose. Oh, yes, and a symbol apiece. Who are they?"

"What an ignoramus," she jeered. "You don't recognize Shakespeare? Don't be fooled by the luxuriant head of curls. Uncle did not like him to have a receding hairline."

"It was the candle that fooled me. But I won't ask its significance. And the other fellow?"

"Milton, of course. Looking quite like his old self, but for the inch or so Uncle took off the end of his nose. And the other in the night gown in Aristotle."

"They bear a remarkable resemblance to each other, do they not?"

"How can you say so? Shakespeare has a moustache."

"Still, they could be taken for brothers."

"There is a certain similarity between all my uncle's pictures. You must develop an eye for the fine points. You will come out looking much like them when he gets around to doing you. You can't escape forever you know."

"You do me too much honour, but I must always be distinguished by my black patch."

"Cretin!" she laughed. "You cannot think he would paint anything so different. You will have two round agates like the rest of us."

He smiled, but picked her up on it all the same. "What a little diplomat you are, Miss Mallow. He wouldn't paint anything so *different*. So grotesque you mean. He only paints over a fault.

But you must not regard me in disgust because of it. The patch comes off shortly."

"It is not in the least grotesque. Quite makes you, in fact. I like it excessively."

"You put me at a disadvantage," he smiled oddly.

"What can you mean? You are going to start finding fault with me. That's it."

"No, but I had hoped to ask you to exchange your cap for my patch one of these days. Today, in fact, or tonight rather, for the ball. My patch will have to stay on till a little later."

"Oh, you go to the ball?" she said, relieved. She had hoped he would be there, that she would have at least one friend.

"I thought *we* were going together. But it was presumptuous of me. No doubt you have made other plans."

"No," she corrected hastily, smiling so there was no possibility of offence taken on his side, and clearly none on hers.

"I should have told—asked you sooner. I meant to bring the invitation myself and arrange it, but I have been busy writing and I see Hettie has bungled it. No matter; you don't know her set yet, and I'll have you to myself this once."

Such gallantry as this set her maiden heart aflutter. There was never any flirtation between them. Their friendship was real friendship and no more, but her heart was not stone and it beat faster at such words as these.

"I had planned to go alone; I shall be happy for your escort."

"You are not living up to your reputation, Miss Prudence Mallow. If you went alone, you would be taken up by the most raffish element at the party. Hettie will have a very mixed company. A brace of the royal dukes, rubbing elbows with nabobs and other parvenus."

"Am I so abandoned-looking? I made sure my cap would protect me."

"Ah, but you are not going to wear your cap, are you?" He

looked at the cap she wore as he spoke.

"I had planned to, certainly."

"I wish you would not. But about your question, no, you are not abandoned-looking in the least. It is only that a new lady coming on the scene is discovered first by the blades. Your finer specimen waits for an introduction, but the caper merchants will be all over you."

She laughed this warning away, believing herself too old and much too plain to attract anything in the nature of a rake.

"I'll hold them all at bay, and introduce you to nothing but bishops and vegetarians." He arose. "I am taking up too much of your time with my foolishness. I'll call for you at eight. Till then!" He raised one hand in a salute and was off.

Her writing block was miraculously cured. She wrote away till dinner time, and over the meal she was able to inform her protectors at what hour her 'beau', as Clarence would persist in calling him, was calling for her, without ever having to reveal there was ever any question of his coming.

Clarence would not miss such an event as his niece setting off for a ball at the home of a countess on the arm of a marquis. In fact, he was so thrilled he too rigged himself in formal black satin breeches and white silk hose to see them off.

"A fine looking couple we have together there," he congratulated his sister. "A pity he is maimed, but I will paint it out. I see Prue has taken off her cap. That will give him the clue she is thinking of accepting him. I shall paint her without her cap. It was a mistake for her to set it on. I urged her not to do it, but girls will be girls. Well, Wilma, will it be piquet or Pope Joan? We haven't played Pope Joan for a week."

Miss Mallow was well aware of the attention caused when Dammler rode out in his carriage, but she was not prepared to fall heiress to such a large overflow of it herself. She looked dignified and pretty in the green gown she had had made, but had she looked a dowd she would have attracted attention due to her escort. Any female Dammler bothered to bring to a polite party was fair game for quizzing by the gentlemen, and jealousy from the ladies. He made some initial efforts to protect her from the wilder bucks, but once she began dancing they separated, and she stood up with anyone who asked her, and was thankful to every man who did so. Two or three times Dammler hastened to her side at the conclusion of a dance to whisk her away from her partner.

"You don't want to encourage old Malmfield," he warned Prudence the first time. "A bit of a devil with the ladies."

"He is old enough to be my father."

"His mistress is young enough to be your daughter. Your best protection from him is that you are too old."

"I hope I am not too old at twenty-four for a man in his fifties!" she laughed. "His present friend, I take it, is an infant."

"I thought you were older than that," Dammler said frankly, regarding her face critically, almost as though he didn't believe her.

"Thank you. I wonder you asked me to remove my cap. You had in mind I should switch to a turban, I collect."

"You mean to say you're younger than I am?" he asked, quite clearly shocked at the idea.

"You never told me how old you are."

"Good grief, and I always took you for an older woman—oh, Lord, I'm making a botch of this. I should be feigning astonishment that you're over twenty. But, really, you look so mature—and very pretty. Oh damn—here comes Clarence."

A vision of her uncle was instantly called up by this admonition. "Clarence who?" she asked, looking to see a redfaced gentleman with a head shaped like a pineapple rolling towards them.

"The Duke of Clarence, Miss Mallow, brother to the Prince of Wales. The one who was in the navy. I wonder Prinney isn't here. You want to watch the whole lot of the royal dukes, if there are any more of them lurking about."

"Aha! A new filly tonight, Dammler?" the Duke said gruffly.

55

Dammler made introductions, and when the music began, the Duke grabbed her arm without a word of request and loped to the set forming for a quadrille. He danced badly, conversed in a sort of one-sided shout which required no answer, and afterwards pressed her to take several glasses of wine. Dammler, with a worried frown, ran them to ground in the refreshment parlour.

"Fine looking wench," the Duke congratulated him in a loud voice. "Has she much money?"

"Not a sou," Dammler answered, shaking his head sadly.

"They never have, the lookers. Pity." Clarence wandered off without saying thank you or goodbye.

"He's broken with Mrs. Jordan. Hanging out for a fortune," Dammler explained.

"And I see you are eager to turn him away from me," she joked. "I have a *few* sous, you know."

"He requires more than a few to support his brood. Ten by-blows at the last count, and that's just with Jordan."

"Oh, well, I draw the line positively at five," she answered. "There must be *some* limit to what I will stand still for, even in a royal duke."

Lady Melvine joined them for a moment, and Dammler recounted to her Miss Mallow's experience and her joke. She quickly relayed it to a Mr. Jamieson, and before the night was over, it was circulated as the witticism of the evening, for the sole reason that it gave people something concrete to say about Dammler's latest flirt.

She met other people, too, some of them ladies and gentlemen of the first stare. At dinner one gentleman, who had asked her to dance but been refused because he was too late, joined them. Dammler remembered that the fellow had wanted to meet Prudence, and was sorry they must sit with him, for he was the very kind of person he wished to keep her away from—a man-about-town, too worldly wise for Prudence, but with a surface of respectability that allowed him to be at such

56

parties as this. Dammler introduced them, but added no little detail to encourage conversation. Prudence thought he had been a little abrupt, and turned to speak to the gentleman to cover it up.

"Is your name Seville, like the Spanish city?" she asked.

"Yes, like the anglicized version of Sevilla, but I am not Spanish at all, as you no doubt know to see me." He was slightly dark of skin, but no more so than Dammler, or any sporting gentleman who was regularly out of doors. He was thirtyish, tall and dark-eyed, and not particularly handsome.

"Interesting, the origin of names. My own name, Mallow, is that of a herb, but I daresay it is really corrupted from some other word entirely."

"You would be interested in words, being a writer. Dammler tells me you write very fine novels."

After a brief conversation, Prudence discovered they had not much in common and turned to her other partner. Mr. Seville made quite a different discovery; Miss Mallow was exactly the kind of cultivated lady he required to lend him a little tone. Before they left the dining table, he asked if he might call on her. She agreed, thinking it mere politeness, and that she would never see him again.

There was one person Dammler was very eager for Prudence to meet, and that was Lady Jersey—"Silence." He longed to see Miss Mallow's blue eyes widen when confronted with that veritable torrent of words. Just before he left he managed to bring them together.

"My dear, I am thrilled to meet you," Lady Jersey began. "I saw you being *bruised* on the floor by poor old Billy the Tar. Clarence, you must know. What an ass he is. You should have *saved* her, Dammler. Oh, have you heard? Billy has been jilted by Miss Wyckham. That is why he is here tonight, to see if he can sniff out another fortune. I take it as very mean for Parliament not to raise his allowance, when he has done so much for the nation. I mean, it stands to reason some of his brood must be talented like their mama, doesn't it? Dorothy is such a charm. So very talented.

"Everyone is talking about you, Miss Mallow. So clever—you draw the line at five! You are broad-minded, but then you are a writer. They are always up to anything. I adore writers. I shall send you a voucher to Almack's if you like. Very select do's we have there, but of course you know that. Hettie tells me you are sending your heroine off to the moon in your next book. I shall certainly read it, and I have thought up a good title for you. Hettie tells me you have a deal of trouble with your titles. *The Girl in the Moon* you must call it. Isn't that clever? Like *The Man in the Moon*, you see. How is your play coming on, Dammler?" Dammler knew better than to attempt an answer, and waited for her to tell him how it progressed.

"Very well, I daresay. I will write my memoirs one day, but there is never time for anything. About a harem, isn't it?" He nodded. "So clever of you. I hope you have lots of lovely eunuchs. I know with you writing it there will be plenty of beautiful young ladies. How you will enjoy casting and rehearsals. Dolly Entwhistle swears she will have her hair dyed black and try out. It turned quite red with grief when her husband passed on you must know. Oh, there is the Princess waving to me. She will be wanting to get my approval to give someone a voucher to Almack's. You must come to us one evening, Miss Mallow. We all agree to have you, and I will be happy to send you a ticket. So charmed to make your acquaintance. I will tell everyone how clever you are." She sailed away, smiling and talking still.

Dammler looked expectantly at Miss Mallow. "I have been waiting weeks to hear you deliver a verdict on her."

"Unlike your friend, I am speechless," she replied.

"I would like to quote that *bon mot*, but I shan't. Old Sally wields a big stick. Will you go to Almack's?"

"Perhaps." After her night of glory, a voucher to Almack's, which would have been a cherished object a few months ago, was not important. Although a dull club, it was the pinnacle of Society. Entrance was severely restricted, and to be offered a voucher was a greater honour than Miss Mallow realized.

As they rode home, Dammler said, "Now that I have given Shilla her head, the play is going nicely. I am learning to be industrious from you. I'll stay home and work on it tomorrow."

This was understood, at least by the lady, to mean she would not see him. She commented that she too planned to work.

"How did you enjoy the ball?" he asked as he handed her down from the carriage.

"I enjoyed it very much."

"Aren't you glad I made you put off your cap?"

"Very glad." She yawned and blinked her eyes. Three o'clock was an unnatural hour for them to be still open.

"You're not used to such late hours, eh, Miss Prudence? Take care or your uncle will have to be exerting his skill to paint the circles out from under your eyes next time."

"Concealing a flaw is his major skill. He threatens to do me again without my cap. Good night, Lord Dammler. Thank you."

"The pleasure was mine, Miss Mallow."

He turned and ran down the stairs two at a time and waved from the carriage. It had been a nearly perfect night, yet there was some little sense of disappointment left with Prudence as he rode away. What had she expected, she asked herself. He had behaved with perfect propriety. Yes, that was it. He would not have done so had he thought of her as more than a friend. Just so would he wave to a male he had been in company with. "What foolish notions are you getting in your head, Miss Prudence?" she asked herself. Remember your name.

Chapter Seven

Clarence's niece rose to a new height in her uncle's favour when it was revealed she had stood up for a quadrille with the Duke of Clarence. She was urged to have a fire in her study if she liked. She hoped he would remember his generosity when autumn rolled around. There was really no need of it in May. She needed all of his good will to jolly him into accepting a new series of activities Dammler undertook on her behalf. They had wasted enough time driving around the countryside, Dammler decreed. It was time they discovered the city itself. It was no childish trip to see the horses at Astley's Circus or Madame Tussaud's Wax Museum he had in mind, but the very depths and dregs of it. They went one day for a drive through the worst slums of the east side, and on another to the middle-class suburbs of such places as Hans Town. Dammler, she noticed, made notes as if he were doing some serious research. Prudence naturally enquired what purpose he had in mind, thinking it was some literary endeavour.

"It's time I was taking my seat in the House," he explained. "I left the country when I was still quite young, and don't know it as I ought. There's no point listening to some long-winded politician read a list of statistics. You have to *see* it for your-self." Prudence could not but wonder why *she* was included in his trips, but having no desire to be excluded, she remained silent. He did mention occasionally that a knowledge of these things would be helpful in her writing. She knew a view of the facade of a row of slums was not sufficient to enable her to write about the destitute, nor had she any desire to broaden her field of writing into sociology; but it was always pleasant to be with Dammler, and so she agreed with him.

He had always some new place to take her. Places she had known to exist only by name, and had never thought to see in person. They went one day with baskets of fruit to Bedlam to see the inmates. Prudence was shocked and horrified to see the conditions under which the insane lived.

"I can't believe people live like that," she said when they left.

"Just as well they're insane. If they weren't when they entered, they soon would be. And virtually nothing is done to cure them."

"Well—but I don't suppose they could be *cured*."

"They don't *all* have damaged brains. Haven't you known people who go off on a crazy spell for a time, but come back to sense later? I have. If it's someone from our class, he is tended privately and as often as not recovers. If it happens to a poor person, he's tossed into Bedlam and left forever."

"Can nothing be done about it?"

"Not by you or me alone. Politics is the answer. A problem of that magnitude can only be handled by society collec-tively—politics, in other words. Newgate is worse, but I shan't take you *there*."

"Do *you* plan to go?"

"Yes, I go once in a while."

"Why do you subject yourself to that?"

"I have been around the world. Now I want to see how other Englishmen live. We writers have to see these things."

"Yes." She had lived in London for four years, she estimated, and had seen nothing but her uncle's friends and a few shopkeepers. She felt herself richer for this spreading of her horizons, even if she never wrote about it.

"I'm going to see the Jane Shores tomorrow," he said that same day. "Would you like to come? It won't be pleasant either, but it is something a lady writer might be interested in."

"Where are the Jane Shores?" she asked, imagining them to be some part of the docks.

"In a Magdalen House. I am talking about the Jane Shores who are in the process of being reformed. Did you think I intended to take you to meet Harriet Wilson?" Prudence only smiled, not knowing Harriet Wilson was the city's leading courtesan.

"There's one beyond Goodman's Field. I've arranged a visit to see how it's set up. Don't wear one of Fannie's bonnets; it would look out of place. Wear that old round bonnet you saved."

Prudence felt a home for fallen women was more to her interest than Bedlam and agreed with enthusiasm to go to see them. This particular house, Dammler told her, catered especially to young unwed mothers. "Try not to show your shock if every second one is *enceinte*," he warned her.

It was a fine looking building outside, red brick, solid and respectable, but inside it was austere. The young girls were about to go to a church service when Dammler and Prudence arrived and they too went to the chapel. Row upon row of girls came in, wearing greyish-brown stuff gowns, broad bibs, and flat straw hats with blue ribbons tied under the chin. Prudence was struck by their youth—most of them could not be more than fifteen or sixteen—and their innocent faces. She had expected to see bold, hardened women, but these girls walked with heads bent, eyes down, and their hands folded. They looked more like novitiate nuns than prostitutes.

The sermon was an embarrassment to listen to—upbraiding these children for their "sins of the flesh," as though they were experienced harlots. Prudence longed to stand up and tell the minister to stop. Glancing at her escort, she saw Dammler's hands clenched into fists, and his lips clamped in a rigid line. Their tour of the house was much more complete than yesterday's visit to Bedlam. They saw the dormitories where the girls slept, their narrow white cots lined up like loaves of bread at a baker's. They saw the girls at work, cleaning the building, cooking, sewing, scrubbing, and also saw them sit down to eat at an uncovered table, each with a bowl and a spoon, and a half a glass of blue milk. Dammler even asked for a bowl of the stew they ate. He took one bite and had difficulty in swallowing it.

After the tour they went to the manager's office for tea, which was served on fine china from a silver pot, at noticeable odds with the girls' meal. Dammler asked a number of questions, a great many having to do with money. Prudence was surprised at his practical streak. She had assumed his interest, like hers, would be in the girls' personal histories.

"How many girls do you accommodate here?" he asked.

"A hundred at a time," Dr. Mulroney answered. He was the minister who had given the sermon, also the chief executive of the place.

"And how long do they stay on the average?"

"About six months, depending, of course, on how advanced their condition is when they come in."

"You mean how soon they give birth to the child?" Dammler clarified.

Mulroney looked at Prudence as though to intimate such matters were not for a lady's ears. Dammler ignored this.

"Yes, just so. We used to have about two hundred girls a year through here—less when I came. Only one hundred and fifty prior to my taking over. I raised it to two hundred, and am aiming for two hundred and twenty-five this year."

"Are you on a commission?" Dammler asked. Prudence wasn't sure whether he was serious, or if it was a setdown.

"Certainly not! I do not undertake work of this sort for any monetary consideration." Mulroney answered, offended.

"What is done to prepare them to leave? If they come out of here without having learned any useful skill, they'll end up back on the streets."

"You have been at the church service, milord. They attend service three times a day, and extra Bible readings on Sunday, and for punishment if they misbehave. We hope to raise their morals to awaken them to the dangers of immortal hell if they persist in their abandoned behaviour."

"You'd do better to raise their ability to make an honest living."

"Each girl is given a Bible upon leaving."

"Yes, she can hawk that, but what does she do the next night, when the shilling is gone?"

Dr. Mulroney lifted his eyebrows at this. Prudence felt Dammler was going a little far, but knew there was no hope of curbing him. "They are not released without having a place to go. They are usually placed in a home as a domestic servant."

"Are the homes carefully selected?"

"Selected—what do you mean? I don't understand the import of your question, your grace."

"It must have occurred to you gentlemen of a sort will come *here* looking for domestics."

"They are well-to-do families we place the girls with."

"Money is beside the point; the girls will see little or nothing of it. What of the *morals*?"

"You can't expect me to ask a gentleman such a question!" Again Mulroney looked at Prudence with an uncomfortable expression.

"No, asking them would certainly be pointless. Character references could be obtained though."

"What—ask character references for the hiring of a servant who is costing the city twenty-five pounds a year to keep? Upon my word, I never heard of such a thing. We are lucky to

64

be rid of these—girls—to whomever will take them off our hands."

"Surely you don't consider yourself an employment agency! Your job is to restore these girls to a decent life. Their success depends on where you place them."

"Oh, as to that, if they are put in too strict a home, they only run off in a month. The fact is, milord, they are no good, nine-tenths of them, or they wouldn't be here."

"They are desperate, ten-tenths of them, or they wouldn't stay in this hell hole," Dammler said and arose abruptly. "Come along, Miss Mallow. I've seen what I wanted to see."

Mulroney accompanied them to the door, trying to pour oil on the ruffled waters, with a very poor success.

Dammler was highly incensed with the visit, and to get him started talking, Prudence asked him what he thought of Mulroney.

"The man is a jackass, and totally unfit for the position he fills. To be speaking of those poor unfortunate little girls—God, did you notice how *young* they are—as though they were hardened street-walkers. You need a man with compassion and understanding for such a post as that. Someone who is concerned for their welfare, who cares about them, and not a dammed accountant. Hastening them through faster and cheaper is all he thinks of, so it will look well on his record. He's pushing to become a bishop, no doubt. Teaching them nothing, and shoving them into any house that will take them. I heard a gentleman—a rake, a pervert of the worst sort—say the other day he was going there to pick up a new maid and he said it with a very meaningful leer, which is why I asked that particular question about selection. Picture one of those pathetic little girls being placed into the hands of a man like—well, never mind his name, but I shall see he doesn't get one."

"How can you do that?"

"By getting rid of Mulroney."

"*You* can't get rid of him, Dammler. You are only a visitor."

"Of course I can. Lucas is in charge of it. I'll speak to him. He's a good man, but so busy he doesn't know what's going on. Let Mulroney go back to preaching his fire and brimstone sermons. He is good enough at that. However, I learned what I wanted to know."

"What, about Mulroney? Is that why you went, to see what he's like?"

"Mulroney? No, I had no idea he was in charge. I know now what charity I am interested in. The insane are pitiful, and half the prisoners in the jails are no more guilty than you and I, but I know I'm lazy and insensitive, and if I'm not deeply interested in a project, I won't follow it through."

"No, you're not lazy or insensitive."

"Yes I am. But I'm interested in those girls—no comments, please. Aren't they enough to tear your heart out? Babies, and already producing more babies. I didn't think to ask what is done with the new babies. That's the proper time to catch them, before they go, or more probably are led, astray."

"I thought you'd burst during the sermon. I nearly did myself."

"Show—all show. That, I fancy, was put on to impress us. As though ringing a peal over them could help. You'd think they'd purposely set out to ruin themselves. More likely ruined by some son of . . ." He stopped suddenly. "I'm getting carried away. But it makes my blood boil. Such a criminal waste of human life and potential. We think ourselves advanced here in England. I didn't see much worse than what I saw today in the most backward countries of the East. Yes, this is a project I can become enthusiastic about."

Two days later Dammler asked Prudence what she did with the earnings from her books. She hadn't seen him in the two intervening days. "I buy hats with them," she replied. She was wearing her navy glazed bonnet with the red rose.

"No, seriously, what do you do?"

The question seemed irrelevant; it did not seem impertinent, which it was. "Well, I pay my bills. What else should I do? And save when I can. I should like to go on a little holiday with Mama. We haven't been anywhere since we came to London, except home to Kent once to visit friends for two weeks."

Dammler said nothing for a moment, but he seemed much struck by her answer. "You're not telling me you *have* to write for the money?" he asked.

"To keep body and soul together you mean?" she asked in a mock tragic voice. "No, we managed to scrimp along before I sold anything, but I confess the extra income has been a great comfort to us. We hadn't much left when Papa died, for the estate, you remember I told you, was entailed."

"But your uncle—you seem to live in a very good style with Mr. Elmtree."

"He has been marvelously kind to us. We should have ended up in some horrid rented lodgings but for him."

"Why didn't you tell me?"

"I told you ages ago. The first time we went out, or shortly after. What, did you think I should be constantly bemoaning my cruel fate? We are very lucky. We want for nothing with my uncle."

"I thought—I just assumed you had money. Stupid of me, of course. I never think of things like that. And you let me take you to Fannie's and bludgeon you into buying two ferociously expensive hats! Dammit, Prudence, you should have told me."

"They weren't so very expensive." He hadn't noticed he used her first name. It had taken a fit of anger to make him do it.

"You can't fool me about Fannie's prices. I am an old customer. Now, I am going to make a grossly indecent suggestion. Prepare your reticule to beat me about the head and shoulders. I want to pay for them."

"Don't be absurd."

"I'm not. Like a cloth-head I dragged you to the most expensive shop in town without considering—*I* have had the pleasure of them, and I want to pay."

"I would really prefer not to discuss this any further," Prudence said in a tight voice.

He dropped the matter immediately, but felt the greatest, blindest fool in the kingdom. And a boor for having mentioned it at all. Poor people were always sensitive about money.

"Anyway, why did you ask the question?" Prudence said, to break the uncomfortable silence.

"I thought you might want to join with me in my project."

"What project?"

"My home for unwed mothers. I told you that was what I had decided to do with my earnings."

"Ah, I thought perhaps *your* earnings too went to Fannie, as you are so familiar with her prices."

"No, I pay for my pleasures out of my own pocket."

"If your *earnings* aren't out of your own pocket, what is?"

"A nobleman, my dear Miss Mallow, does not work for gain. *Infra-dig.* We lords are too toplofty to engage in common labour for a wage. The taint of having earned money by the sweat of our brows can only be removed by donating it to charity. No, we are allowed to keep anything we wring out of our tenants by starving them in a hovel, but honestly earned money must be got rid of immediately."

"How ridiculous you make it sound."

"The truth often has a ridiculous ring to it. Well, I don't have to tell *you*. It's what your books are all about, isn't it?"

"I never thought so."

"You may not have known you thought it, but you wrote it. There was your Lady Allyson de Burlington, remember? The illiterate who kept the house full of books to hide the truth; and your Sidney Greenham—half greenhead and half pig I assume—who would never allow pork to be served at his table as he had his humble beginnings in a sausage factory. Hiding the truth at every turn, because it is unpalatable. In any case, I am not allowed to keep my hard-earned money, and I mean to give it to my favourite people—ruined females."

He made a joke of it, but Prudence knew he was serious about helping the girls, and was proud of him. "Where will you set up your Magdalen House, here or in Hampshire?"

"I have pretty well decided on Hampshire, not too far from the Abbey, so I can keep an eye on it personally. I refer to the running of it—the finances and employees and most of all, where the girls are placed when they leave."

"Which brings to mind old Mulroney. Had you any success with that man—Lucas was it?—who was to get rid of him?"

"He's on his way out. We have managed to get him a rung up on the ecclesiastical ladder in a nice rich town, where he can't do much harm. He'll never dare to scare the wits out of a bunch of fat squires with his sermons and Bible readings. Let him herd as many people as he can to swell his church attendance and give him a good record. He'll concentrate his accounting skills on getting some stained glass windows and an organ for St. Martin's and have something to show for his efforts."

"You mentioned your home would be in Hampshire so you could keep an eye on it. Do you plan to return to Longbourne Abbey soon then?"

"Yes, after the Season."

"Oh." She tried to keep the disappointment out of her voice.

"I'll be in London a good deal, of course. I plan to take my seat in the House."

"This sounds like a new Lord Dammler about to emerge. What of the poet?"

"He'll have to keep his nose to the grindstone to support his women. I refer to my charity girls," he explained with a lift of the eyebrow.

"My, with all your women of one sort or another, you'll be busy."

"I'll still find time for you," he said with a smile. "You'll have to come to visit me at Longbourne Abbey some time."

Comforted with this promise, she accepted the inevitable.

Chapter Eight

Mr. Seville had called on Miss Mallow two days after the ball and found her out with Dammler. When he returned two days later, he found her at home and asked her to drive out in the park with him. It was not the same exciting adventure as going out with Dammler, but it was better than sitting home with Clarence, and her escort exerted himself to be entertaining. He was not a serious man; Prudence had his measure within a quarter of an hour. He was a man of the world. His conversation was of balls and the *ton*, of horses and fashion. He didn't seem to think a lady capable of discussing more weighty matters, or perhaps he was incapable of it himself, but he was amusing.

"Have you heard the latest *on dit* about Clarence and the Princess?" he asked, leaning closer to her.

How very odd that she should know him to be referring to the Duke of Clarence, and either of two other princesses not of English royalty.

"Lieven or Esterhazy?" she asked, with a feeling of being very much in on things.

"Lieven," he replied, not finding her answer remarkable, "was being shown to her carriage at the Pavilion t'other night by Billie, and what must the old slice do but pop in on top of her and try to make love to her."

"He is a courageous man," she answered, laughing at the picture called up by this incongruous couple.

"Aye, *false* courage—in his cups certainly. But Lieven is awake on all suits. She told him the Congress of Vienna was giving Hanover to Prussia, and England going along with it for a wedge of Westphalia. You may imagine his reaction—a confirmed Hanoverian. Lovemaking was forgotten. 'God damn! Does my brother know this?' says he. She assured him he did not, and he turned the carriage about to go back and tell Prinney the news. Famous it was. Prinney twigs him about it ten times a day. All a hum, of course."

"I hear Miss Wyckham has given him his *congé*," she remarked, remembering Dammler's gossip.

"She'd snap him up fast enough, but the Cabinet won't hear of it. It'll be some dull old Austrian princess for him, poor soul. But he's had the best of Jordan, so he don't need *my* pity."

"Rather pity Mrs. Jordan."

"Clarence will provide, never fear. He'll come down heavy. Thinks the world of his family—as any man should, of course," he added hastily. "The least he can do. I have no opinion of men who seduce and abandon, as the saying goes."

Prudence found the tone of this conversation displeasing and attempted to divert their discussion. "Lord Dammler is writing a new play," she said as an opener.

"You are pretty thick with Dammler, I believe?"

"We are friends. Both being writers you know . . ."

"Professional thing, is it? Just a common interest."

"A little more than that perhaps. We are friends."

"He ain't your lover?"

The bluntness of this question shocked her even more than its content. "Mr. Seville! Indeed he is not. The notion is absurd."

"No offence, Miss Mallow. No offence in the world. But you ain't seven years old, and his affairs are no secret. He's not a bit too good for you. Not in the least."

She was silent a while after this interchange. "Now I've gone and hurt your feelings, and that I didn't mean to do. I would never have suspected it myself, but it's only what's being said. Wouldn't have asked you out if I'd thought it for a minute. Just wanted to be sure. A man can't be too careful of such details."

Poor Prudence, reared in a retired village and unused to the ways of high life, took his concern to be for being seen with a lightskirt, when he was only worried that he was stealing Dammler's property. The talk went better after that, and when he deposited her at her door she had concluded that these *ton* people talked a little warm, but in their hearts they were strict moralists.

She was flattered to receive next day a bouquet from Seville, and not ill-pleased at the note with it requesting her company at the opera two nights hence. She had been there twice with her uncle, but not in a box with the upper members of Society. Her taste of high living had whetted her appetite, and she sent off a note accepting his offer. So this is all there is to it, she thought as she had her hair dressed and the gold gown worn to Mr. Wordsworth's dinner party slipped over her head. One had only to meet a few of the right people and she was on her way to balls and the opera and drives in the park. She read both the Society column and the Court column to be up on the trivia that passed for conversation with Mr. Seville.

Before she left Uncle Clarence, decked out in garments suitable to escort her, though he was in fact staying home to play piquet with her mama, handed her a black leather box. "I want you to wear my dear late wife's necklace," he said.

She accepted with thanks and put it on—a small set of diamonds no bigger than grains of rice, but real diamonds, he assured her. "Ah, there is nothing like diamonds to make a lady sparkle," he said, standing back to admire the chips. "Dammler will be sorry he lost you." There had been a two-day interval since his last visit.

"We are still friends, Uncle. That's all we ever were."

"Ho, you are the slyest girl in town," he ran on. "You think to make him jealous by parading yourself before him with another man. I hope it may turn the trick for you. Seville is well enough, but no title at all. He is just plain Mr. Seville, even if he has the name of a city. It was not named after *him*, you may be sure. Well, well, you look very nice. You are in looks tonight with Ann's diamonds."

"You will have to paint me thus, Uncle," she teased in a merry mood.

Her amazement was great when he did not concur. "There is no painting a diamond," he acknowledged sadly. "A *pearl* now comes out nicely with a dab of white for a highlight, but a diamond cannot be painted. None of the old masters had the knack of it. I've tried all their tricks, but a bit of red or blue or green doesn't begin to do it. *I* can't do it, and in short it can't be done. It only comes out looking like a sapphire or a garnet. Well, water is the same. Water can't be painted either. Turner thinks to hide his deficiency by always putting what he is painting upside down in the lake as a reflection, but he fools no one. We are all on to him. I'll just step along to the saloon and meet Mr. Seville. We want him to know you have a family to protect you. A young lady on her own might be taken up as fair game. I shall just mention Sir Alfred and Lord Dammler to let him know we are not quite nobody." He mentioned them so often that Seville could not but conclude they were indeed acquainted, intimately.

Seville had a box at the opera by the season. It held six seats, but only the two of them were in the party. Prudence had supposed she was only one of his guests; she was surprised to find herself quite alone with him, and worried a little at it; but they were not stared at or scorned, so she thought it must be all right. Several persons acknowledged Seville, and a few nodded and smiled to her.

At intermission she espied Dammler across the auditorium with a large party, one member of which occupied his whole attention. She was a lovely vision in white chiffon and diamonds, with a riot of some unnatural but lovely shade of curls on her head. She wore a very low-cut gown, and she never took her eyes from Dammler for a fraction of a second. They seemed indecently engrossed in each other, unaware that half the crowd was ogling them. Prudence knew from Dammler's conversation that he had a very active social life quite apart from his afternoons with her, but other than Hettie's ball she had not actually seen him engaged in it. She found it a distressing sight, but such an interesting one that she could not draw her eyes away from his box.

"I see your friend Dammler is here tonight," Seville remarked, noticing her staring at him.

"Yes. Who is the lady with him, do you know?"

"Some Phyrne or other," he answered, raising his glass to examine her more closely with a smile of appreciation. Cybele, of course, but it wouldn't do to let on to Miss Mallow he was interested in the girl.

"Not a maidenhair fern, I take it," Prudence said, wondering by what adulteration the girl had achieved such a stunning hue to her hair.

She was at a loss to understand Mr. Seville's bark of laughter, and why he should say, "That's a good one, Miss Mallow. A very good one indeed. You are an Original!" No more did she think it worth repeating when a whole bevy of callers came to their box, everyone of them gentlemen. But they all agreed it was a gem of the first water.

This sudden influx into their box attracted a certain degree of attention to it. Lady Melvine, one of Dammler's group, noticed

74

and called it to his attention, but by the time he was looking at them, Prudence's attention was directed at their guests. They all seemed extremely lively and good-natured. Two of them were being called milord, but she didn't catch the name, which Uncle Clarence would like to know when she got home.

"Can that possibly be Miss Mallow with the Nabob?" Hettie asked Dammler, levelling her glasses at them. "Yes, certainly it is. How well she looks when she smiles. Only see the collection of old roués with them—Seville should know better. For that matter, Miss Mallow should know better than to be here with him alone. Well, well, she's flying high."

"There's Barrymore. Dash it, Seville shouldn't present her to *him*," Dammler said, frowning.

"Why don't you drop in on them before intermission is over?"

"To lend the party an air of respectability? It would have rather the opposite effect, I'm afraid."

"How true. To rush from one light o' love to another. Too titillating. The cats would love it. I daresay Cybele wouldn't."

"Miss Mallow is not in the same category as . . ." he slid an eye to his fair charmer, who pouted at him, demanding attention.

"You'd better slip her word when you next see her. Not the thing."

"I will," he said, with a last scowl across the hall, then he turned to his female.

Prudence did some soul-searching that night alone in her bed. After spending several hours in Mr. Seville's jolly company, she immediately forgot him and considered another. She was becoming fonder of Dammler than was wise. For romance he would naturally favour Incomparables of the sort she had glimpsed this evening. It was a byword that every beauty in town was after him. How absurd for her to entertain the idea he felt anything but friendship for herself. He never had, and she had known it from the start. The wonder was that he found anything in her to attract him as a friend. Well, you prudent girl you, she said to herself, time to put all that prudence to use and get yourself in line. Don't sit waiting at your desk for him to come. If your *friend* drops by, you will be happy to see him. Too happy, but never mind. You won't show it, and it will never occur to *him*. He half thinks you are a man.

The next afternoon, Miss Mallow was honoured once again with a call from Dammler. It was raining, and she assumed they would not be going out. "Hard at it, I see," he said, seeing she was at her desk, with her hair tousled and her fingers stained with ink. "With all your skylarking you must make use of any odd minute the suitors leave you. You make me realize how hard *I* should be working."

"I am not entirely given over to dissipation," she said, striking an expression that did not go a jot beyond the limits of platonic affection.

"You are on the pathway to hell, milady," he jeered, waggling a finger at her and smiling more widely than she allowed herself to. "We will have to be rechristening you if you keep up this pace. Hobnobbing with nabobs—too many *obs* in there—your finely tuned ear won't like it."

"That's all right. We may say what we daren't write."

"And sing what is too foolish to say."

"How is Shilla doing? Leading you a merry chase, I hope."

He sat in a casual fashion just short of sprawling which she felt instinctively he would not do if he wished to appear at his best with a lady in whom he was interested. "We were wrong to let her bolt on us. The hoyden has fallen in with a caravan of unholy men, and how Wills is to get a dozen camels on stage is beyond me."

"The excitement occurs off-stage, does it not?"

"Damme, *something* must happen on stage. She's become so brazen there's not a move she makes that can be seen in polite company I can't have the Mogul wringing his hands and cursing in frustration for two hours. I may have to bring her back to the harem and start all over. But I'll put her into a novel later and let her go her length. I am too fond of her to give her up."

"Cutting into my territory, I see. Take care or I'll put Clarence into a play or a poem."

"Good idea, but you are diverting me from my errand. I am here to ring a peal over you, Miss Imprudence. No my girl, widening your big blue eyes at me won't save you from a scold. You know well enough you were the talk of the opera last night, with every rake and rattle in town drooling over you."

"How nonsensical you are," she said, happy to know he had seen her moment of glory.

"And as to making *me* a laughing stock with that curst viper's tongue of yours. My Phyrne was furious; she is justly proud of her locks. You may be sure she heard of your wit."

"There was no wit in it. I only said . . ."

"I know well enough what you said, and what you *meant*."

"I only meant she coloured her hair."

He sat up and stared at her. "Oh, no, you didn't," he contradicted flatly. "You *said* it very nicely, I grant you, but you called her a Phyrne. We all admit tacitly to these things, but we don't run around broadcasting them, calling names."

"Dammler, *tell* me so that I shan't blunder again. Is her name not Fern?"

"Prudence Mallow," he said, shaking his head, "you are either the biggest greenhead in town or the best actress."

"What did I say?"

He hunched his shoulders, and threw up his hands in the gesture of helplessness so characteristic of him. "Where do I begin?" he asked himself. "Phyrne, sweet idiot, is not a *name* like Mary or Joan—it is a title, like Princess or Prostitute. Rather more like the latter, if you follow me."

Prudence was stunned, but she had resolved some time ago

to match her new acquaintances in sophistication, and she tried gamely to rally. Still her shock was quite evident to him. "I see," she said.

"You are disappointed in me."

"No," she answered quickly. "Why should I be?"

"Why indeed, I never led you to believe I was a saint. Oh, Prudence, why did I ever meet you? You are giving me back my conscience. I was well rid of it. I haven't felt such a reprobate since the first time I got drunk and Mama cried for two hours."

"*I* am not crying," she laughed at his boyish despair, and a little, too, at his using her first name without realizing it. "I am just a little surprised that you would be seen in such a public way with a—one of those women."

"Well, everyone does. Half the females there last night were prostitutes. I hold them to be every bit as respectable as a married woman who commits adultery—more so, in fact. They're not hypocrites. *They* have not promised to love, honour and obey anyone's desires but their own. Why should it add to a woman's virtue or reputation to deceive her husband with a lover? Surely that compounds the trespass. No, no, I won't allow anyone to tell me I must restrict my amours to married ladies."

"You ought to restrict yourself to an appearance at least of respectability."

"Where did you get the bizarre idea my Phyrne is not respectable? Top of the trees. She has none but the most elevated of lovers, and only one at a time. Unlike the married ladies, who require at least two, and preferably three or four. It is better to consort with a Phyrne than with a married lady. There is no question of it in my mind. Tell me you disagree. On what logical grounds can you possibly refute me?"

"I don't. There is much in what you say, but that is not to say that consorting with either one is good. You set up a home for ruined girls on one hand, and ruin them on the other. There is no logic in that."

"Prudence, we're talking about two *very* different species. Those little girls—young, ignorant without the sense to know what they're getting into . . . My Phyrne—the mistresses of gentlemen, are in a different class entirely. They knowingly go into this sort of a life because they don't want to work. They prefer a life of leisure and luxury, they have a beautiful body to buy it with, and they sell it. It is a business transaction."

"Oh, don't try to tell me it is a good thing to keep a mistress."

"I didn't say it was good."

"You said it was *better* to have a mistress than to take another man's wife. Surely better is a degree of good. Take it a step further, you lover of logic, and you must agree *best* would be to take no lovers at all. A chaste married lady or a spinster is better than either a Phyrne or an adulteress, surely."

"Not to me she isn't," he replied unequivocally. "Oh, all right, if you're talking theology or religion or some damned thing. I thought we were talking about real life, and not philosophy. In actual practice, it is *less immoral*—does that satisfy you—to keep an unmarried mistress than to go poaching on your friends' private property."

"Yes, I'll accept that partial victory, before you convince me I'm a scoundrel for not selling my own old ramshackle body to help my uncle pay the bills."

"Oh, I don't go quite that far, Prudence," he replied, throwing his head back in uncontrolled laughter. "And to think, I came here to read you a lecture! How did I end up giving you the notion you should take to the streets? We—Lady Melvine and myself—do not approve of your consorting with the Nabob."

"Is Mr. Seville so rich then?"

"Full of juice. An uncle from the East India Company died and left him a million, literally."

"*I* have no objection to the fact. Do you disapprove of money *per se?*"

"No, I am excessively fond of it, but . . . ." She looked, waiting. "Your Mr. Seville—ah—likes the ladies. Of a certain sort."

"The sort who use the title Phyrne?"

"Yes, those certainly, and those who use the title Duchess or Baroness even better. It is generally considered he is looking for a title, to ease his own way into the peerage. He cannot mean to *marry* you; he is well into negotiations with Baroness Mc-Fay, and for entertainment he prefers the muslin company. Why do I feel like a child molester telling you these things?"

"I don't know, but you misjudge him. He is not like that at all. He has very strict notions of propriety." She toyed with the idea of telling him Seville had feared she was Dammler's lightskirt, but decided against it.

"Seville! He has no more notion of propriety than a jack-rabbit."

"How can you say so? He's your friend. You introduced him to me."

"Yes, and that is why I am worried. I never thought you'd catch his eye. You aren't his type. I wonder if the old fool has decided to take up with the literary society. Might think it would lend him a vicarious air of intellect. God knows he could use it. He is *very proper* in his dealings with you?"

"Of course. Oh, he gossips about the *ton*, but you may be sure he does not take me for any loose piece of baggage."

"There—I've depraved you. For Miss Mallow to be speaking of herself in terms of loose baggage! Well, he is up to something, but apparently it isn't what we feared. I don't like the company he introduces to you, however. I wish you would see less of him, or at least not go about with him without some other company. Some respectable married couple, or some such thing."

"I am not really fond of him. I don't expect I'll be seeing much of him—we have little in common."

"If the old Benedict gets out of hand, call on me, and I'll come galloping *ventre à terre* on my white steed to rescue you. Promise me, Prudence."

"Promise." She found herself aping his shrug, and felt foolish.

"What a lot of bother you women are. Whoever would have thought I would end up playing Dutch uncle to a little greenhead of a spinster." Prudence gave a mental wince at this, but concealed it quite well. At least he had come to realize she was not a man.

"Now I have shocked you with my heedless tongue again." She realized she had not concealed it as well as she thought. "You are only twenty-four, and not a spinster any more, I suppose, since I foolishly induced you to take off your caps. Do me a favour, Miss Mallow, put them back on and start pretending you are forty or so again, so I can stop worrying about you."

"Don't worry about me. I have a family to protect me. Worry about Shilla and her Mogul. When is she due to tread the boards?"

"Not this season. It isn't half done." He arose. "I'm off, Miss Mallow. May I call you tomorrow? I'd like you to look over Shilla for me and see what you think of her. There is no one whose opinion I respect more."

"I should be happy to," she answered with real pride. Her womanhood had been laid low by his thoughtless words, but how fine to have a poet of Dammler's stature pay her such a compliment.

Chapter Nine

The next morning Prudence received two notes, one of them accompanied by a spray of violets, which she had happened to mention liking, from Mr. Seville. He requested her company for a drive that afternoon. Just as well I cannot go with him, she thought, remembering her appointment with Dammler. The other envelope bore a crest, and when she opened it, it was a scrawl of two lines from Dammler. "Miss Mallow: I can't bring Shilla to you this p.m. after all. She has other plans, and we daren't buck her. See you soon. Be Prudent about S. Dammler."

She felt a letdown of no small magnitude, then read the note again for any hidden compliment or insult. It was facetious—but he was always joking. Some business had come up that detained him. There was no one whose opinion he valued more than hers. He would come soon. "Be Prudent about S." Seville, of course. Strange he hadn't said what detained him. Had it been herself breaking the appointment, she would have felt a complete explanation necessary. And no explanation occurred to her either which could be important enough to break a date with Dammler. From suspicion she slid easily into jealousy, and she was soon possessed of the idea that Shilla should more accurately read Phyrne. That would account for his not giving her the reason. No doubt a gentleman friend would have understood at a glance what he meant and accepted it. Her eye fell on Mr. Seville's spray of violets. It never occurred to Dammler to send her a flower. Why should she sit home while he was out enjoying himself? She picked up her pen and accepted Mr. Seville's offer. A drive in the park was quite unexceptionable, and she was *not* doing it to spite Dammler. Not the highest stickler could take exception to it, and she hoped she met Dammler head-on with his Phyrne.

Mr. Seville called at three o'clock, carrying a large bouquet of flowers. Her innate sense of taste and comedy laughed at this second shower of blooms in one day, but she accepted the roses with a good grace. "I see you wear my violets next to your heart," Mr. Seville teased, his brown eyes dancing.

"Be Prudent about S" darted into her head. "Oh, but a spray of flowers is generally worn on the jacket, you know, and the left side is less in the way than the right."

"They are lucky violets," he said with a sigh as they went out the door. He let his eye rest long on them, or possibly the bosom beneath them.

"Shall we go, Mr. Seville?"

"Yes, there is no privacy here, in your uncle's house." Clarence, informed that Mr. Seville was a nabob, had been fawning.

"Uncle likes to meet my friends," she explained.

"Yes, that is natural. He seemed not to dislike me," he said, in an excess of understatement.

"He likes you very much," Prudence assured him.

"Still, it must be difficult for you, under his roof, with no privacy to meet your friends at your own ease. You, who move in literary circles, must often feel the want of a place of your own."

"I sometimes feel I could work better if I had a place of my own, but Mama and I are in rather straitened circumstances since my father died."

"It seems a pity, if money is all that stands in your way."

"But money is important, especially when you haven't much of it."

"A lady like you shouldn't have to worry about money. You should be dressed in fine gowns and jewels." Prudence looked down at her very best blue outfit and thought the remark uncalled for. "Real diamonds, I mean, not those little chips you wore the other evening."

"I am not likely ever to have diamonds. I manage to get along without them."

"Did you never have a desire to dress yourself in silk and jewels?"

"Occasionally," she admitted, a vision of Phyrne in her chiffon and diamonds passing through her head.

"You'd take the shine out of them all, Miss Mallow. Countenance—you have countenance. It is your being a literary woman, and so dashed clever. Able to drop a droll word into any conversation and make it sparkle. Better than diamonds. Diamonds can be bought, but wit is inherited, like a title."

"Or money," she laughed in agreement, thinking he was not so bad after all.

"Yes, by Jove, like money. Well, there's more than one way of getting the blunt, what?"

"Yes, one can earn it by hard work."

"An attractive lady wouldn't have to work too hard to earn it. A man of means would be happy to share his with her." Mr. Seville reached out and grabbed her gloved hand. She hardly knew what to think, but she quickly decided to be prudent about S; and recovering her hand, she edged a little closer to her own side of the carriage.

"What a smart phaeton that is," she said, pointing out the window to where a high-perch phaeton was being tooled past by a very dashing lady. Prudence looked closely to see if she recognized her, but she was having no luck in spotting Dammler and his friend.

"Would you like to have such a rig?"

"Yes, indeed, I'm sure anyone would, though I shouldn't know how to handle it so well as that lady does."

"Her nags are nothing out of the ordinary. I have a pair of matched bays, high stepping fillies—smashing they'd look harnessed to a bang-up little phaeton or dormeuse."

"That sounds very nice. Why don't you get such a carriage for them, Mr. Seville?"

"I will, by Jove," he answered promptly. "Anything you like."

"Only if *you* like, I meant," she countered in a little confusion.

"I think we like pretty well the same things," he said, smiling with satisfaction at his progress.

"Shall we get out and walk a little?" Prudence suggested as they were entering the park, and the carriage suddenly seemed too small.

The Nabob was all complaisance with her every whim. He was gratified to see several eyes turn to watch them. Miss Mallow was becoming known in Society, more through her association with Dammler than through her writings, and Seville was not the only gentleman who was beginning to look in her way. He lacked distinction and knew it. He wanted a mistress who would set him above the common herd, and thought he had hit on a capital idea in having Miss Mallow fill the position. She was not a common lightskirt but a rising star in the literary firmament. As a writer, and such a worldly creature, she would not be aghast at the idea of union out of wedlock, though he fancied he would be her first. The uncle and mother might be a bit of a nuisance, but it was clear as a pikestaff she couldn't stand the uncle, silly old fool, and the mother could be bought off. Well, the girl had as well as said he'd have to come down heavy. Diamonds and a rigout for the horses were only the beginning of it. He'd have to set her up in style, and let her entertain her friends. Not Dammler, though. He'd draw the line at that.

Before he took her home, he invited her to a play the next evening, but she was wary of going into public with him again alone and claimed a previous appointment. He took this in good part as coyness, and felt the time had come to begin distributing his largesse.

The next morning yet another arrangement of flowers arrived, and concealed among the stems was a blue velvet box. Miss Mallow was struck dumb, upon opening it, to see a fine set of matched diamonds sparkling at her. She lifted them out and beheld a necklace. Her first thought was that it was a mistake. The box had somehow been put in with her flowers by accident. She ran to her mother, asking if she should not go back to the flower stall and return them. Clarence had to be called in on such a momentous decision as this to give the male viewpoint.

"What would a set of diamonds be doing at the flower stall?" he asked reasonably.

"They must have been meant to go in some other arrangement of flowers," Prudence suggested. "They are likely a wedding gift or some such thing. Will you come with me, Uncle? I dislike to go into the streets carrying anything so valuable, and we cannot send a footboy on such an errand."

"That must certainly be the explanation," her mother agreed, fingering the stones lovingly.

While they talked, Prudence opened the little card that accompanied the flowers, and her eyes widened. Mr. Seville had laboured long over a suitably discreet message to send along with his bribe and come up with the words, "Pray accept this small necklace as a token of my esteem, and an indication of my intentions." She handed the card to her mother. "It is no mistake," she said. "Mr. Seville sent the necklace."

Mrs. Mallow had time to read half the message before

Clarence had the card out of her hands. "The fellow is a rascal!" he charged angrily.

Mrs. Mallow retrieved the card and read the rest of it. "It is no such a thing, Clarence," she answered. "See, he speaks of his 'intentions.' It is an engagement gift."

"We are not engaged," Prudence said, horrified. "Why, I scarcely know the man. It is ludicrous to speak of an engagement on such short acquaintance."

Clarence was again examining the card. "You're right, Wilma. 'An indication of my intentions,' he says. He means to have Prudence."

"I don't mean to have him!" Prudence replied.

"Not have him? Nonsense," Clarence declared. "He is a fine fellow. Knows everyone. Ho, what a joke it is, us thinking he meant it as an insult. He would not dare to insult Prue. He knows pretty well I am connected with Sir Alfred and Lord Dammler. Well, this will teach Dammler to shilly-shally around with his courting. Snapped right up under his nose. Serve him right."

"Uncle, I do not mean to accept Mr. Seville or the necklace."

He was deaf to her protests. "Wait till Mrs. Hering hears this. Her feather is dry. I'll take her picture round to her myself this afternoon and tell her what my niece is up to. Real diamonds," he said, opening the blue velvet box. "It is a pity I couldn't paint them. I must do a portrait of Mr. Seville. Some little symbol of Seville being named after him can be slipped in. A corner of the old Gothic cathedral perhaps, or the Alcazar. I daresay I have a picture of it somewhere about the house. I might do him in costume as a grandee—Lawrence is always dressing his models up in costumes of some sort or other. I don't like to satisfy him to copy his trick. No, I will do Mr. Seville in modern dress, with the Alcazar in the background, and a nice piece of gold in his hand. Gold paints up nicely."

"I will return the necklace," Prudence said.

Her mother regarded her in uncertainty. "It seems a pity,

Prue. Can you not care for him? He seems a very nice gentlemanly sort of a man, so lively and good-natured. You are getting on . . ."

"No, Mama. I will not be bought."

Clarence, holding the necklace to the light muttered to himself. "There's yellow and orange in them. I never tried yellow and orange to do a diamond. And blue and green and purple. It's a rainbow is what it is. A prism. There is the secret of doing a diamond! Come to the studio, Prue. We will paint you in the diamond necklace, with Seville in the background—the city I mean."

"I'm giving them back," Prudence said, snatching them from his fingers.

"Think what you are about, Prue," he warned. "You'll never get another offer like this. The man is rich as Croesus. You'll never have to write another word. Burning out your eyes with that scribbling . . . You will be dashing off to balls and coronations and Spain."

"He is a mere commoner, Uncle," Prudence reminded him, to mitigate the blow of her refusal.

"I daresay he is a marquis or some such thing—whatever sort of a handle they use in Spain, if the truth were known. They wouldn't have named a city after him for nothing. On your honeymoon you ought to nip over to Seville and look into it. He has a Spanish look about him, now I come to think of it. The eyes are dark, and the face quite swarthy."

"There will be no honeymoon."

"And even if he ain't," Clarence rattled on, deaf to any drum but his own, "he can buy up a title. They are for sale if the pockets are plump enough. Everyone knows that. He might start off with a simple 'Sir' and work his way up to a lordship."

"I am returning this necklace immediately," Prudence said, and left with it in her hand.

Her mother rushed after her. "He will be calling today, after this. Wait and hear what he has to say, Prue. Think about it a little. Be wise, my dear. You were always so prudent before."

"I am being prudent now, Mama. I do not wish to marry Mr. Seville. Indeed I do not. I don't care for him in the least—in that way I mean."

"My dear, you must not hope Dammler means to have you. He is quite above your touch. He thinks of you only as a friend. It is clear from his manner."

Prudence looked aghast. She had not thought she was so transparent as that. "I think of him as a friend, too."

"A little more than that on *your* side, I think," her mother said gently. "I do not mean to force you. Such a thought would be quite repellent to me. You are all grown up now. You must do as you think best, but don't be rash, my dear. Think of it a bit. It would be very fine to be independent—not to have to worry about the future. We are very comfortable *now*, but Clarence will not live forever. Sooner or later his son George will be taking over, and he will not want to be saddled with us."

Prudence did not change her mind, but she agreed to think about it before acting. Every word her mama said was true. They faced a bleak future of comparative poverty. It could be removed by her accepting an offer from a gentleman she did not actively dislike—one who could and would give her everything she wanted, and more importantly, would let her give Mama what she wanted. But the price was too high. She could not consider it independence to be bound leg and wing to Mr. Seville. She did not admit to any other reason for refusing him in her ruminations.

In the afternoon he called, and to remove him from Uncle Clarence's congratulations, she grabbed her wrap and went out with him.

"You had my little gift?" he asked, as soon as the coach bowled away from the house.

She had it right in her reticule to return. "I cannot accept it, Mr. Seville."

"It is a mere bauble. When the matter is settled to our mutual satisfaction, I will give you a real necklace. I am not a skint, Miss Mallow. You will not find me clutch-fisted."

"I know I would not. You are very generous, Mr. Seville, but I cannot feel we would suit."

"I know I am not clever like you, but you would be able to smarten me up if you felt it worth your while. We would be happy together. A nice apartment—house if you wish—either in the city or country. All would be to your orders."

She repined, but she did not weaken a whit. "No, really. I think of you only as a friend. I had not thought of any closer association."

"If it's money that worries you . . ."

"No, it's not that. I know you are wealthy—generous."

"A cash settlement beforehand. Everything in order right and tight."

"No, please, it sounds so very mercenary. I do not wish to haggle over it. I am flattered—honoured, but I cannot accept your offer."

"Is it your family that worries you?"

"Oh, no, they thought it a very good thing. They were not in the least averse. It is quite my own decision."

This easy capitulation of the family bothered him. "I felt your uncle would not mind, but mothers sometimes throw a rub in the way."

"Mama is anxious to see me settled. She worries about the future."

"I would take good care of you."

"I cannot feel it would answer." She took the velvet box from her reticule and handed it to him.

"Keep it," he said magnanimously. "I don't despair yet. I will have at you again, Miss Mallow. I don't give up easily."

"No, it would be improper in me to keep it when I don't mean to marry you," she said, and shoved it to him.

Looking with downcast eyes at the box, she did not see his eyes start at the dread word 'marry.' He could scarcely believe his ears. No mention had been made of marriage. What had she got into her head—to think he would marry a little nobody without a connection in the world? He feared Miss Mallow was making sport of him. But when she did finally look up, the innocent lustre of her eyes disabused him of that idea. He felt weak, and very fortunate indeed to have escaped so easily from his unprecedented predicament. Only think if she had accepted! He took the box without a word and stuck it into his pocket.

"I expect you would like to go home?" he said a moment later.

She nodded. "I'm sorry," she said, before she descended from the coach. "I hope we may continue friends?"

"You should be more careful in your friends, Miss Mallow," he ventured to warn her. Why, the chit was not up to snuff at all. Leading him on—no one with the least bronze would have mistaken his intentions. Her, gallivanting with Dammler and the wildest bucks in town. Who would have thought her still wet behind the ears?

"I am careful, Mr. Seville," she answered calmly. "Goodbye."

He didn't bother going with her to the door, though he descended and handed her down from the carriage. He brushed his brow when she was gone, and thanked a merciful providence at his close escape.

Prudence longed to go to her room, to lie down and worry whether she had done the right thing, but no such luxury was allowed her. Clarence and her mother had to be told the whole story, and berate her with words and glances respectively for her folly. To escape them, she said that now she had chosen a career over marriage, she must get to work, and went to her study.

"I hope your daughter knows what she is about," Clarence said to his sister. She was not his niece today, turning off a Nabob.

Prudence closed the door behind her and sighed. What a

dear refuge her study was! Shakespeare, Milton and Aristotle chided her silently from matching frames with their subtle smiles, but she ignored them and pulled out her manuscript.

It was a quarter of an hour before she was sufficiently calmed to work, and immediately she was interrupted. But it was a happy interruption. Dammler tapped on the door and stepped in, having dispensed with even the appearance of formality by telling Rose she needn't bother announcing him.

"Hello, Miss Mallow," he said smiling cheerily. "Shilla and I bring our humblest apologies for missing our appointment, but we have an excellent excuse."

An excuse she felt was the right word for it, for the *reason* she still held to be Phyrne. "But before we get on with the good news, I will convey the bad," he said, assuming an aspect of severity that was at odds with his jaunty manner. "It has come to my burning ears that you did not heed my warning. You've been gallivanting with the Nabob again. Don't deny it!" His finger waved at her in a playful manner. "Riding in the park with him yesterday and hanging on his arm in the most vulgar manner. I mean to be firm with you and Shilla in future. Give you an inch and you take a mile. You girls are all alike. Next thing he will be offering you a *carte blanche*. There I go depraving you again. I daresay you think a *carte blanche* is no more than a little white card."

"You overestimate the depths of my innocence."

"Say height rather."

"Say what you like, you do Mr. Seville an injustice."

"I wonder. He is trotting after you pretty hard, and his intentions you know . . ."

"Don't judge everyone by yourself, Lord Dammler," she shot back angrily.

"Oh, ho, I've touched a nerve! This bower of bliss in which you create, I suppose was provided by the Nabob." He looked around at the vases of flowers, two of which had been put in her study. "When a man starts sending too many flowers it is time to beware. He is up to no good. Next it will be a diamond bracelet, and from there—it is well known no lady can resist diamonds—it is the love nest, and a garish turnout for the park with matched horses. Are you sure you're not hiding a diamond bracelet up your sleeve?" He grabbed her hand, and looked at her wrist, his eyes narrowed in playful suspicion.

"I see you know the procedure well, milord."

"I am familiar with the moves of the game, shall we say?"

"By all means, let us talk at cross purposes. We wouldn't want to sink into too clear an understanding. But you look in the wrong place for diamonds. It was a necklace offered, not a bracelet. Mr. Seville meant to treat me more lavishly than you treat your flirts."

"You are joking, of course. He wouldn't dare . . ."

"His daring knows no bounds. He dared to offer me his hand in marriage."

"Prudence!" It was a shout of abundant but undefined passion. He looked to see if she joked, but read a contradiction on her face. "You hussy! You didn't bring the Nabob round your little ink-stained thumb! Good God, how Hettie will stare. So you are an engaged woman, and truly rid of the opprobrious title of Spinster."

"I do not find it opprobrious, nor am I so anxious to relinquish it as you seem to think I should be."

"Well, you surely never *rejected* him?"

"I have not accepted his flattering offer."

"Prudence, you fool! It would be the making of you."

"Et tu, *Brute*."

"I lag Clarence in my sentiments, I collect? But he's right, you know. It would be no poor thing for you to be set up so richly for life. I can't credit it yet that it was *marriage* he had in his mind. Quite sure you understood the nature of the offer?"

"There is no doubt in my mind, and I find it unflattering that you choose to doubt it."

"You needn't rip up at me. It is only what anyone would think."

"How can you think I should have accepted, if he is so ramshackle?"

"Oh, well, if it was marriage he meant all along, that's different."

"You called him a jackrabbit!"

"A very rich jackrabbit. I should have known when he treated you so *very properly* it wasn't a left-handed marriage he had in mind. What a feather in your cap. Are you holding out for a title then, or why did you refuse?"

"I don't love him."

"Oh *love*, what is that? Everyone prattles on about it, but I don't think there is any such thing in the whole world. I never met a man yet who was in love for two days running with the same woman, nor any woman who did much better."

"Strange talk for the Romancer of the Western World."

"Romance, that is something quite different. Fiction, in fact, of the sort you and I in our different ways deal in. It's easy to be in love with a paper character. I adore Shilla—have been in love with her for a week—a new record for me. We can make them into our idealized version of a mate, with the dull and annoying bits left out. We have them at our beck and call, and if we choose to let them run amok a little, we know with the stroke of a pen we can bring them to their senses. What has that to do with love?"

"We don't see eye to eye on the matter. I conceive of love as something quite different."

"What?"

"Caring for someone else more than you care for yourself."

"But that's not love—it's a maternal instinct or devotion or some such thing—another form of self-love really. Our children are parts of ourselves. I'm talking about mature love between a man and a woman."

"So am I."

"Then you're talking nonsense, and I expect you know it very well, or you wouldn't be blushing like a schoolgirl. Never mind, I never did understand women. But I know this, when they talk of love they only want you to take them out to show off to their friends, or to buy them some new jewels or an annuity. They're after something."

"If a woman is interested in a man at all, she takes what is offered by him. If those are the terms in which you couch your offers, then you can't blame a woman for accepting them. For myself, I shouldn't have thought it had anything to do with *love*."

"You're either a fool or a very wise woman, I don't know which. In any case, your Seville seems to share my opinion on the matter. It *was* diamonds he offered, was it not?"

"Yes, and they were not accepted. I didn't mistake them for love."

"You can't know so much of the matter as you let on. You never have loved anyone but that jackanapes of a Springer, and you didn't love him enough to accept him in the long run. I'll not be bludgeoned into taking lessons in love from a sp—ahem, *fellow writer*."

"It wasn't intended for a lesson, but an opinion. A solicited opinion, I might add."

"My apologies, ma'am. You have put me firmly in the wrong, as usual. Now shall we proceed to the good news? You put it out of my mind with your conquest of the Nabob. It is a conquest of a different sort for you. A literary conquest."

"What, have you been to Murray?" She thought a new edition might be required as her books were selling better now.

"No, Murray came to me yesterday, with Dr. Ashington in

tow. It is why I had to break our date."

"Ashington of the *Blackwood Magazine*? Does he mean to do a piece on your cantos?"

"Yes, but that could not be good news for *you*. He is doing your books, too. He's devoting an issue to new young writers. You are to represent the novelist, myself the poet, Sheridan the dramatist though he's not *young* any longer, but he's the best living dramatist they could come up with. Hunt and Hazlitt are running in tandem for the essayist. We're in good company."

"*Me*? But he cannot have heard of me. I am not a serious writer."

"No more am I, but they mean to make us serious by lionizing us. They'll be reading philosophy and politics and religion into our stuff till we won't know what we meant when we scribbled it down. I daresay you'll turn out to be a cynic when he's through with you, and here you take yourself for a romantic."

"And you a moralist, when you think you're a rake."

"He wants an introduction. That's why I am come, to see when it would be convenient to bring him. You have no objection, I take it?"

"I'm thrilled out of my wits. Does he mean to come here?"

"Yes, if you don't mind. I'll bring him along and introduce him, then shab off to let him pick your brain in peace. Don't let him talk to Clarence, he'll discover your trick and you'll be revealed for the nasty little baggage you really are."

"I can't believe it—Dr. Ashington. What is he like? Is he old?"

"Yes, a dull old stick—too old for you to charm. You'd better count on your considerable powers of conversation, and not your big blue eyes. He has no use for Scott, by the by, and thinks the world of Coleridge and Southey, if you want to butter him up a bit. I can't see how he reconciles two such different sorts as that last pair, but then if he likes your stuff and mine, he must have catholic tastes. Or more likely Blackwood has urged us on him, to get Ashington out of the past. A classicist by inclination. Just think, Miss Mallow, we'll be bound up for eternity in one magazine together. Does it appall you? I see you are underwhelmed at the idea, but you'll have Hunt and Hazlitt to spell you from me. They are both sensible fellows, and Sherry can provide the comic relief. I don't mean that in any disparaging way; I wish I had half his comic genius."

"I can't believe it's true—Dr. Ashington—the *Blackwood Magazine*—it's like a dream come true."

"You had dreams of such conquests, had you? And when you wake up, you can consider having wangled an offer of marriage from the Nabob. No mean feat that. I still can't believe it. It surprised me more than Ashington's article. Quite took the wind out of my sails, in fact. Will tomorrow be all right to bring the Doctor along?"

"Yes, any time he likes."

"Don't be so available. Impress him with your heavy calendar. We'll make it the day after tomorrow."

"No, tomorrow! He might change his mind."

"You underestimate yourself, but if you like, it will be tomorrow. I'll drop by Hettie and tell her the news."

"She'll never believe I am to be interviewed by Ashington."

"Ninnyhammer, she'll never have heard of him. I meant the news about your other victory."

"Oh, no, I do not mean to tell it around, since I refused him. It would not be at all the thing. I wish you would not tell anyone."

"Just let me tell Hettie. She won't tell anyone if I ask her not to."

"But she prattles—you said so yourself."

"She can be as discreet as a diplomat when she likes. Why, the stories she could tell about *me* if she wanted to . . . but she will love to hear it."

"Very well, but let her know it is a secret."

"Yes, Miss Prudence. Well now, you've turned him down, so we shan't have any excuse to come serenading you." Prudence naturally looked mystified at this, and he explained. "Did I not tell you what I did last night? Oakhurst is being married soon, you know, and I was telling him of the custom in Spanish countries of serenading the bride-to-be. The groom hires a group of minstrels and they serenade her under her window. She comes out and throws some flowers at them. We decided to get a band of us together and go serenading Miss Philmont. Had a merry time. Philmonts had us in after for a drink. Oakhurst and some of the others went on to a club, but I went home to work on Shilla. I'm hard at it revising, and didn't bring her along for you to see today."

There seemed a certain pointedness in his telling her of his innocent evening's entertainment, conveyed more by his conscious manner than by the words themselves. "When shall I see her?" she asked.

"I can drop her off with Ashington tomorrow, and perhaps you will be kind enough to scan her over the next day or so. Let me know if she's too risqué. She is developing a streak of propriety, I'm happy to say. I believe she's given up Mrs. Radcliffe's stuff and taken to your novels. She is beginning to talk up marriage to me."

"To the Mogul?"

"No, she's got clean away from him and is reforming one of the unholy men in that caravan I told you about. She's after me to make him a prince in disguise or something. She'll be wanting a cottage with a picket fence next. I absolutely draw the line at a batch of chickens. Don't you agree?"

"It doesn't seem to go with a prince."

"King George would disagree with you. Made everyone of his princes take a turn cultivating a garden and rearing fowl, but of course they are commoners in disguise as princes. And with that piece of treason I shall leave you." He laughed and left the room.

Hettie was amused but incredulous at her nephew's tale that Miss Mallow had brought Seville up to scratch. "No, it cannot be possible. I have heard in a dozen different quarters that he is chasing the Barren Baroness—McFay you know, that doughty old Scots lady who is a baroness in her own right; the title dates from Queen Anne. She has two husbands in the grave already, and never a babe in the basket, which is why they call her the Barren Baroness, of course. With such a wife in his eye, it is easy to understand Seville's wanting a love o' life, but he surely never offered *marriage* to Miss Mallow."

"Oh, no, an offer in form she tells me. I trust the lady knows the difference."

"Is it possible you trust too much in her worldliness?"

"She tells me I overestimate her innocence."

"Does she indeed? Well, she sounds brassy enough, if *that* is the sort of conversation she carries on. I hadn't thought her so bold."

"No, no, she is not bold; just bright and clever. Quite a greenhead, actually."

"Is she a greenhead, or is she not? You can't have it both ways, Dammler."

"She is a strange combination of innocence and worldliness. But in any case she says old Seville always treats her with respect and propriety, which he wouldn't have done if he'd had in mind to set her up as his mistress. She hardly seems the mistress type, you must confess."

Lady Melvine sat digesting the matter. "I recall her little joke at the opera—your Maidenhair Phyme, you recall. Their conversation cannot have been entirely innocent if that is the sort of thing they were discussing. And there was her drawing the line at *five* bastards at my ball, too. I personally should draw the line much higher, and I do not consider myself naive."

"That was joking, Hettie. She is always joking—it is her liveliness that leads her on to say things a little out of line sometimes. Well, I do the same myself."

"And as *you*, of course, are as innocent as a new-born lamb—*voilà*! It is settled. She is as innocent as Lord Dammler—a minx, in other words. And would have rubbed along very well with Seville. The wonder of it is that she turned him off, if it was *marriage* he had in mind."

"She doesn't love him."

"If *that* is her only reason, she has reached a pitch of innocence almost beyond pleasing."

"It pleases her," he answered, and from the satisfied look on his face, Hettie thought it seemed to please Dammler pretty well, too.

Chapter Ten

Having whistled Mr. Seville's fortune down the wind was in part forgiven when Lord Dammler returned, and when Prudence gave the news that she was to be interviewed for a famous magazine, she was once again Clarence's niece, riding high in his favour.

"So we are to read about you in the *Morning Observer?*" he said, smiling fatuously.

"No, not a newspaper, Uncle, a literary magazine. It is called *Blackwood's.*"

"*The Observer* is sure to pick it up and give it a column or two. They won't pass up a story like that. Your name in the papers—next we will be seeing cartoons of you in the shop windows, like Dammler."

"It is not that sort of a magazine—not a *popular* one, you know, but very prestigious in literature. Other writers and educated people read it, but it will not lead to cartoons in shop windows."

"You are always putting yourself down, Prue," he chided her. "You let on Mr. Seville and Dammler were only friends, too, but they see fit to send you diamonds and speak of their intentions."

"Only Mr. Seville did so."

"Dammler will take the hint and get cracking. I hope you *told* him."

"Yes, I mentioned it."

"That was *prudent*," he joked across the table at Wilma, who smiled her agreement.

"Well, well, what a merry chase you are leading us all. How should we dress to meet Dr. Ashington for the interview tomorrow?"

The word "we" struck her ear a cruel blow. "I think I shall put back on my cap. Dammler says he is an older man—conventional, I believe."

"There will be no need for us to do more than welcome him," Wilma told her brother. She realized Prudence's discomfort at her uncle's intrusions. "We will say how do you do, and then leave them alone for the interview. It is literature they will be discussing. We know nothing about it."

"*I* have been reading a good deal lately, and I will pick up a copy of the *Backwoods Review*, too. Odd name they have chosen for it."

Mrs. Mallow rolled up her eyes, and Prudence swallowed her mirth. "Your ordinary clothes will be fine. The occasion doesn't call for formal wear."

"I shall get a new suit of formal wear made up all the same. We are doing a deal of running about lately, and my satin breeches are getting tight. So you mean to put on a cap to impress the Doctor, do you? Sly puss, I don't know why you ever took it off. It is more appealing than anything else on a young lady, with pretty ribbons to give some colour, of course. I like it excessively."

Prudence saw she could do no wrong, with or without her cap—or her gown for that matter. She was doing exactly right so long as she brought fame and glory to the house. She wouldn't have been surprised to see a rug laid on the study floor for her. It had at present a thread-bare scatter mat, but with the shelves and the oil paintings this antique was looking out of place.

The next afternoon Dammler came, but Ashington was not with him. Clarence, Mrs. and Miss Mallow were surprised when he entered the house alone. "Ashington is at a meeting and will meet us here shortly. I came on ahead to await him and make you introduced. I see you have put on your cap to impress him with your age and seriousness," he teased Prudence.

"Aye, she looks well in her cap I am always telling her so," Clarence assured Dammler.

"And here *I* have been leading her astray and advising her to remove it," Dammler replied.

"Yes, I frequently tell her she looks too old in her cap," Clarence said, with no awareness of his own contradiction.

"How does the painting go on, Mr. Elmtree?" Dammler asked, his motive not so innocent as his polite face would suggest.

"I have invented a new way of painting diamonds," he answered wisely. "It is not done as Rubens and the old fellows thought at all—making it transparent like glass, with just a little dab of white or blue. And it isn't done like a garnet or emerald either. It is a prism—that's how it is done. All colours of the rainbow. I discovered it while holding my niece's diamond necklace to the light. You heard about Seville offering for her?" Dammler nodded. "A great box of diamonds he sent her, big as eggs, but she didn't care for him, being a foreigner, you know. There are queer knots in all foreigners, say what you will. He was pretty cut up, poor fellow, but he'll get over it."

"You were actually speaking to him about it yourself?" Dammler asked. This was proof positive that Hettie was wrong. He was relieved to hear it.

"We talked it over a dozen times," Clarence told him misleadingly, with no intention of lying, but from a constitutional inability to distinguish fact from what he wanted to think. "He was always hinting around that he wanted to marry her."

"The acquaintance surely was not a *long* one?" Dammler asked. Damme, Prue hadn't known the fellow more than a couple of weeks.

"No, not long, but he was here all the time. Quite lived in her pocket."

Some recollection of having seen Prue most days of the first week of her acquaintance with Seville caused Dammler to view Clarence's words with suspicion, but the full extent of the inaccuracy of Elmtree's story did not occur to him. He thought Seville must have spoken to Clarence once about the offer.

"That must be Dr. Ashington at the door now," Prudence said with infinite relief.

He came in and was introduced, and when Dammler took his leave, Clarence and Mrs. Mallow left the room with him. Ashington was an intellectual-looking gentleman, almost an aesthete. Tall and cadaverously thin, with hollow cheeks, he had eyes that were bright and penetrating. His hair was brown, just turning grey. Prudence placed his age at forty or so. When they were alone, he said, "I did not expect to be meeting a *young* lady. Your books led me to expect a woman of more advanced years—well, let us say *mature*. I do not mean to imply they are old hat."

"I am twenty-four," Prudence said.

"You have accomplished a great deal for your age. Three books to your credit, and another in the works Lord Dammler tells me."

"Yes, I am at work on another."

"Good, good. Regular output, that is what it takes to establish a reputation. Oh, I don't mean churning them out like sausages as Scott does, but a book a year or so to keep yourself in tune, to flex your muscles and learn your craft. I see an improvement, a logical growth in your books."

"Thank you," Prudence said, wondering what he meant. "I was surprised to hear you mean to write an article about my books. I did not look for such recognition from such a famous magazine."

This artless praise went down well. "I confess I was not acquainted with your work till Dammler called it to my attention. There are so many novel writers you know, and in general one does not look to *female* writers for any purpose more serious than amusement."

As Prudence's sole interest had been to amuse, she was lost for a reply. She said "Thank you," again, and as she said it, she pondered his other comment. *Dammler* had called her to his attention. She owed this interview to him.

They talked for some time about her work. She was questioned closely as to her *theme*, when she had never thought an inch beyond plot and characters, and decided between them that her theme was no less than the whole fabric of upper-class English society, and what held it together. Next she was interrogated as to her views on Miss Wollstonecraft and feminism.

"I am scarcely familiar with her works at all," she confessed. "I have glanced at her *Vindication of the Rights of Women*, but do not consider myself a feminist."

"You do not advocate higher education for women then?"

"Good gracious, no! I only attended a seminary for five years myself. If the occasional few women want it, and it does not interfere with their lives—their duties—but in general, you know, I cannot think Latin and Greek of much interest to women." She also thought it quite a waste of time for *men* to spend years learning a couple of dead languages, but wisely kept it to herself. The Doctor had a nasty habit of throwing a Latin phrase at her, and there was no point in antagonizing him.

He smiled benignly at her answers. "I notice you do not concern yourself with the broader problems of modern society—war, politics, economics, the general revolutionary trend of Western society."

"My canvas is small. I have often heard it said that a writer should stick to what she knows, and my life has been sheltered. But I write for women—women are interested in the home, society in the limited sense of friends and neighbours, and in the case of *young* ladies, finding a husband. That is my subject. I leave the other fields to men."

She spoke the simple truth. When he talked of "revolutionary trends" and "liberal minds" she scarcely knew what he meant. She just wrote about people—their minds and hearts as Shakespeare and other writers before her had done. Her answers pleased him. It allowed him to admire her achievement without fearing he had a feminist and an intellectual on his hands. He disliked feminists intensely. He was dyed deep in conventionality, felt threatened by women who challenged men's preserves, and was all for keeping them in the home. As a literary man, he liked a woman who read a little, and it was admissible in his scheme of things for a few women to write stories for the others to read. If they wrote it well, so much the better. He was willing to admit Miss Mallow wrote in a lively style. She had no pretensions, and he liked her. He liked that she lived with her family as a decent Christian, that she wore a cap, was modest and deferential to himself. He also liked her blue eyes and her trim figure, but that was quite a different matter. He stayed two hours, took tea with her, and left with a high opinion of Miss Mallow.

So high indeed that he returned the next afternoon with a few more questions, and an invitation to her to take tea with himself and his mama on Sunday. She accepted gladly, and never once suspected that beneath Ashington's stiff facade a heart not quite old was beating a little faster.

On Saturday morning Dammler dropped in to see how the

interview had gone, and at last to bring Shilla, whom he had forgotten when he came to introduce Ashington.

"How did it go with the Doctor?" he asked.

"Quite well, I think," she answered.

Clarence and her mother were also present on this occasion.

"Ho, she is always putting herself down," Clarence took it up. "He stayed forever. We had to add hot water to the tea twice, and finally drive him from the house."

"Indeed!" Dammler answered, looking at her quizzingly.

"And was back the next day to go at it again," Clarence added. "He is taking her to meet his mother tomorrow. *He* will be popping the question too before a week is out." This good-natured hint was a warning to Dammler of the sort of competition he had.

"Another suitor, Miss Mallow?" Dammler asked with a twinkle.

"No! That is, he did drop by the next day to clear up a few points..."

"And about the tea?"

"Well, his mama is an invalid, you know, and cannot get about much."

"No, I didn't know. Strange he did not ask *me* to take tea with her."

"He is sweet on Prue; there is no doubt of that. None in the world," Clarence declared in a conclusive manner.

"Lord Dammler is not interested in all that, Clarence," Wilma cautioned her brother.

"Indeed, I am interested," Dammler countered playfully. "I came to see how the meeting went on, and am delighted it went so well. He can be a crusty old devil if he's rubbed the wrong way."

"Prudence is well named. She rubbed him the right way," Elmtree asserted.

Dammler's eyes just met Prudence's at this remark, with a

shared flicker of amusement. "I also came to see if you would take a look at this first act of my play," he said, and arose to give it to Prudence.

"Why don't you go into the study?" Clarence suggested. Prudence was surprised at her great fortune in being offered a release, till she realized her uncle meant to accompany them and show off his shelves and paintings.

"We are getting this little cubbyhole fixed up for my niece," he said. "A private spot for her to work in. There are shelves there for her books, and a desk."

"Very nice. Handy," Dammler said, then as more praise seemed to be expected he added, "It's good to have a desk to write at."

"And a few fellow writers to keep her company," Clarence pointed out. "My work."

"I recognized the style. I have praised those portraits to your niece on a former occasion. Very nice."

"There is a lamp there you see, and a brace of candles, too, in case she wants to work nights."

"Yes, she is ready for anything, rain or shine." He looked over his head to see the lucky girl also had a roof over her head to pamper her. "You have no excuse to be slacking off, Miss Mallow, with such a room as this."

"She never slacks off. She is always scribbling, when she is not out skylarking."

"I never waste a minute," Prudence said. "Well, I am wasting one now, am I not? Show me your manuscript, Dammler."

Clarence finally took the hint and turned to leave, stopping at the door to admire the sight of his niece with a famous lord and poet, looking at home to a peg in her snug little study. For a wild minute he wanted to paint the whole scene for posterity—study, books, desk, poet, niece and all, but the moment passed, and he went instead to call on Sir Alfred and relate all the vicarious busy-ness of his day.

"Have a chair, Dammler," Prudence offered. "We are denied

no luxury here in my study. Walls, floor, windows, everything."

"Your success goes to your uncle's head," he answered, sitting down and throwing one leg over the other.

"The day he sees me as a cartoon in a window, I fully expect a set of matched diamonds. A pity he couldn't paint them."

"You're not so up on *his* work as he is on yours. You must know the trick is a prism."

"So it is, it slipped my mind."

"Now come and tell me how you seduced the Doctor. I want to hear all about it."

"Why, the secret is simple. You have only to nod and smile and say 'yes' to all his ideas, and he will turn you into a font of wisdom. Only fancy, Dammler, I have a *theme*, and didn't guess it till he told me."

"I think the cap helped, and the blue eyes, too. And your skill in rubbing the right way, of course. Which *is* the right way to rub the Doctor, Prudence? I seemed to get his hackles up right from the start."

"Why, gently, of course, as though he were a cat."

A smile, not quite pleasant, flickered over Dammler's face and was gone in a minute. "What is your theme, in case he should ask me about it?"

"Ah, well, nodding and saying 'yes' is one thing, but explaining is something else. It has to do with the whole fibre of life, you see. Heavy stuff; no trite banalities for me. Wordsworth may content himself to say let nature be your teacher, and Dammler to urge a life of action on us all, but when you get into *my* tomes, you must dig deeper to discover the eternal verities."

"He's a humbug, and so are you, Prudence Mallow. Common sense, there's your great theme. You take pretensions of all sorts and hold them up to ridicule."

"Truth to tell, he spouted Latin at me half the time. Very likely that was what he meant, only I was too ignorant to realize it."

"But he liked you—he will write well of your works?"

"I believe so. He said I had accomplished a good deal for one so young. I seem young to him."

"You have accomplished a good deal."

"I understand I am indebted to you for the article. No, don't deny it; he let the cat out of the bag, and I mean to thank you."

"He asked my opinion of the best new novelist the past couple of years, and I told him. Odd he hadn't come across your work himself, as he is an expert in the field. I hold that a serious lapse on his part."

"He does not look to a mere *female* writer for any seriousness of purpose. He admitted as much."

"Who else does he think will explain their wily minds to us? No man begins to grasp their complexity. Scott, though I admire his work, hasn't a notion of a woman, and Wordsworth deludes himself with writing about his sister."

"Mmm, and Dammler's opinion is best left unstated in polite company."

"You don't mean to forgive me for telling the truth, do you? But I spoke of only one aspect of the female mind, if you recall."

"Yes, the grasping aspect. I'm glad you don't mistake your conception of love as having anything to do with the *heart*."

"What a sharp tongue she has. I'll bet Ashington was not treated to it. No sir, rubbed gently. You save your jibes for helpless victims like myself."

"You recall the name is Prudence."

"We are never allowed to forget it. Here, Spinster, see how the other half lives." He tossed his manuscript on the desk.

She opened it and scanned the first page. "Gracious—my poor innocent eyes! You debase me entirely, Dammler, with such language. 'Sensuous body,' 'voluptuous curves,' 'full lips,' 'amorous eyes'—and this is only the description of your Shilla. I tremble to hear the minx open her full lips."

"Oh, God, did I write all that claptrap? She has changed. She's undergone quite a metamorphosis since I began. I mean to rewrite that initial description. Skip over it and go on to the dialogue—that was just to help Wills in casting."

"I know just the lady to fill the description given. Ah, no, but Shilla is an Easterner with *black* hair."

Prudence turned a few pages without looking up to see Dammler's scowl, then she continued to tease him. "She hasn't much idea of propriety, has she? 'Lounging at ease in a sinuous pose on an Ottoman.' What is she doing lounging on a Turk? She sounds a very hussy."

"An Ottoman is also a sort of sofa—a thing without a back on it. Like a bed, without the curtains, and sort of curved." I brought one back with me from the East."

"I wager you did. It sounds the right place for her, but I think you'd best add the curtains if she means to carry on in this fashion. Hmm, and preferably close them before the stage curtain rises," she added, reading on with great interest.

He tried to grab the pages from her fingers, but she held him off with a straight arm, laughing and reading aloud, "With a melting glance of languorous longing . . . Oh, really, Dammler. For shame!"

He grabbed her arm in a tight grasp and wrested the pages from her. "All that is mere stage direction It is not meant to be spoken aloud. God, how dreadful it sounds. I must have been bosky . . . I'm going to rewrite those first few pages. Start here . . ." He flipped through a few pages and pointed a finger to a passage of dialogue.

Prudence read for a few minutes, nodding and smiling. "Yes, I like her better as I get to know her. She is not quite so brash as those amorous eyes would indicate. She has a sense of humour I see. 'I don't mean to be a *bonne bouche* for that pot-bellied Mogul.' Would she know a French phrase?"

"She shouldn't, of course. She picked it up from her reading,

I expect. I'll have to change that. She becomes more English as it progresses. She'll be wanting a spencer and a half-dress before it's over."

"Yes, and I wish you would give them to her, to cover those voluptuous curves."

"Have pity on the male half of the audience. But I wanted your verdict on the tone, the way she thinks. Is it feminine? It's hard for a man to know. The male writers usually fall down badly in that respect. I can't think of one who presents a credible lady."

"Not when they set out consciously to do it. I make no distinction between the way men and women think in general. We are all people. We speak a little differently, but we want the same things as men, and outside of a few conventions—usually to the man's advantage, I might add—our minds operate in the same manner."

"I'll leave it with you. That's the entire first act. I'm into the second and shan't need it right away. Overlook that terrible description of her at the beginning if you can, and try to imagine her looking more . . ." He stopped and threw up his hands in a helpless gesture.

"*Less* Phryne-like?" she suggested daringly.

"Viper. She is not supposed to be anyone's maiden aunt. That remains unchanged." He picked up his hat and cane. "When am I to see your new work?"

"When it is printed between covers."

"You don't have this problem then, with your characters changing on you?"

"No, not at all, neither in appearance nor behaviour. They don't always do what I want them to, but they stay in character. They don't go reforming or turning bad on me without a good and sufficient reason that is inherent in the plot."

"It never happened to me before. But this is my first attempt at developing a character. In the cantos the characters slipped in and out so quickly as Marvelman toured all over that *he* was

112

the only constant, and *he* was in no danger of reforming. Well, I'll pick Shilla up in a day or two. Be kind to her."

"Still in love with her?"

"I become steadily more infatuated." He bowed and left, softly closing the door behind him.

Prudence sat down and read the whole first act without a break. It was good—witty and sparkling, as Dammler's work always was, but the problem was glaringly obvious. Shilla started out a hussy and in one act was changed into a conventional girl. The early pages would need a good deal of revision, but it would be a sensation. The settings and costumes would be exotic and different, and with the magic of Dammler's reputation and some staggering beauty playing the lead, it would be the talk of the Season when finally presented.

Chapter Eleven

On Sunday, Prudence went to tea and met Mrs. Ashington, an invalid, half crippled, who obviously doted on her clever son.

"Lawrence tells me you are a writer," the woman said in awed accents, though in her position she must surely have met many writers.

"Yes, ma'am, I write novels."

"Very good ones," Dr. Ashington added. "Very good indeed for a woman. I shall bring Miss Mallow's works home for you to read, Mama. You like to read a good lady's book."

"Oh, yes, I read all Miss Burney's books. Such nice stories, and Hannah More's. Lawrence has written a very good piece about you, Miss Mallow. I copied it out for him. He says you write very well. Quite complimentary."

"Perhaps Miss Mallow would like to scan the article before it goes in for publication," Ashington suggested. Before he took her home, he gave her his own copy, and as soon as it was possible she read it with great eagerness.

There was not a single word of abuse in it, yet when she put it down, she was disappointed. It sounded as though he were reviewing books for children. The whole tone was condescending. She wrote "very well for a lady," "did not concern herself with the serious problems of society," "had a knack for turning a telling phrase," "stuck to what she knew and did so well," and "was a careful craftsman." Had she been reading the article without knowing herself the subject, she would not have been tempted to run out and buy the books. She felt a bit dispirited. She gave it to her mama and Clarence to look over, and they expressed a view exactly contrary to hers. They were delighted with the criticism, and congratulated her on her good luck in being brought to public attention.

She was talked around to thinking she was fortunate. She had expected too much. She knew her canvas to be small, that point was well taken. To a learned man like Dr. Ashington, her stories must indeed seem childish. Any lingering sense of pique she felt against the Doctor was banished when he called to pick up his copy a day later and invited her to a dinner party. Coleridge would be there, and Miss Burney, he told her.

"It is time you met the other writers of your generation. One cannot write in a vacuum."

"I have met Miss Burney," she replied.

"Indeed?" He did not appear pleased with this. He had wanted to confer the treat himself. He stayed to tea, and impressed the family with his talk of philosophy and history, half of it in Latin quotations. Goethe and Kant rolled off his tongue, too, as easily as Smith and Brown and Jones. He mentioned rare tomes of which he had the only copies in existence. His library numbered five thousand volumes, he announced.

Clarence didn't bother mentioning the two shelves he had installed in his niece's study, or take the Doctor to see them. In fact, Clarence was reduced to near silence, saying only 'indeed,' or 'you are quite right,' or 'I have often thought so' at suitable pauses, or nearly suitable. He sometimes erred, being Clarence. Prudence was invited to view the five thousand books and glean what knowledge she could from surveying their Morocco leather bindings and reading a dozen titles. Within the hour three books were opened for her inspection, but as they were in Latin, Greek and Russian, she could do no more than comment on the clarity of the print and say she wished she could read those languages. Ashington smiled grandly, saying that he would be happy to translate any passage she was interested in, as *he* was quite familiar with all three tongues, and three others. But one set of foreign symbols looked very much like another, and she selected no passage for translation.

"A lady is better off not bothering her head with these things," he said, nodding in approval, and they went to take a glass of sherry and a stale macaroon with his mother.

When Prudence arrived home, she was told that Dammler had called, and taken his manuscript with him.

"He will speak to you about it another time," Clarence told her. "He is anxious to hear what you have to say about it. I told him he would do better to hand it over to Dr. Ashington for criticism. *He* would know whether there is anything in it, but he declined. He was in a bad skin about something or other. Didn't stay a minute."

"Did he say when he would come back?" Prudence asked.

"No, but he will likely come by later in the day, or tomorrow. We had a little chat about Goethe and Kant, but he only stayed a minute." Prudence's eyes rounded at this, and she wished more than ever that she had been home, instead of inhaling dust and wisdom in Dr. Ashington's library.

"I have been thinking, Prue," Clarence continued, "we ought to add another row of shelves in your study. I see you have those two shelves all filled up, and I daresay there are a dozen more books lying around the house that might be there. I have a Bible in my room, and there is a dictionary somewhere that Anne used to use, to say nothing of the *Backwoods Review* I have subscribed to. We will want to keep those issues to refer to."

"Have you subscribed to it, Uncle?"

"Indeed I have. I have been letting up on my reading a bit lately, but there is nothing like books when you come down to it. I daresay all the titles would be listed there, and a word or two to tell you about them. I shall certainly put a book in Dr. Ashington's hand when I paint him. what a lot of books the man reads. He is worn to the bone with them."

Two days later, the day of Dr. Ashington's dinner party, the monthly copy of *Blackwood's Magazine* was published and the Doctor personally brought a copy to Prudence. He caught her at work with her cap off and looked a little surprised. "Well, Miss Mallow," he said, "I have caught you *en déshabille*. But we are old friends now, and you needn't blush at my finding you so."

She looked questioningly at him, and he stood staring at her pretty little face, as he found it. "You are without your cap," he chided.

"Oh, yes, I sometimes work without it." Especially when I am expecting Lord Dammler, she thought. He hadn't been to see her in several days.

"I shall leave the door open," he said, carefully opening the door wide behind him. Prudence felt he was surprised that she didn't call her mother to chaperone them. Strange, even with the door open, the place seemed stuffy today.

"You see what I have here?" he asked, handing her the magazine. "Your name in print."

She accepted it and thanked him. "I came to bring it to you, and to tell you there is no need for you to have your uncle's carriage wait for you this evening, or return for you. *I* will be happy to conduct you home after the evening is over. You will hear some good talk. Coleridge is an interesting speaker, and Dammler makes a good joke."

"Is Dammler coming?" she asked. Not having seen him lately, she had not heard this before.

"He did not send in an acceptance till yesterday. He is a bit careless of the formalities, I fear. I should have been out in my numbers had he not accepted, but someone could always be found at the last minute. There are many writers who would be happy to accept a last-minute invitation from me, and would not feel ill-used to do so."

"I am sure they would be happy to come."

"I shall leave you in peace to peruse the article. Till tonight then. I quite look forward to having you at my table."

His smile was warmer than formerly, and Prudence had a sinking feeling that there was some significance to all these marks of attention the great man was bestowing on her. But she was curious to see how the same words she had read in handwriting looked in print, and soon forgot it. She read the whole thing again, and set it aside with not a smile, but not a frown either.

In his rooms in the Albany, Dammler was similarly occupied in reading his copy of the review. He read his own first, shrugged his shoulders and turned to Miss Mallow's. He began with a smile that rapidly faded, then became a frown. His indignation turned to wrath as he read, and when he flung it aside he said, "The swine!" in a contemptuous voice.

He was in a foul mood when he left for Ashington's, and his mood did not improve to find Prudence there before him, seated between Ashington and his mother, and being treated as quite a member of the family. Nor did she seem the least incensed at the carving Ashington had given her work, but was smiling agreeably and hanging on the old fool's every word, as if he were Solomon, spouting off some words of wisdom. The final straw was that she wore her damned cap, and a grandmother's gown that made her look forty. She was fixing herself up to appeal to that great pretentious ass of an Ashington. He wanted to shake her.

"Ah, Lord Dammler, we are just discussing the latest issue of *Blackwood's*," the host said, making him welcome.

"Can we not find a more interesting subject?" Dammler

asked with a charming smile and a bow to all the assembled company. He was the last to arrive.

Ashington's eyes narrowed at this remark, and Prudence's widened. "It cannot be of interest to the other writers among us—and *non*-writers," he added, acknowledging Mrs. Ashington and a Mr. Pithy, neither of whom was in the field of writing. There was another woman present to whom no one introduced him.

"I hope Mr. Coleridge and Miss Burney are broad-minded enough to be interested in writing other than their own," Ashington said in reply.

"Do you?" Dammler asked, and took up the last spare seat in the room. "You expect too much of people, Doctor. One would not have thought from your writing that you expected the ladies to be interested in anything but food and frocks."

"Oh, more than that, Dammler. You are too hard on me. They may legitimately lay claim to an interest in society and human relationships. I fancy they know as much about that as any of us."

"A good deal more than some of us," Dammler replied haughtily. "But as you are speaking of the magazine, let us hear what Miss Mallow thought of her review."

"I was pleased with it," she answered promptly.

"Very complimentary," Miss Burney took it up. "You were quite right in pointing out her craftsmanship, Dr. Ashington. Certainly Miss Mallow has mastered her craft remarkably well for such a young writer." She saw she had been too hasty in cutting Miss Mallow, and had full intention of taking her up again.

"That would be just praise for a good carpenter," Dammler parried, "but Miss Mallow does not deal in wood, fashioning tables and chairs. Craftsmanship in a writer is the polish on a diamond. You forget the quality of the stone, Doctor."

"I disagree with you, Dammler," Coleridge spoke out in stentorian tones, looking very like a statue with his egg-shaped head and Grecian nose. "Craftsmanship is all in a writer. *My* subject matter has been considered odd by some, but the manner of writing has always given me a good audience."

"It is more important in a poet. Poetry must be musical, lyrical, for the truth of the matter is we aren't saying anything of much import, but a serious novelist has a point to make, and if the point is well taken, the craftsmanship is the icing on the cake."

"But a *female* writer is not working with serious ideas, but merely a story," Ashington pointed out.

"What, no *theme?*" Dammler asked, quizzing Prudence, who lowered her brows at him, with a face like a thunder cloud.

Observing this, he behaved civilly for a short space, till he happened to glance over and see Ashington patting Miss Mallow's hand, and she not scolding him as she ought for his patronising gall, but accepting it calmly. He arose abruptly, just as Mr. Pithy was about to impart to him his views on the latest session of Parliament, and walked over to Prudence. "I haven't managed to find out from you what you thought of my first act, Prudence," he said, casually throwing in her first name, as he never did but when they were alone. "So odd the way the chairs are set up in this room, as though the company were not meant to converse except in little clusters."

"I was about to see if dinner is ready," Ashington said, and arose with a cool glance at the interruption. "I believe *this* is the seat you want, is it not, milord?"

"How discerning of you, Doctor," he smiled icily, and sat down.

"My opinion of your *first act* upon entering this room, Dammler, and *every* act that has followed it, is just what you are about to hear. What has gotten into you tonight?"

"I referred to Shilla and the Mogul."

"I know what *you* referred to, and I trust you read me as clearly."

"What a boring party this promises to be." He looked around the room with disdain, not answering her question. "Coleridge waiting for a chance to give us all a lecture on his new literary philosophy that is now twenty years old, and that long-nosed Burney toadying to anyone she thinks might do her any good. And as to you and Ashington . . ."

"Be quiet. His mother will hear you."

"I don't care who hears me. I won't have you fawning on him in this manner. It's disgusting!"

Fortunately, dinner was called. Ashington made straight for Miss Mallow and took her arm, while Dammler looked on, seething, and offered his arm to the crippled mother. Mr. Pithy was required to bolster her up on the other side, which left a Miss Gimble, who appeared to be a deaf-mute relation of the family, to enter unescorted.

Conversation at the table began auspiciously enough with Coleridge entering on a longish tale of how he and Wordsworth had come to hit on their idea of writing in a more modern, everyday manner than had been fashionable when they began to write. He was roundly applauded by Miss Burney, who evened out her praise by mentioning that Dammler had taken it a step further in his *Cantos from Abroad*.

But from there, the party disintegrated. Ashington, a confirmed classicist who acknowledged other writing only under duress from his colleagues, stated that he did not like to see form abandoned so entirely as it was by the modern poets.

"If you refer to myself," Dammler took him up, "it cannot have escaped your notice that I write in the classical rhymed couplet of Pope."

"We are comparing apples and oranges," Ashington objected. "Pope was a philosopher, a scholar. His theme was classic. A very serious writer, he did not tell wild tales of imaginary trips around the world."

"*Bad* apples and oranges you mean?" Dammler asked with a

raised brow. "It is news to me that my trip around the world was an illusion. I was quite convinced it took place, and have the scars to prove it."

"As to illusion," Coleridge mercifully interrupted, to regale them with his writing of the "Kubla Kahn" while under the influence of opium. A discussion of opium in all its uses and abuses followed, to get them over the first course.

The second course brought fresh problems. Ashington was at pains to select some particularly fine prawns for Miss Mallow and place them tenderly on her plate. Observing him, Dammler was at it again, but more obliquely this time. "What do you think of this fellow Shelley?" he asked, knowing the name was anathema to the doctor.

"He is a scoundrel and a knave," Ashington charged bluntly. "He should be run out of the country, or locked up. To be seducing innocent young women and preaching atheism and anarchy . . . I suppose *you* approve of him, your grace?"

"I like him excessively," Dammler agreed, smiling in anticipation.

"What is it you like so much, his defiance of the existence of God, or his embracing free love?"

"Of *those* two, his atheism, of course. I am an atheist myself, thank God." There was a satirical gleam in his one flashing eye.

Prudence gasped, and Miss Burney emitted one sharp hoot of laughter. The rest of the audience was stunned into a moment's silence.

"You have just contradicted yourself," Ashington pointed out when he recovered from his shock.

"How clever of you to have noticed it *already*," Dammler laughed. "But I spoke of him as a poet, whose morals are nothing to any of us. It is his odes I particularly admire. In poetry, *though the same does not hold true for a novel*, the mastery of craft is important. He is a true poet."

Ashington reined in his temper, and relief came again from Coleridge, who set his posture to a good lecturing pose for a prolonged expounding on the matter. From there, he proceeded to air another of his views, having to do with the idea that Shakespeare hadn't written a word of his own plays. He had delivered a series of lectures on Shakespeare and Milton to the Philosophical Society and was eager to repeat them. "It is clear from his background the man could not possibly have written them," he propounded. "Look at who he was—a deer poacher, a profligate, an *idiot*."

"What leads you to suppose he was an *idiot*?" Dammler drawled in his affected voice.

Interruptions were not welcome when Mr. Coleridge was lecturing. He scowled and continued, "Bacon, possibly, or Marlowe may have written such things . . ."

"Certainly Bacon was an idiot," Dammler interrupted again. "Put a deal of faith in the philosopher's stone. Spent years studying it. And as to profligacy, Donne, you know, was no angel—his sermons were to the contrary—nor Thomas Aquinas nor St. Paul, nor any of the great writers."

"Your adherence to the principle of profligacy is pretty well known, Lord Dammler," Ashington said, with a winning smile to Prudence, "but one may be a profligate without being a poet, and a poet without being a profligate."

"Or one may be both, like William Shakespeare."

"Shakespeare *did not write* the plays attributed to him!" Coleridge resumed. "As I said in my lectures in 1811 . . ."

"And have repeated *so often* since," Dammler added.

Coleridge stared, as at a worm. "Well, it is generally acknowledged among intellectuals that he was incapable of writing anything of the sort."

"Have you been speaking to some intellectuals?" Dammler asked in a bland manner. There was an uneasy pause before Dammler went on, "*Repetitio est mater studiorum*", as we scholars say. Shall I translate for the ladies? 'Repetition is the mother of learning.' If Mr. Coleridge tells us often enough the works of Shakespeare were not written by the author, but by some mysterious syndicate too ashamed to own up to their writing of the greatest masterpieces in the English language, we shall all learn it. Very well then, they were not written by Mr. Shakespeare, but by some other gentleman who happened to have the same name."

Prudence had to suppress a smile, but there were heavy frowns from the literary gentlemen present, and she soon turned serious.

"As to their being the greatest things ever written," Coleridge went on with his mangled lecture, "I firmly believe Milton stands head and shoulders above Shakespeare."

"That old trump?" Dammler asked disparagingly. "He was a Puritanical sham."

"You confuse his personal life with his works," Coleridge said.

"Not an uncommon error. *Some* confuse *Shakespeare's* personal life with his works."

"*Whoever* wrote the plays," Fanny Burney intervened, "he did a marvelous job. Did you see Kean's *King Lear?*" She managed to divert the irate gentlemen, and peace reigned till the meal was over.

How neatly she handled that, Prudence thought. She knew in her bones this squabble was all to do with herself. Dammler and Ashington were like two dogs fighting over a bone, and with about as much concern for the object over which they battled. If she were at all experienced, she would have known how to handle them, but dinner with Uncle Clarence and her mama had not developed any latent powers of diplomacy she possessed, and she waited in dread to see what the next horrible development would be.

Within half an hour, the gentlemen came to join the ladies in the saloon. Prudence died inside to see both Dammler and the Doctor walk at a jealous pace towards the one seat beside her. She arose at once, and flew to a chair beside Miss Burney, to engage her in a spirited discussion of bonnets, from which the gentlemen were excluded. A dozen times she heard slurs and innuendos exchanged between them, and at the end of an hour she arose with a very real headache to say she must leave.

As the party was going so poorly, the others quickly seconded her idea, and there was a general commotion of thanking and leaving.

I'll take you home, Prudence." Dammler said.

"*I* am taking Miss Mallow home," Ashington stated triumphantly.

"You will not want to leave your mother alone," he countered.

"She is not alone. Miss Gimble lives here for the purpose of looking after her."

"There is no need for you to put your horses to for nothing. I know very well where Prudence lives, and will be passing by her door."

"*I* shall be stopping at her door," Ashington topped him. "And step in to say good evening to Mr. Elmtree and your dear mother, Miss Mallow, if it is not too late. Shall we go?"

"Well, Prudence?" Dammler said to her, throwing the whole decision of choice on her unwilling back.

"It was arranged beforehand that Dr. Ashington would take me home," she said, and gave the Doctor her arm, with an apologetic smile at Dammler.

"I'll see you tomorrow then," Dammler replied, and turned away with an air of the keenest indifference to offer Miss Burney his company. She had her own carriage coming, but sent it away empty for the honour of a drive on Dammler's tiger skin seats.

Ashington did not accompany Miss Mallow into the house, nor ever have the least intention of doing so, only to be cornered by Elmtree and be made to drink a glass of wine. His sole purpose in claiming he meant to do so was to take Dammler down a peg, and claim his ownership of Miss Mallow. Prudence, naturally not unaware of the bickering between the two the whole evening, undertook an apology on her absent friend's behalf.

"I fear Lord Dammler was not himself tonight. He seemed in a very bad mood. I have never seen him so out of curl."

"It is typical of him. His head is swollen with all the praise heaped on him for those shoddy verses. I would not have written him up but for Blackwood wanting a piece on him. Dammler was in his cups, very likely. It is the only thing to account for such behavior."

"It did not seem to me he drank to excess," Prudence offered as a pacifier.

"I think he was foxed before ever he came. He was grossly offensive from the beginning. You will not want to have much to do with him. He makes himself too familiar, using your first name."

The party, so looked forward to, had been a disaster. Dammler had behaved abominably, and incomprehensibly, as well. Why had he taken such a dislike to Ashington? The strange thought entered Prudence's mind that he was jealous of her. He acted very like a jealous lover, but that was not possibly the reason, unless it was jealousy of her writing, and not herself. Yet he had implied Ashington's article did not do her writing justice. That he was not jealous of her as a woman was clear—he had thought her mad not to accept Mr. Seville's offer of marriage. *That* had not bothered him in the least. There was some other explanation, and she was curious to hear it. He had said he would see her tomorrow. She could hardly wait. And she would also tell him what she thought of his performance.

Chapter Twelve

On the morrow, Dammler did not come. Anger with Prudence and shame with himself for having acting so badly kept him from making the promised call. To hell with her, he thought, and resumed his life of dissipation which he had been making some genuine efforts to curb since her lecture to him on love and degrees of goodness. What did she know or care about anything? Silly little chit—bowled over by that doddering old doctor. He shouldn't have let himself spout off so to Coleridge though, and with Miss Burney there, too, to broadcast it.

Instead of Dammler, it was once again Ashington who came to call on Prudence. His excuse was a book—a translation of Vergil into English for her to read, as she had expressed an interest in his books. He said he would like it back when she had perused it, but had another treat ready to thrill her. He was giving a speech at a lecture hall that night, and wished her to attend.

"It will be of some interest to you, I hope—a little talk on the decline of drama. We have fallen a distance from the days of Aristophanes and Marlowe to what passes for drama nowadays. Drivel written by Dammler and the likes, about a harem in the East. I hope you don't mean to attend it."

"It is not being presented this year."

"Is it not? I had hoped . . . Well everyone knows what it is about anyway. It will be all violence and lust and such things as should be prohibited. He and Shelley are a fine pair of atheists."

Prudence did not much want to attend a lecture, but Clarence was having his cronies in for cards that evening, and a lecture might at least be instructive if not amusing. When Ashington mentioned that he had given Fanny Burney and Coleridge tickets the evening before, she decided to go. The glitter of famous names was still new enough that she enjoyed associating with them.

Clarence was disappointed that she would not be on display at his card party, but if there was anything that could bring him to accept it, it was her being so marvelously occupied elsewhere, in such company. The names of Coleridge and Burney and Ashington would be more mentioned at the card party than hearts, spades and clubs. Those notable persons might have been at the lecture, but if they were, Prudence saw none of them but Ashington. She sat alone in the front row of a sparsely filled hall on a chair of uncompromising hardness. The lecture was tedious and very long. Ashington knew a great many names of plays and playwrights, their plots and dates, and was determined to mention every one of them. From the Greeks to Sheridan, he could have not omitted one, in any language. The lecture began at eight-thirty; at eleven-thirty he was still at it. It seemed he would never end, but just before her eyes closed completely, he was bowing to light applause and walking towards her for congratulations.

There was not even a stop for refreshments to repay her for her long vigil. It was 'right home and to bed' for her, Ashington smiled gaily. How he still found breath after his harangue was a wonder.

His jolting carriage lumbered along the streets from the lecture hall in an out-of-the-way part of town to Grosvenor

Square, passing the lively entertainment section on its way. How many carriages were out, the occupants laughing and wearing evening clothes, and on the streets groups of friends met and chatted and laughed, planning more revels before 'home and bed' for them. Prudence felt a twinge of envy. What was she doing with this old man, when she would much rather have been out at a play or at the opera? Mr Seville's company was preferable to this. One particularly rowdy group of black-coated gentlemen and gaily-gowned women, the latter of whom Prudence suspected of being Phrynes, one and all, was ahead of them, about to cross the street at the corner.

"That is Dammler there, is it not?" Ashington said, looking out the carriage window.

This speech was the most interesting thing he had said all evening in his companion's opinion, and she quickly leaned out her window. She sat across the banquette from Ashington, the better to see and hear him. She had no difficulty in spotting Dammler, because of his conspicuous eye patch. She thought she would have known him anyway by his walk. Her glance sped to his partner. It was not the blonde Phryne this time, but a gorgeous redhead of the same calling.

Ashington rolled down his window and hailed Dammler. "Good evening, milord," he called in a loud voice, to attract his attention.

"Good evening, Doctor," Dammler said, smiling and raising his hand in quite a friendly way that led Prudence to suspect on this occasion he had been drinking freely. His eyes turned to the other window, and the smile froze on his face.

"Miss Mallow has been to hear my lecture on the Drama," Ashington said. "Pity you did not come."

Dammler continued staring at Prudence, and said not another word. When Ashington rolled up the window and the carriage proceeded, he was still standing in the street, with a redhead pulling at his arm and pointing out that the others were yards ahead of them.

"That scheming weasel!" Dammler said.

The next afternoon he fulfilled his promise a day late and came to call on Prudence. His eye patch had finally come off, revealing no disfiguring scar, but a slight tilting of the left eyebrow at the outer tip, and a small white mark beneath. He wore no smile on this occasion, but entered the room with an angry face.

"Oh, Lord Dammler, you have your patch off!" Prudence said. "How well you look without it."

"I am *Lord* Dammler now, am I?" he asked in a curt tone. "A new sense of formality, to go with your cap and your hoary Doctor."

"Come in," she said, peering down the hall to see if they were being overheard by anyone.

He strode in and slammed the door behind him with a bang. "You are busy writing an extract on the good Doctor's lecture I presume?"

"No, I was wondering whether they have hedgerows in Cornwall. My heroine is gone off there on a visit, and as I have never been there myself, I am having trouble describing the countryside. Have you been to Cornwall?"

"I think I have, but I may have imagined it, as I have a habit of doing. You had better check with your mentor."

"Dammler, for goodness sake sit down and quit glowering over me. What has got you in such a temper?" If anyone deserved to be in a temper it was herself, but she was behaving beautifully, she congratulated herself.

"What do you think has got me in a temper?" he shouted, ignoring the offer of a chair. "You, putting on your cap and grandmother's gown and your prim manner, nice as a nun's hen, to please that damned jackanapes of an Ashington."

"So that's it!"

"God, how I wanted to go across that room and box your ears. The gall of him. The consummate effrontery to treat your work as though you were a clever little schoolgirl writing a

130

pretty description of a garden, and *you* smiling and simpering like a Bath miss. He hasn't the least notion what you're all about. He thinks you write . . ." The hands flew up in frustration. ". . . love stories or domestic comedy. I don't know. Dammit, Prue, you should have given him a taste of your tongue, instead of sitting at his feet as though he were a tin god."

"I *do* write love stories, domestic comedies. He is used to reading Greek tragedies and philosophy. He has five thousand books!"

"And knows everyone of them by heart, complete with name and date, to bore his hearers and pretend he has a thought of his own."

"You are unjust. He knows a great deal. Why, he speaks *six languages.*"

"He hasn't an interesting word to say in any of them. How *can* you be humbugged by that great bloated, self-important bore?"

"He is thin as a rail!"

"I am speaking of his egotism."

"Well, he is important! It was inexcusable the way you behaved last night—the night before I mean—at the dinner party."

"Yes, now we get down to it. I suppose he had a good deal to say about last night. He made a point of calling your attention to me."

"He only stopped to say good evening to you. It was well done of him, considering the way you had behaved."

"Well done? Oh, it was marvelously done. It was pure spite. He wanted you to see me making a damned fool of myself. He wouldn't let that chance pass."

"It's not *his* fault that *you* were out carousing and drinking and—and so on."

"Especially so on! That must have tickled him, to catch me red-handed."

"And redheaded," Prudence said, laughing at his chagrin.

He looked at her, and in a moment was laughing, too. "Prudence Mallow . . . you, putting on your cap and prissy face. You're a baggage at heart, passing for a lady. You did it all to butter up the old slice, didn't you?"

"I did not! I have a high opinion of Dr. Ashington."

"A high opinion of the good he can do you, hussy."

"I am not so *conniving* as that. He is an eminent authority on . . ."

"Everything. He's a rasher of wind. Don't bother to let on you admire him. You have more sense than that. Do you think I care if you put the old goat to good use? Get what you can from him, and welcome. You may be sure he'll get back what he can by asking you to copy his essays for him, to save him the four pence a sheet to have it done. I'm pleased to see you taking advantage of him."

"I am not! It never entered my head to butter him up so he would give me a good review. It sounds a horrid, dishonest thing to do."

"You can't mean you're taken in by his insufferable air of knowing everything. Only see who he had to dinner—that old court card of a Coleridge, and cardess of a Burney."

"And Lord Dammler," Prudence reminded him.

"I only went because you were to be there. Till he let that slip out I had no intention of going. I daresay he wrote that to me in his note to get me there."

"And you didn't accept till the last minute either—*more* bad manners."

"He has been giving you a list of my virtues, I see. But truly, Prudence, you can't *like* him."

"I respect him. He knows so much more than I do about everything—literature I mean."

"In six languages—two of them dead, and the other four rapidly expiring at his hands. *I* speak six languages, too, and I don't see you showing me this great respect."

"Do you? What languages do you speak?"

"English, French, German, Spanish, Italian and Russian—a bit of Hindustani and Chinese—well, a dozen phrases in each. And I don't include the dead ones, you see."

"I didn't know that. How very stupid I am compared to you two."

"What—am I elevated to Ashington's stratosphere with my six languages? I should have told you sooner. And I have 10,000 books, more or less. That must give me a rung up, eh?"

"Uncle Clarence speaks of setting up another shelf," she said with exaggerated modesty. "To hold the *Backwoods Review*, you know."

"He *didn't* call it that! I esteem your uncle. When will he paint me?"

"At the drop of a hint. You have only to name the three days you have available. With your patch gone, there will be nothing to it," she laughed lightly. How very comfortable it was with Dammler. He might get angry and scold and rage, but in the end she could say anything to him without fear of giving offence, and he took the same liberty with her.

"Are you really an atheist?" she asked suddenly.

"I don't trot off to church every Sunday, but I certainly believe in God. Can't you tell when I'm being facetious? I only said it to get a rise out of Ashington."

"You shouldn't be facetious about God."

"Why, do you think He has no sense of humour? You're slipping into your friend's mistake of picturing Him in the image of Dr. Ashington."

"Why were you so angry at his party?"

"Initially because of that nasty piece he wrote about you, but it didn't improve my fit of pique to see you two so close. I think Clarence is right. The old devil would have you if he could."

"Well, you know Uncle Clarence. Any single gentleman is suspect on the first visit, and a confirmed adorer on the second."

"What must he make of me?"

"Oh it is all *my* fault. I am not giving you the sort of encouragement you want, being so shy and behindhand in your dealings with the fair sex."

"I'd better smarten up if I mean to have you," he laughed, very much in the old joking way.

"You still haven't told me why you antagonized poor Ashington so. You didn't object to Mr. Seville's offering for me. You can't compare the two. If Ashington is interested in me, he is in *every* way superior to Mr. Seville, except in wealth, of course."

"I acknowledge nothing of the sort. Seville *liked* you. He would have treated you like a queen, and given you anything you wanted, asking in return only that you look pretty and say smart things to show a clever lady could tolerate him. Ashington is a different article altogether. He wants you to adore him, to spend your time helping him puff himself up, yes, and he'd make you his copy girl in the bargain."

"He likes a little praise to be sure, who does not? But he would never ask me to waste my time copying for him. He thinks I write well."

"For a *lady*. And speaking of praise, how did you like Shilla? Isn't she charming? I like her better all the time."

"Yes, once I got over the description of her wanton way of draping herself over an Ottoman, I took to her a good deal. The first part must be radically altered though. You have put so much of an English nature into her, I doubt you'll pass her off as an Easterner at all. Could she be an English orphan who somehow got marooned in Turkey?"

"Possibly. That might be an idea. Have I told you her latest spree?" Prudence shook her head. "She's through with her prince, fickle creature. I no sooner get a crown rammed on his head than she turns pious on me, and is at present making up to a fakir the caravan chanced upon in Constantinople. An older man, and a hypocrite to boot. Fills her head with religious mumbo-jumbo, but he's only after her tender body."

"The beast. If she is to be a *bonne bouche*, as she calls it, for anyone, she would do better to stick with her prince. Do you think if you relented and gave her the chicken coop . . ."

"We've been all through that," he shook his head. "I even promised to throw in a couple of geese and a duck, but she took it for a canard." The hands went up in derision at his own poor pun.

"What a fowl—that's *f-o-w-l* thing to do."

"You don't have to spell it out to *me*, Miss Mallow. You are falling into bad habits with your new suitor. But I had better withdraw that, before you have a few words to say on the subject of bad habits yourself. Reverting to Shilla, it was my letting her away from the harem in the first place that did the mischief. All your fault. I followed your intuition."

"I had an inkling it might be laid at my door. I wonder you still care for her. Her attachment to the Fakir seems enough to turn off any sensible fellow."

"I am conspicuously lacking in sense where women are concerned. I am taking her away for a holiday to see if I can bring her to reason."

"Usually works, does it?"

"Shrew. Wills is anxious to get her on the boards for the fall Season, and she's a long way from finished. There are too many distractions in London."

"Are you going home then, to Longbourne Abbey?"

"No, the Malverns have asked me to Finefields. I finished the last batch of my cantos there earlier."

"I see." It was pretty generally known that he had done more than write his cantos there. Even Prudence had heard of his affair with Lady Malvern. "Are you sure you won't find distraction there waiting for you?" she asked pertly.

"Yes, Mama, quite sure. And I shan't drink to excess or stay up too later either. You refer, I collect, to the Countess. The rumours of my indecent affairs are grossly exaggerated, Prudence. I am not quite the lecher I am made out." He looked at her long and searchingly as he said this, as if to reinforce his meaning.

"It is none of my business. I had no right to infer . . ."

"No, and no right to look at me last night as though I were a ghost either. You looked—*awful.*"

"I was merely surprised—coming on you so suddenly and unexpectedly. And I was very tired, too."

"So was I. In fact, I went straight home to bed. Alone," he added the last word deliberately.

"Dammler!" she said impatiently, colouring quickly. "You know you should not say such things to me. It is quite improper." Her eyes slid to the carefully closed door. Improper, too, for her to be here alone with him, cap or no.

"Surely my specifying I was alone saves it from any taint of depravity," he said, following her eyes to the door and smiling.

"It is exactly what makes it wrong, and you know it well. The question ought not to have arisen."

"I thought it *had* arisen in your mind, however, and wished to remove the doubt. The statement, in short, was unexceptionable, and the fault lies in yourself. 'Honi soit qui mal y pense,' as our polyglot friend the Doctor would say, if he had the wit. We have established by repeating two or three times with no foundation that you are a baggage, Prudence, and you have just confirmed it. If you were half the prude you let on you are, your mind would not have coloured my innocent statement red."

"I was a prude—a proper lady, I mean," she corrected as his smile widened into a grin, "till I met you. It is you with your voluptuous harem girls and double-entendres *and so on* that has been the undoing of me."

"I wouldn't say you're quite undone yet," he said rather seriously, but he was never serious for long, and was soon back teasing her. "Have I not a dozen times hinted you off from rakes and roués, and pointed out the danger of an excess of flowers and diamonds?"

136

"Yes, and brought more mischief into my study than ever you kept out of it."

"I *do* apologize for Ashington. I ought not to have inflicted that bore on you."

"He is the least reprehensible person you have introduced me to."

"God knows he is reprehensible enough."

"If you pass me in the streets two years hence hanging on some Cit's arm, wearing the title Phyrne, I hope you will feel at least a pang of guilt."

"My sweet conscience, don't say such *appalling* things to me," he laughed uncomfortably. "Emotional blackmail is the lowest form of trick. Still, I had rather see you in that title than Mrs. Ashington. I would not think you so utterly lost to any chance of temporal happiness."

"I suspect our ideas of happiness are as divergent as those of love."

"You are bringing me round to a more proper notion of love. You and Shilla between you. I remember what *you* said, and she might give me her views while I am at Finefields with her."

"And Lady Malvern."

"And *Lord* Malvern. Your baser nature obtrudes again, Prudence. I'll escape before you make me sign a pledge of chastity, like a priest or nun. May I see you once again before I leave? Tomorrow . . .?"

"Yes, surely."

"Morning or afternoon—which is convenient for you?"

"Either one. Say morning."

"Morning. Don't I say it well? Obedient as a puppy, you see. Adieu, Prudence."

She shook her head at his foolishness and they parted, restored to perfect amity and only an empty feeling of sadness clinging with Prudence at the prospect of her study being deprived of mischief in the near future. Looking around at it, she remembered their different visits—strange how it shrank to a prison when Ashington was there with the door wide open, and expanded to a universe when Dammler came in and closed the door behind him. She hardly knew what to make of this last visit. His anger was still not explained to her complete satisfaction. He obviously hated Ashington—she had not known that when the matter of the articles had arisen, but was coming to understand it after her evening at the drama lecture. She was beginning to dread the sight of Ashington herself, and his learning was impressing her less than formerly. Why was his company so dull, when he knew so much? But then, whose company would not be dull after Dammler. A vision of his laughing face floated before her eyes. She would always picture Dammler laughing. So happy, joking, even swearing when he shouldn't before her, and saying outrageous things. But with a serious side, too—his charity girls, his talk now of politics, and leaving . . . He wouldn't ask her to Longbourne, of course. Once he got away he'd forget her, find new friends. She was merely a part of one episode of his life—of this one spring. She'd never forget or regret it, never be the same person after knowing him and all the different aspects of life he had exposed her to. Well, she was the better for the experience, but how she dreaded the future.

Chapter Thirteen

Dammler had every intention of calling on Miss Mallow before leaving for Finefields. To amuse her, he even drew up a ridiculous charter of behaviour, promising not to drink, gamble or *so on* during his visit, and intended to extract a similar document from her. He had it in his pocket when he went to see Murray to consult with him on business before leaving, and became involved in a longer meeting than he hoped for. It was suddenly lunch time, and too late to call on Prudence before afternoon. She had not seemed particular when he came, so he went to a club with Murray without a worry of missing her. Back at Grosvenor Square, Prudence sat waiting impatiently, pretending to work while looking at the clock every ten minutes. What a fool I am, she thought. He will not come at all. It won't be the first time he has broken an appointment. He has lied to me before too—she recalled his pretending to have read her book when she knew well he had given it to Hettie unread. As to saying he meant only to work at Finefields, that surely had not even been intended to be taken seriously. Why should he go to Finefields to work, when his own place would be more private, surely more agreeable for *work*. She felt her anger to be unfair. If a famous celebrity, a bachelor and a lord, chose to conduct his life in the same manner as his peers, who was *she* to take offence? It was impertinent of her to take such an officious interest in his private life, and impossible not to.

She was called to lunch, and before she left the table a note was given into her hands. Her heart hurried at receiving it, and settled back to a dull thud when she discovered the spiderly scrawl of Dr. Ashington.

"Which of your beaux is sending you a billet-doux?" Clarence asked.

"It is not a love letter, Uncle. It is from Dr. Ashington."

"Wants to do another piece on you, does he?"

"No. It is a curious note. He wants me to meet him at Hatchard's. What can it be, I wonder? It sounds quite urgent—'as soon as possible'—he 'would not impose on my good nature but for knowing my interest in his work.' It must be someone he wants me to meet—some writer, I suppose, or something of the sort."

"Lord Dammler has not come yet," Mrs. Mallow reminded her.

"No, he was to drop by this morning. Odd he did not come, but this sounds quite urgent. I think I must go. Perhaps—I hope I shall be back before Dammler comes."

"We'll ask him to stay," Clarence assured her. "It will be a chance for him to see around my studio."

Prudence dashed off without even finishing her lunch to Hatchard's in her uncle's carriage—always available to her when her errand involved a well-known person. Dr. Ashington awaited her at the door of the shop and asked her carriage to wait.

"Miss Mallow, how kind of you to come!" Ashington took her arm and led her inside.

"What is it you want, Doctor? Why did you ask me to come? I am agog with curiosity."

"I should not have asked you. I feel guilty about it but I hoped

140

you might help me out of a difficulty."

"I shall be happy to if I can." She was more curious by the minute. What could it be?

"The fact is, I brought Mama out to select some books, and she has taken a weak spell. She seldom leaves the house, and it was too much for her."

"Oh, is she ill? I hope she has not fallen."

"No, no, it is not that bad. Just a fainting spell, but the matter is, I have an appointment, and am unable to take her home. Her falling ill has detained us and upset our schedule."

Prudence assumed he had an important meeting he must attend, and while she thought, when she saw his mother sitting at her ease and leafing through a novel, that she might safely have been sent home in a hackney, she was not entirely insensed. Ashington had been kind to her. She agreed with no ill humour to take his mother home, happy that she would be home within three-quarters of an hour herself, and not likely to miss Dammler. This always was at the back of her mind.

"I had planned to drop by your place later on," Ashington added. "This will save me the trip." He offered her a largish sheaf of papers. "These are some notes I have dashed off on my lecture the other night. You liked it, I hope?"

"Yes, it was very enlightening," she congratulated, not for the first time, but she hoped for the last. She thought the notes were meant for her further perusal, and took them with a heavy heart.

"How kind of you to say so. I hope it shed some light on the subject. We are publishing it in the magazine next month."

"I see. How very nice." Why did he not wait and let her have a printed copy—easier to read than these notes, which were quite crossed out and jumbled up, with lines and arrows all over, and a disheartening number of footnotes, she saw at a glance.

"Again I must impose on your kindness. Would you be so good as to act as my amanuensis?"

"I beg your pardon?" The last word was not known to her.

"They need to be copied out. They are quite a mess, but you will sort them out. You are a clever girl."

The meaning of the unknown word was becoming clear. "Do you mean you want me to copy them out?" she asked, her anger rising, and the full imposition of not only this but the use of her as a delivery woman for his mother also descending on her with clarity.

"If you will be so kind. Reading them will help settle it in your mind. There is a good deal of material there. It will be helpful to you."

"Yes, a *very good deal!*" she said. "Too much for me to possibly copy I'm afraid." She handed it back to him.

He did not seem to understand. "Oh not *today,* Miss Mallow. I will not need it for a day or two—do it at your leisure— a little break from your story writing." He shoved it back at her.

With great firmness and a martial light in her eye there was no pretending to ignore she pushed the papers back. "I do not copy out material any longer, Dr. Ashington. I finished with that some time ago." During her talks she had mentioned to him her early work as a copier. "I know a few people who do that sort of work at four pence a page, if you would like their names."

He was greatly offended. "Well! Well! This is gratitude, I must say," he declared angrily.

"You may accept my taking your mother home as my gratitude for any slight favour you may have done me," she charged back. "You do not ask Mr. Hazlitt or Lord Dammler to do your copying for you, I notice."

"Well, but they are *men* . . ."

"They are *writers,* like myself. Good day, Dr. Ashington."

She climbed into the carriage without his assistance, and the coach bowled down the street.

"So kind of you, my dear," Mrs. Ashington smiled, not having heard the altercation through the window. "Lawrence appreciates it. It wouldn't do for him to miss his appointment. He must get his hair trimmed, for he dines with the Philosophical Society tonight."

"Dr Ashington is on his way to get his *hair trimmed?*" Prudence asked. Her voice was cold, but a volcano was forming beneath it.

"Yes, he always goes to Rolland—so hard to arrange an appointment with him, but it is worth waiting for, he does it so well. He would have had to wait two or three days if he hadn't made it this afternoon. Otherwise he would never have disturbed you, for he is so very thoughtful."

"Yes, I appreciate his *thoughtfulness,*" Prudence answered with awful irony that went undetected. Until she had half carried his invalid mother in to Miss Gimble's waiting arms, Prudence could not give full vent to her anger, but when she was alone, she beat the seat of the carriage in frustration. So *that's* what he thinks of me. Calling me on a fool's errand, interrupting my lunch and speaking of *urgency,* when he means only to get his hair trimmed! While that old fool gets his hair cut, Lord Dammler sits cooling his heels . . . And Dammler using her like dirt too. Saying he would come when he had no intention of doing anything but dashing off to Finefields to see the Countess. Her cheeks were rosy and her eyes flashing when she entered the house.

Dammler preceded her by a quarter of an hour, coming directly from his luncheon with Murray. Clarence had informed him of the note and the urgent flight to Hatchard's. He confided that she was to meet some great famous person of unknown or at least unstated name. But the name Ashington had registered clearly, and Dammler was already in a certain mood himself, the charter in his pocket forgotten. Clarence's inconsequential chatter, usually amusing, irritated him and the quarter hour that he waited seemed much longer.

When she entered, he arose and said curtly, "It was a short interview. We are all curious to know who Ashington called you to meet. Odd he did not see fit to bring the person here."

Prudence was still furious, but not about to admit to the ignominy of her meeting. "It was no visitor, but his mother who fell ill. Quite ill."

"Fortunate he is a doctor," Clarence said. "Speaks six languages. He would know just what to do."

"Yes, call a young lady who speaks only one," Dammler returned.

"But why did he call *you*?" her mother asked. "A doctor surely . . ."

"A doctor will be called, certainly. I took her home," Prudence explained.

"Why *you*?" Dammler asked. "You went with them in the carriage, I suppose. A woman's presence might have been helpful, but I should have thought Miss Gimble . . ."

"Miss Gimble has her in charge now."

"He never called you from your luncheon on such an errand as this," Mrs. Mallow continued. "That is very odd—why, I don't think that was very considerate of him, Prudence.

No more did Prudence, but she disliked to appear such a footmat in front of Dammler. "Who else should he call?" she asked angrily.

"Why, one of his family."

"Well, he called me," Prudence replied, and felt as foolish as she looked, with Dammler regarding her, with some expression between a grin and a frown on his face.

"Very strange. Very strange, indeed," Clarence decided, then went on to figure it out in his own fashion. "But Prudence is practically family. That is why he turned to her. Mrs. Ashington is very fond of Prudence."

It was discussed a little longer in this useless fashion, then Dammler decided enough time had been wasted. "Can you show me that passage from Rousseau we spoke of yesterday, Miss Mallow? You have it in your study, I think. I have only a moment to stay."

Mrs. Mallow suspected some chicanery here, but the study visits had become an accepted thing, and she did not object. She hardly knew how to handle a daughter who had grown up and become half-famous.

Prudence didn't hesitate a second, but jumped up smartly to go with her deceitful friend to look up a passage in a book she did not possess. "It is well Uncle doesn't know you have ten thousand books," she chided. "Just as well he doesn't know I have no Rousseau, too."

"Have you not, Miss Mallow? I'll give you mine—but it is in the original French, of course."

"Of course—I didn't think you linguists would weary your eyes reading plain English. Your French book is of no use to me. But tell me why you wanted to escape into my study."

"Just to see you before I leave." Prudence didn't point out the obvious, that she was as highly visible in the saloon as she was in her study. "Why does Clarence say you are practically one of Ashington's family? Does the Doctor plan to adopt you?" he asked with a jeering look.

"You know that was not his meaning."

"Marriage, then—that's it?"

"Yes, that is what my uncle meant, and if he thinks for one minute I'd have that . . ." She stopped abruptly. Oh dear, she hadn't meant to reveal her disgrace.

"My dear girl, *what* has got you in the boughs? I am consumed with curiosity to discover the whole truth of this urgent business. It was shabby of him to call you only to get his mother home, but in an emergency you know, he might have lost his head."

"It was no emergency, and he didn't lose his head, not by a hair."

"What then?"

"You were right about him! There, I didn't mean to tell you, but I can't keep it to myself a moment longer."

"You haven't told me a thing. Come, cry on my shoulder. If

he's insulted you, I will be charmed to call him out."

"Well, he *has*, but it's not the sort of thing he can be called to account for. He meant it for a rare compliment, I expect, for me to be his 'amanuensis,' as he calls it. And I suppose you know what that fine word means?"

"I do," he said, and seeing that the nature of the insult had not been serious, and particularly as he had foreseen it himself, he fell into unholy mirth. "Am I right then in assuming you and the Doctor have had a falling out? I see you brought no papers with you to transcribe."

"You may be sure I did not! I only wish I had scattered his lecture on drama to the four winds, all over Bond Street. It would serve him well. Not that the wind would carry such heavy stuff. It would sit in a heap on the corner and break through the cobblestones with the weight of all his facts and figures."

A smile showed triumphantly on Dammler's face. "The lecture too was a failure, was it?"

"It was a disaster. I wished I had a cup of coffee to keep me awake, or better a glass of undiluted laudanum to put me happily to sleep."

"But how ill was his mother? That was just a pretext, was it?"

"She had some slight dizzy spell, and as the Doctor had to get his *hair cut*, *he* naturally could not break his appointment."

Dammler sat down, put his elbows on his knees, and his chin in his hands. "Does he have any hair left to cut, or did you yank it out on the spot?"

"I would have, but we were gone by then, his mama and myself. *She* let it out—he didn't have the nerve." Prudence paced to and fro as she spoke, too angry to be seated.

"And it's all my fault. I brought him down on your innocent head, thinking he might do you some good."

"How could *you* know what he's like? He keeps up a decent face to *men*. He would not try such a stunt with a man."

"Sit down," Dammler said on her next passage past his chair, and he grabbed her wrist. "We've wasted enough time on the Doctor. I must leave in a moment." She sat on a chair beside him, still breathing hard.

Her mind was full of her insult, and she could not let it go. "My writing is nothing you see, deciphering his hen's scratching was to be a pleasant diversion for me."

"What is it you're writing anyway?" he asked to change the topic. "You're very close about it. The *theme* I know is too large to be put into words, but the plot, the characters, what of them?"

She tried to shake off her agitation. "It's about a young girl who *thinks* herself in love with a very handsome fribble of a fellow, only because nature gave him straight teeth and a fine head of hair, and because everyone else is in love with him. But she is brought to her senses and realizes, just in the nick of time, of course—that it is really a plainer but more worthy fellow she has cared for all along. I plan to pretend, if any critic asks me, that my theme is the age-old one of distinguishing between appearances and reality. That has a good sincere ring to it, don't you think? It seems to me to encompass most of experience."

"Yes, vague enough for anything. And your heroine, she is not fooled by the teeth and the hair. She prefers a butter tooth and a lank of mousey lock in the end?"

"How foolish you make it sound. The second hero is not so inferior as that. His teeth are left to the imagination, and the hair is just dark, not rhapsodized over. I hope by chapter ten the hero's flashing smile and tumbling black locks will begin to pall on the reader, and she'll use all her powers of imagination to make the second hero into a good likeness of the first, with virtue thrown in. Mere looks are not enough."

He listened closely, nodding his head. "Tell me, Prue, do you find, as you write, that the people you know and see regularly begin to creep into your characters? Have you any particular straight tooth and tumbling lock in mind?"

147

"None in the world. I don't write about real people."

"There was your cat in the garden, and Aunt Clarence, the composer."

"No, no, only characteristics, not characters."

"I see. It's different with me. Strange the way the imagination works, isn't it?"

"Do you know what *I* think?" Prudence asked suddenly.

"What?"

"I think he just pretended his mama was ill to get me to go to Hatchard's, so he wouldn't have to bother bringing his writing here."

"I wouldn't be a bit surprised," Dammler agreed, happy to abet any ill she had to say of Ashington, though it interrupted his own interesting line of thought.

With Prudence in such a mood his little charter of good behaviour seemed inappropriate, and he left it in his pocket. The visit was not going as he expected, but he was happy to see she was on to Ashington. "So while you are opening your heroine's eyes to the glories of bad teeth and hair, I shall be trying to cajole Shilla back to her prince, or her Mogul. I wonder how she would like your hero?"

"We'll ask her when my *Patience* comes out. That is the title I have chosen, for her and the book. She has been dipping into my novels, I think you said."

"*Patience*, eh? Will we by any chance be reading that she is well named?"

"I may have borrowed a little something from the similarity," she admitted. "Having listened all my life to it, I decided to put it to use; but she is not me."

"No, your printed reincarnation will of course be as a man—that is your method, is it not? I will keep a sharp watch for you. If I read of a young gentleman being put upon by an aged female critic, I shall know what to make of it."

"You won't read it! I mean to put him out of my mind entirely. Such a person is best forgotten."

"Well, I mean to get busy and finish my play in a week, if possible." He thought again of the charter in his pocket, and wondered if he should produce it. "I need the money for my charity girls. I didn't go out at all last night. Stayed home and got the second act written in rough."

This was the second time he had mentioned in a seemingly casual fashion the innocent nature of his nights, and Prudence decided to chide him about it. "I wasn't hellraking last night, either, but I hadn't meant to brag to you about it."

"Oh, what a heartless wench she is! You complained loud enough when I was out carousing. Won't you say a kind word on my improvement?"

"I did not complain! Don't cast me in the role of guardian of your morals."

"Well, I hoped to please *you* by improving. No one else ever was kind enough to worry about me, or care whether I ran to perdition."

"What a plumper! Your mama cried for two hours when you got drunk."

"But she's been dead for ten years. I started drinking young. And my father has been dead for fifteen years. Just a poor orphan waif really. Couldn't you pat my head and bless me, or must I lie on the floor and hold my breath to excite any interest?"

"Indeed it is not necessary to choke yourself. Good boy," she reached out and patted his head, and felt sorry for him, in spite of his shameless bid for pity. "And if you do a good job on Shilla, I'll buy you a sugar plum, and possibly an ice."

"How do you put up with me?" he asked. "I think I must try the patience of a saint. Hettie would rant to hear me call myself an orphan. She has begged me a dozen times to move in with her."

She was glad he hadn't. "She is not exactly motherly, is she?"

"Lord, no. But *you* are. Do you think Clarence might adopt me? I would make you a very good brother."

She felt a wave of despair wash over her. She had graduated from male friend to bothersome female, only to end up his sister! "I suppose it is my luxurious study you have your eye on by this ploy," she laughed, to hide her disappointment.

"No, he'd have to build me one with more shelves—I bring a dowry of ten thousand books, you recall."

"And an Ottoman. Such heathen articles have no place in Grosvenor Square."

"But this heathen article feels very much at home here. Too much so. I let on I was in a hurry when I lured you in here. I'd best leave, before Clarence gets his eye to the key hole to see if I'm having any luck putting my ring on your finger."

He arose as he spoke and walked to the door. "Remember now, we are agreed to work hard this next week. Till our next chin," he waved, and smiling a rather sad smile, as though he were in no hurry to leave, finally he went.

Prudence sat on alone, contemplating his visit. She hadn't realized he was so alone in the world. Just Hettie, and while she was jolly company, she would be no sort of defender for a young man like Dammler. Quite the contrary—she would spur him on to anything. Perhaps this explained his not going to Longbourne. To go to a house empty but for servants could not be pleasant. He was really nearly alone in the world as far as family ties were concerned. Was that why he kept coming back here then? To feel he had a family? It was odd he expressed affection for Clarence, when she considered it, but not so odd he found a sister in her. Their shared interest in writing had started the friendship and from there it had come to the sort of hellish fraternal relationship he spoke of. That would explain his ire at Ashington's poor review of her work. She admitted now it was an insult. Explained too his not minding seeing her married to a wealthy man such as Seville. Oh yes, it explained everything, except what she was to do about being in love with this self-imposed brother.

Chapter Fourteen

Dammler was off to Finefields with Shilla and Lady Malvern (and Lord Malvern), and Prudence was left home with Uncle Clarence and her mother. There was no correspondence between them, and when Fanny Burney called one day a week later, Prudence agreed eagerly to accompany her to call on Lady Melvine. She hoped to hear from his aunt how he progressed, and more importantly, when he was to return. His whereabouts had purposely been kept secret from the press. As Prudence carefully set the buff chip straw bonnet from Mademoiselle Fancot's on her curls, she had a hope Dammler might even be there. One week was the duration mentioned for his stay, and Hettie was surely the first person he would call on. His only family—a tender pity for him had been growing during the past week. It was this rootlessness that she held to be responsible for his wilder extravagances.

But her hopes were dashed; he was not there, and what she heard of him was of a nature to discourage her completely. The writing was not going well, Hettie told her, there were too many distractions. Prudence felt only one of the distractions was necessary to keep him from his play. He had written mentioning prolonging his visit another week. Possibly two.

"Was it really *work* he had in mind when he went to Finefields?" Miss Burney asked archly.

"Now Fanny, don't ask embarrassing questions," Lady Melvine retorted. She looked to Prudence with a smile as she spoke, trying to understand the girl. Dammler spoke of her a good deal, but whether she was a young innocent thing or a scheming, designing woman always remained unclear. Prudence forced out a worldly laugh, and Hettie said to herself, innocent is it? She is the slyest girl in town. And jealous, too, though she tries not to show it. "He did take his manuscript with him, or said he did," she added.

"Strange the aura of secrecy surrounding the visit. But they would not want company descending on them," Miss Burney mentioned.

"No, Dammler is beginning to hide his amours and put on a respectable face. He never tells me of his *chères amies* any more. I sometimes wonder if he is thinking of marriage. He asked me to write him of all the births, deaths, marriages and important court decisions while he is away. You don't suppose he is waiting for that perfectly dreadful Lady Margaret to get her divorce?"

"Or for Lord Shelhurst to die?" Fanny laughed.

The specific names meant nothing to Prudence, but the import was clear enough. He had been carrying on with these ladies, while prating to her about improving to please her. In a snit she said, "Perhaps it is the births he is interested in."

"Miss Mallow, you are too horrid," Lady Melvine approved happily. She personally had no use for missish women, and felt much more at home with Miss Mallow, the worldly sophisticate. "I shouldn't think he would marry anyone like Lady Margaret or the Shelhurst woman," Hettie said consideringly. "They are well enough for flirts, but when it comes to settling down it will be some prim-faced little duke's daughter with a fat dowry he will settle on. His sort always does. No, he can't have marriage in mind at all, or he'd have gone to Longbourne Abbey to get things in shape. He said he was purposely *not* going there as he had such a lot to do at the Abbey he wouldn't find time to write if he went there."

Here was another blow for Prudence. That Dammler would look to a high-born, well-dowered lady for a wife had never occurred to her. Here she had been wasting her time being jealous of the Phyrnes, who were actually to be pitied. Naturally it would be a title and a fortune he would eventually marry.

This visit plunged Prudence into gloom, and she could not find solace even in her writing. The sanctity of her study without a little enlightening mischief from Dammler proved too pure. She made any excuse to get out of it. Two days later she wanted to go down town with her mama. She foolishly imagined the carriage would be at her disposal, but was informed otherwise. With never a prestigious caller for nine days save a lady writer Clarence had never heard of, and who looked suspiciously like a nobody, his carriage was busy sitting idle in the stable.

The *Backwoods Review* arrived and sat unopened on the table. The building of the third shelf to hold it and its brothers was put off, with no one to admire it. "Strange Dr. Ashington does not call," Clarence said a dozen times a day. He also reverted to the halcyon days of the Marquis de Sevilla. "That Spanish grandee who sent you all the flowers and diamonds, Prue, what do you hear of him lately?"

"Nothing. I do not see him at all."

"I read in *The Observer* he has joined the Four Horse Club. He is making his way in the world. He would not have been a bad catch for you. I think your daughter was too quick in turning him off, Wilma."

Prudence sighed wearily, and her mother, interpreting it, said, "Lord Dammler should be returning soon, should he not, Prudence?"

"No, he has prolonged his stay at Finefields. He does not

write his aunt of returning soon."

"I expect he is working hard on his play," the mother said.

"Ho, playing hard is more like it," Clarence corrected. It rankled that he had never got that form on canvas. Thrice he had hinted, and thrice the hint had been ignored on the pretext of work, but he always found time to sit around laughing with Prudence, keeping her from her writing. "I am happy he has stopped badgering Prude. There was no getting anything down with him borrowing all her books twice a day. I suppose he took that French book off with him, did he?" he asked sharply.

"No, he didn't," Prue assured him with a slightly wistful smile. Nor was there ever any French book for him to take.

"Well, it seems to me those shelves are half empty, and they used to be full. Why, we spoke at one time of requiring another, but it is not necessary now. They are only half full. Dr. Ashington, now, has five thousand books." Clarence had taken this statistic for his own, and broadcast it among his friends, sometimes as five hundred, sometimes as five hundred thousand, either of which was equally impressive to him as being an incalculable, unreadable number. Dr. Ashington, still in London with his name appearing in the paper to be pointed out to Mrs. Hering and Sir Alfred, loomed larger in Clarence's thoughts than Dammler. His title of Doctor, while not raising him to the peerage, was as far removed from Elmtree's ken as a dukedom, and as valuable.

"He was an interesting man. You should call to see how his mama goes on, Prue. She always liked you. I daresay it is her being so ill that keeps him away from the house. He would appreciate your calling. I read in *The Observer* that he is giving a lecture on Plato and Aristotle and some other Italian tonight. You will take it in, I suppose?"

"No, I do not plan to attend."

"The carriage will be free if you would like to go. Wilma will be happy to go with you. She is interested in that sort of thing."

Prudence exchanged a silent, speaking glance with her mother. The only thing more foolish he could have suggested would be that he was interested himself, but he wasn't quite so eager for the return of the Doctor as to put himself out an iota. "It is busy this afternoon, however," he remarked. "John Groom has to give it a wash and polish. It is covered in mud."

"Mama and I will take a hackney down town," Prue told him.

"I am feeling a little peakey, dear," her mother said. She did look pulled, Prudence noticed.

"Never mind, I'll stay home. I *did* want to select a frame for my portrait though," she added cunningly, hoping to eke at least a footman out of her uncle.

"Oh, well, if that is why you want to be off gallivanting, I daresay one of the boys can be spared to go along with you and carry it," Clarence told her, a little mollified.

It was just outside the framing shop that she ran into Lady Melvine, and stopped for a chat. After the initial exchange of courtesies, Prue asked if she had heard anything more from Dammler. He was the main link between them, and she thought the question not encroaching.

"He does not write me often, naughty boy. No mention of returning to town. But I fancy we know what is keeping him busy." Neither of them fancied the play for Drury Lane had anything to do with it.

Prue laughed in a manner she considered worldly, and added daringly, "And he promised me he would be a good boy, too. Give him a scold for me. Tell him I disapprove of his distraction."

"That I shall. Do you go to the play this evening? It promises to be good. Kean—always a delight."

"No, not tonight," Prudence answered, intimating she would put it off till another evening, though, of course, she would not be going at all. "We are busy elsewhere tonight," and added to herself, busy playing Pope Joan at a penny a hand.

"You have your distractions, too, I see," Lady Melvine teased gaily. She heartily approved of a pretty young dasher who knew her way about town.

"It doesn't do to become stale."

"Much chance! Tell me who he is," Hettie asked eagerly.

"Oh, just a friend," Prue replied as airily as though it were true.

"Tell me, does Seville still pester you? Dammler told me of his offer."

How strong was the temptation to lie and say he did, in hopes that it would be relayed to Finefields, but she contented herself with concealing the truth. "I never accept an offer to go out with him," she said, truthfully but misleadingly, as no offer was ever made.

"You could do worse, my dear. Full of juice. He has been accepted into the Four Horse Club, I hear. Buying Alvanley's greys for a thousand pounds might have had something to do with it, though he is a fine whip, Dammler tells me."

"Yes." Looking up, Prudence was aghast to see the tall form of Seville approaching them. Guilt and shame overcame her—she would be revealed for the liar she was. She doubted Seville would do more than lift his hat in passing. To forestall any idea that they were on such cool terms, she hailed him merrily as he passed by.

"Why, Mr. Seville, congratulations are due to you. I hear you are in the FHC. Not wearing your outfit I see."

He stopped and smiled civilly. "No, we do not meet today. Thursdays, you know, in George Street, Hanover Square, to trot over to the Windmill. How do you go on, Miss Mallow? I haven't seen you since . . ."

She jumped in to prevent exposure of the date of their last meeting. "From Hanover Square you leave? I must go down and see you off one day. I have never seen it. I hear it is a famous sight."

"There is usually a pretty good turnout to see us off."

Seville was astonished at this change in her behaviour. Quite throwing herself at his head. It occurred to him she regretted her decision in refusing him. Her brash manner also led him to suspect she had known all along it was not marriage he had meant. She had been pulling his leg—having a little joke at his expense. He always thought she was up to all the rigs. But she was too late—negotiations were nearing completion for his nuptials with the "Barren" Baroness, and even more interesting plans afoot for teaming up with a pretty little dancer from Covent Garden.

"I will be in the crowd next time. Look out for me," Prudence said, to keep up the appearance of friendship.

"I won't be there next time. I am off to Bath tomorrow for a week's visit."

"Oh, I have never been to Bath. I should like to see it some time. Is it nice? I thought it was quite dull nowadays."

Why, the minx was clearly throwing herself at his head. If that wasn't a hint! "A little quiet. One must make one's own excitement."

"I'm sure you are well able to do that."

"I hope to keep from being moped to death," he answered, then turning aside to Hettie, he addressed some few remarks to her. Happy to think she had brushed through not too badly, Prudence took her leave of them both with a wave of her hand, as though she had a million things to do. She was only looking for a hired hack to climb in and take home the frame she had selected for Clarence's approval.

"Miss Mallow is so charming—a pity she turned you down," Lady Melvine continued on talking to Seville. "But one hears you will soon be making an announcement of a match with someone quite different."

This was the first intimation Seville had that Miss Mallow had told anyone of his offer to her. Since she had *appeared* to misunderstand it, he was relieved she had kept it to herself. The old Baroness would fly into the boughs if she heard of that tale. He hardly knew what to say—to deny outright having made her a *proper* offer would be ungentlemanly, and to confirm it would be a disaster to himself. "I hadn't realized she was bruiting it around," he parried for time.

"No, now I come to think of it, I believe she told only Dammler, and in the greatest secrecy. He told no one but myself, and I have not breathed a word. But it is no secret to *you* that you offered for her, so no harm done.

"Is that what she says—that I offered for her? Ha, ha, well it never does to contradict a lady, what? But don't spread it around. A certain Baroness you know, would not like to hear it."

Lady Melvine's suspicions were naturally aroused at this veiled statement. "Why, you rascal, Seville, I believe you deceived the poor girl."

"Deceived *her*? There was some deceit in the business I begin to think, but you must not be too hasty in placing the blame."

He left, eager to extract himself from the unpleasant predicament without being too specific. But his words fell on fertile soil. Miss Mallow was not seven years old, and she must have known as well as everyone else in the city that Seville was dangling after the Baroness. Why, he had offered Prudence nothing but a *carte blanche*, and she had elected to turn it into an offer in form, and for no other reason but to make Dammler jealous. All her sly questions and comments about being displeased of the Countess Malvern. What a clever little article she was, to be sure, and making herself out the picture of innocence. She, with her drawing the line at five by-blows, and her Maidenhair Ferns, and its being the *births* Dammler was interested in. Such wily behaviour as this was sheer joy to Hettie. She went straight home and penned a long letter to Dammler telling him the whole amusing story, together with every other bit of gossip she could think of, then set it aside and forgot about it until, two days later, Bishop Michael's wife left him. This was written into another letter, and when she prepared to send it off, she discovered the first one still on the desk, and slipped it into the envelope also.

"Our *innocent* Miss Prudence has been bamming us all," she had written. "Seville's offer may have been in form, but not the form she would have us believe. It was nothing else but his mistress he meant to make her, as I told you all along. Yes, and I think she regrets turning him off, too, for she was fairly throwing her cap at him today on Bond Street. But he escapes her and goes to Bath (with his *chère amie*, I fancy). How surprised he will be if Miss M. follows him down. She claimed a great interest in seeing Bath. But I may be mistaken—I believe she has some other beau in her eye, as well. She is full of engagements. She tells me to inform you she is not pleased with your 'distraction' keeping you from work. What *can* she mean, I wonder!"

She reread it with a chuckle before sealing it, unaware that she had done anything more than give her nephew a good laugh. He seemed always to be laughing over something Miss Mallow had said or done.

Prudence went home in a state of nerves. Not only her study but all of London was becoming intolerable to her. The book was going poorly, and she wished for a change. Dammler had claimed to want peace and quiet to work—she wanted a noisy holiday with not even the pretence of work. Brighton, where the *ton* would soon be going with the Season coming to a close, was too steep for her poor resources. Mr. Seville's mention of Bath came to her. Mama had been feeling poorly lately; the waters might do her some good.

The major flaw in the plan was that Mr. Seville would be there. She did not like to give the impression she was trailing after him, as he might be forgiven for thinking after the saucy way she had hailed him on Bond Street. But he was leaving tomorrow—staying only for a week. By the time she had arranged through an agent for lodgings and got herself and Mama there, the week would be up. In fact, she would not go *before* a week was up. That this also gave Dammler more than double the time he had claimed to require at Finefields had nothing to do with it. He might stay as long and be as distracted as he liked. It was nothing to her.

The subject of the trip was broached at home, with some little trepidation lest Clarence might object to letting his horses take such a journey on their behalf. But to her relief it proved the very thing to put her back in his good graces. Her manner of introducing it may have had something to do with it.

"I was speaking to Mr. Seville today, Uncle," she said cleverly.

"Seville? Were you indeed? Well, that is nice. I think you gave the marquis short shrift. I am happy to see he is dangling after you again. A Spanish title is no small thing when all's said and done. So, Seville is back after you, is he? I am happy to hear it."

"He is going to Bath," she added. "He spoke very highly of it. I quite wished I were going myself. I shouldn't wonder if the waters would be good for you, too, Mama."

Mrs. Mallow was delighted to see her daughter divert her thoughts from the impossible direction of Lord Dammler and she too thought the waters would do her a world of good. The very thing. Even more good to see Prudence settled with Mr. Seville. She had no illusions as to his having a title up his sleeve.

"So you are off to Bath with Seville, eh?" Clarence ran on, making up a story to please himself and Mrs. Hering.

"Not *with* Mr. Seville, Uncle. He leaves tomorrow. But I should like to go along a little later."

"You will be needing the carriage then. I am happy I had John Groom give it a good scrubbing down for you. We will hire an extra team and send you off in style with four. We wouldn't want Seville to think us skints."

"I am not going there for the purpose of meeting Mr. Seville,"

Prudence pointed out very precisely. "It was not his idea, but my own."

"Ho, you are waking up now, milady. You are well named. Very prudent of you to tag along after him. Well, I don't expect he will be surprised to see you show up all the same. The idea will not be displeasing to him." Before many more such sentences, it was Seville who was following her there, a week before her.

A trip to Bath for a month's holiday might have been a small undertaking for some, but for the Mallows, who hadn't spent a night away from Mr. Elmtree's house since their moving in with him but for their two weeks' visit with friends in Kent, it was an operation of major dimensions. There were many trips to the agent's office to determine where they would stay, whether they must take their own linen and plate, what servants, if any, were provided, and a dozen other details. A week was hardly long enough to arrange it, but the great day was finally looming close before them.

Prudence was anxious to know one more thing before she left. When did Dammler intend to return to London? She also wanted to tell someone he knew and whom he would be seeing where she was going. She didn't hope he would actually drive all the way to Bath to see her, but she wanted him to know she was there, in case he should be in the vicinity. Lady Melvine occurred to her only to be rejected; they were not close enough to make such a quizzing visit possible. A much better person would be Murray, their publisher. She must tell him she was leaving. If she went in person, he might have news of Dammler. She went to his office the day before she left, and it was he who mentioned his most famous writer, but alas, he didn't know when he would come back.

Nor at Finefields did Dammler know himself when he would be returning to town. He had arrived in a peaceful state of mind, happy to be away from the hurly-burly of London to get down to serious work. The first two days went amazingly well. Shilla agreed to part with her fakir with no reluctance at all—almost seemed glad to get rid of him. He knew his choosing Finefields for a retreat had raised eyebrows in certain quarters, but his and Lady Malvern's relationship was not what it appeared to the world. She had quite a different lover hovering in the neighbourhood, but he was not known or glorious, and she was happy to give the illusion of being better occupied than she actually was. Dammler was content to let the world think what it would; it gave him some measure of relief from the other importunate females who badgered him. They met only at meals, and for a ritual flirtation under her husband's nose for half an hour after dinner. Old Malvern took it as a personal insult if you didn't fall in love with his lovely wife. He was more jealous of her suitors than she, and more demanding. He would not have approved of Mr. Varley, the present possessor of Constance's heart.

Dammler wrote in the mornings, rode or hunted in the afternoon, for he was an active person and couldn't stay cooped up all day, and returned to his work at night. But after almost two days of successful writing, he came to a halt. Shilla, having parted with her Fakir, dug in her heels and refused utterly to return to either the Prince or the Mogul. Under duress, he forced her back to the first, then the other, but she wouldn't say a clever word. He could not think a sullen, scowling face would please the audience at Drury Lane for two acts. He wished Miss Mallow were there for him to talk to. Shilla had a lot of Prudence in her, he realized. What would Prudence do in such a circumstance? She had turned off her hypocritical Doctor friend, just as Shilla had given her fakir the boot. He wondered if the Ashington incident had influenced him. Very likely, and here he had thought it a fine inspiration on his part.

Sitting at the Louis XVI desk in Lord Malvern's spacious study set aside for his use he found himself thinking about Miss Mallow more than his play. Well, they were related—he had really turned Shilla into a good likeness of Prudence. The same sharp tongue, the same innocent mind in a milieu too sophisticated for her, though Prue would die sooner than admit it. Their many conversations replayed themselves in his head. Well then, quit deceiving yourself; Shilla is anyone but Prudence. Give her her head, and let us see what develops. Miss Mallow's heroine—surely herself in disguise—did not sit down halfway through the book and content herself with turning off one lover without having a better one in view. He needed a new character to be acceptable to Shilla-Prudence. Now why was it himself in his literary guise as Marvelman that darted into his head? Why was it himself and no one else he wanted to put into the last acts to rescue Shilla from her woes? Would Prudence approve? "Patience," he thought, would not. "Looks are not enough," "a handsome face," "a fine tooth and a tumbling lock of black hair" were soon replaced by a worthier hero.

Dammler looked into the large gilt-framed mirror across the room, and the first thing that struck his eye was the black lock falling across his brow. Oh, yes, she was too polite to say it, but it was this lock of hair she took exception to. "A fashionable fribble" she had called Hero Number One, and had replaced him by chapter ten. His black jacket, tailored by Weston, set to perfection on his fashionable shoulders. His white cravate was immaculate and tied intricately. Even alone, working at his desk, he was not dishevelled. How often he had gone into Prue's ascetic little study and seen her head over her work, ink on her fingers, and her hair tumbling about her ears or tucked up under that cap! "You are quite the 'Tulip,' ass!" he told his reflection. He had flaunted his Phyrne in her face, and called her prude. Shilla vanished from his mind and it was now only of Prudence and himself that he thought. His thoughts were not pleasant company. Prudence could hardly think worse of him if he had purposely set out to disgust her. Not a redeeming trait. Women and warm talk, urging her to have Seville, running down Ashington in a fashion she disliked—in a jealous, spiteful manner. How had he not realized, when he wanted to kill Ashington, that he loved Prudence? He had some thought of it the last time he had seen her. More outrageous behaviour! Had whined and begged for sympathy by parading his poor weak attempts at virtue before her, and telling her he was an orphan. What a fool! What a snivelling, underhanded way to try to get around her. But she wasn't fooled for a minute. "*I* wasn't hellraking last night either, but I hadn't meant to brag to you about it."

So, jackanapes, you are in love with a clever little prude, and like the simpleton you are, have turned her against you. You will have to get busy and do a *volte face* to win her over. After a day's deliberation, he did put Marvelman into the play. Wills would like it—Marvelman had gone over well, and his appearance would ensure some interest in the play. But he'd have to keep Wills from putting an eye patch on whomever played the part. He worked hard, often with success, but as often with worries scuttling through his head that had nothing to do with the play. He postponed his return to London in hopes of finishing it and of being free for romance when he got there.

In the second week of his visit, his man of business found a building he considered suitable for his Magdalen House, and he took a few days off to inspect it. While in the vicinity, he also went to Longbourne Abbey to begin putting it in shape. He didn't want to have it in a shambles when they arrived. Presumption! In his mind it was quite a settled thing that Prudence would accept him.

And then Hettie's letter arrived to send his plans all to pieces.

Chapter Fifteen

The letter arrived in the morning, dated several days previously, he observed at a glance. Hettie was up to her old trick of waiting for the good fairies to post her letters for her. He started to read it through, his interest quickening as he saw Prue's name flash out at him down the page. He could scarcely believe his eyes—read it twice, then a third time to be sure he had it right. It was fatally easy to believe Seville's offer had not been an offer of marriage, Clarence's exhortations to the contrary. The man was clearly unreliable, but that Prudence for one moment thought it to be anything else he could not credit. The remainder of the passage threw him into a spasm of fear. She had decided to have Seville after all, then—God knew *he* had given her *every* encouragement to nab him! What foolish thing would she be likely to do? "Throwing herself at his head" had a bad ring to it, and a strangely uncharacteristic one. He couldn't envisage Prudence to be so lacking in pride. Turned into a virago when Ashington offended her *professional* pride. What nonsensical things had he said to her that day they had discussed it? He'd rather see her Seville's mistress than Ashington's wife—that at least was the gist of it. So she wouldn't deter her folly on *his* account. But surely she thought it was marriage Seville meant.

He read the letter yet a fourth time. Seville was going to Bath with a *chère amie* (possibly), so Prudence was safe for the present. But he knew he would get no work done here with this business tearing at his insides. He had his valet throw his things into a bag, made a hurried apology to the Malverns, and a quick departure to London. He arrived in the late afternoon, and stopped first at Hettie's place.

"What is the meaning of this letter you wrote me, Hettie?" he asked at once.

It had been penned days ago. She scarcely knew to what he referred. "The one about Bishop Michaels?" she asked.

"No, about Prudence Mallow."

"Oh, Miss Mallow and Seville! Isn't it shocking? So brass-faced and clever of her. I quite dote on the little minx. If it is a rich lover she wants, I mean to help her find one."

She sat benumbed at the reaction this friendly intention called forth. Dammler jumped from his chair and looked ready to murder her. "She is not a minx! She's as innocent as a lamb, and if Seville has ruined her, I'll kill him."

"Dammler! What foolishness have you got into your head? He never offered her his name, and she knows it well. She only said so—to impress *you*, I fancy, and it seems to have worked remarkably well, too."

"She does not know it! Is he spreading this tale around town?"

"Lord, no, he's scared to death the Baroness will hear it. I doubt he has told a soul. But if you had seen her making up to him on Bond Street last week you would be less sure of her innocence. It was compliments and promises to go down and see him off with the Four Horse Club—yes, and as broad a hint for him to take her to Bath with him as she could well make with *me* standing by."

His mouth set in a grim line, and his fists clenched. "This is all my doing. Is he gone to Bath?"

"I believe so. I haven't seen him since that day, or Miss Mallow either, now I come to think of it. It seems to me there is more between you and Miss Mallow than either of you have let on. All her questions, and sending you word she disapproves of the Countess . . . And how does it come you promised *her* to be a good boy?"

"How does it come *you* were telling her I was not a good boy—revolting phrase. I suppose you told her I wasn't getting a line down on paper. She'll think I was carrying on with Lady Malvern."

"It is what everyone who knows where you have been thinks. Weren't you?"

"No—only the flirtation Malvern requires from all his male guests. I was *working*, Het."

"Dammler, are you telling me you are having an affair with Miss Mallow?"

"No!"

"You are so—I know the signs. Both of you jealous as green cows, and she with her little messages to send you. Oh, she *wanted* me to tell you she was after Seville in order to get you back. She is up to anything! And how well it worked!"

"That is the first encouraging word I've heard since I set foot in this house. Did she seem jealous?"

"Yes, and bound and bent not to show it. So she *is* your mistress."

"No, but she will soon be my wife," he said firmly.

He left the room with long strides and bolted his horses straight to Grosvenor Square. Hettie sat reeling on her sofa, wondering if she had heard aright.

Dammler received with dismay the information that Miss Mallow was not at home, and would not be home in the near future—she had gone to Bath. He requested an interview with

Mr. Elmtree, who pretended to his sitter, a Mr. Sykes, brewer, that he was peeved, but in fact he was in alt. "It is Lord Dammler, the marquis, you know—he writes rhymes. A great friend of my niece. He has been off visiting an earl, but he is always about after my niece when he is in the city. He is sweet on her."

Dammler's return, not only to town but to Grosvenor Square in person, did much to re-establish him as an eligible parti. "Well, well, I had best see what he wants. As he has sought an interview with me, he is probably ready for his sitting now. We are trying to work out a mutually agreeable time, but I am very busy these days. Lawrence's taking up his time with the Royal Family throws a lot of extra work on my shoulders."

He took his time about wiping his hands clean, relishing the thought that Dammler would see how busy he was. He left on his frock, as a hallmark of his profession, and excused himself for it as he entered the saloon.

"You catch me hard at work, Lord Dammler. I am doing a portrait of Mr. Sykes—the brewer, you know. His face is a little red, but I will tone it down for him with white. He will have a nice genteel complexion when I am finished with him, he needn't fear, and the symbol, you know, can be a spray of hops. There is no need to go putting a glass of ale in his hands. No one will connect it with ale—a spray of hops looks much like a mulberry . . ."

"I came to see if you could tell me where I might find Prudence," Dammler interrupted impatiently. "They tell me she is gone to Bath."

"Yes, so she is. It was Seville's idea. He talked her into it. They left this morning—set out in a carriage and four. They were to stay the night at Reading and continue the trip tomorrow."

Dammler knew Clarence well enough to realize Prudence had not actually set out in a carriage with Seville, to stay the night at Reading. "Who went with her?" he asked.

168

"Her mother is with her, of course. She could not go with him alone."

"Is Seville actually in her carriage, or she in his?"

"No, no, he went on a few days ahead. He is waiting for her there. And how did the rhyming go at Finefields?"

"Well. She is not really *with* Seville then?"

"No, he dashed on a day ahead of her. She is meeting him there. He was very eager for her to go."

"So you told me. Do you have her address?"

"Yes, she stays at Laura Place. I have it written down here somewhere." But 'there' proved to be not in the saloon, or study, or anywhere else he could remember. The butler came to his help. He had it written on a card for the purpose of forwarding mail, and eventually a copy of it was handed to Dammler.

Clarence supposed from Dammler's manner that he was in some rush, and it was not long dawning on him that the reason for urgency was jealousy. He was right for once, but could not keep his knowledge to himself.

"You will be trotting after them, will you?" he asked bluntly.

"Yes, I leave immediately. They stop at Reading, you say? Do you know which inn?"

"They stop *tonight* at Reading. They left at nine o'clock this morning. You will not catch them up at Reading."

"I will if they stop the night. Do you have the name of the inn?"

No, he didn't have the name, nor did the butler, there being no point in forwarding mail there, but he thought she had mentioned "The George."

"You mean to drive all night then?" Clarence asked, well impressed with this eagerness.

"Yes."

"Well, well. You are pretty anxious to catch up with her. This will put Seville's nose out of joint, for her to land with you in her wake. A *real* marquis . . ." The only thing as variable as the value of a Spanish title was the choice of husband for Prudence. Whichever man or name was before him was the best by a long shot.

"If it doesn't, I will," Dammler said tersely, and turned to go, his hat still in his hand, for in his haste, he hadn't handed it to the butler.

"You mean to try your hand with her, do you?" Clarence confirmed, trailing him into the hall.

"Yes, certainly. I mean to marry her."

"Well, well, I shall know what to tell Ashington if he calls."

"Does that bleater still come around?" Dammler asked angrily.

"He is always chasing after her," Clarence answered promptly, harking back to a time some weeks before. "But she has given him the slip. It is Seville who pesters her now. It is the Spaniard you must watch out for. There are queer knots in all foreigners, say what you will."

Dammler returned to his apartment, exchanged his travelling coach-and-four for the faster curricle and his fresh team of greys, determined to be at Reading before morning, if he had to drive all night. He dined alone at home on cold meat and left at seven o'clock, tired even before he began the drive, from his trip from Finefields and his worries. It was nearing midnight when he pulled into "The George" at Reading, so tired he could hardly walk, and knowing he would not see Prudence before morning. He felt he had been a damned fool to come pelting after her in such haste. As he signed the register, he glanced to the names above his to see if she was there. He saw her neat signature, and her mother's. The very sight of them cheered him, till his eye slid up a little higher on the page, and he saw the less pleasing sight of R.J. Seville, Esq., in a dark, bold hand.

His blood surged through his body till he was breathing faster. "I see a friend of mine, Miss Mallow, stops here. Would you be kind enough to give me her room number?"

"I'm afraid I can't do that Mr . . ." The clerk glanced at the register. "Lord Dammler!" he shouted. "Oh . . . oh, well, in *that* case I'm sure it is all right. Miss Mallow is in the suite at the *east* end of the first floor."

"And Mr. Seville? I notice he too is registered. Another—friend of mine."

"He is next door to Miss Mallow."

"How very convenient," Dammler said in a controlled voice, and turned away to take the stairs two at a time, toward the door at the east end of the hall.

Chapter Sixteen

Prudence was so eager to be off to Bath that she scarcely closed an eye the night before, and was up at seven o'clock to check again her luggage to see if she had packed all her essentials, plus a good many items she suspected of being superfluous. But one couldn't be sure of getting Gowland's lotion and Longman's soap at Bath, and it was best to be prepared. Clarence wouldn't miss their taking off for the world. He put on his new blue coat of superfine to bid them farewell, and tied an Oriental for the occasion. He went outside to tend to the tying on of the trunks, and to let Mr. McGee next door have a look at his coat and cravat. He would later stop around to tell Sir Alfred that the ladies had got off bright and early. Mr. Sykes was not coming for his sitting till eleven o'clock. Very fortunate he had gentlemen lined up for the next few paintings. After that he would try his hand at a couple of country scenes in Richmond Park. It was the season for it. June might mean Bath or Brighton for most, for Clarence it meant three more landscapes of Richmond Park. Well, well, it would be good to have the place to himself again for a few weeks. Quite like old times.

At nine o'clock Prudence and her mother pulled away from

the door and settled back to enjoy the luxury of getting away from Clarence, London, and the stale familiarity of home. It was a fine day. Once free of London they enjoyed the brisk trot provided by an extravagant team of four horses, and the view of emerald countryside, dotted with trees and flowers.

"We should do this more often," Prudence said. "Now that we have a few pounds from my work to spare, we should go to Bath every spring."

"Mr. Seville will not be there every spring," Mrs Mallow replied coyly.

"I certainly hope not! I am not going because *he* is there, Mama. In fact, I hope he will have left before we arrive."

"I don't think that is very likely," her mother laughed, rather complacently. She was glad to be getting Prudence away from London and her memories of Lord Dammler. Impossible that *that* would ever come to anything but heartbreak.

Strangely, Prudence did not mind in the least that both Clarence and her mama thought she was running after Mr. Seville as hard as she could. Had they inferred for a single moment she was flinging herself at Dammler's head, she would have been incensed, but to their little jokes about Seville she was impervious. They had a pleasant nuncheon between London and Reading, and remounted for the afternoon's journey, and both felt themselves fortunate to be lurching along in a quaint old vehicle twenty years old, with four fast-tiring nags to pull it, to a fashionable resort for a four week's stay in rented rooms hired sight unseen at a low cost. Their spirits were still high when they arrived at "The George" in Reading in good time for dinner. They took a walk to stretch their limbs before eating, and splurged on hiring the smallest private parlour in the establishment for dinner. Breakfast they would take in their room. There must be some limit to their high living they agreed.

But for this one meal there was no limit. They ordered two courses and a small bottle of wine. As Prudence was treating herself to buttered lobster, Mrs. Mallow too decided to be daring and order up a dish of oysters. She thought they had a funny taste, but since Clarence never served oysters, the sensation was new, and so she said they were delicious and forced herself to eat every one, as Prue was paying such an exorbitant sum for them. Before the sweet was served she felt ill, and before she managed to wobble to her bed she was sure she was dying. She wished she *would* die and get it over with. She was weak, terribly sick, with a cold sweat over her whole body and an ache in every joint and muscle.

Prudence became alarmed, and dashed to the desk downstairs to enquire for a doctor.

"There's Mr. Mulcahy who sometimes comes to tend patrons," she was told. His address was looked up in a desultory and condescending manner.

"Send for him—please, at once!" she said.

"*We* don't send for the physician. You must do it yourself, ma'am," the clerk said.

"I cannot leave Mama. She is very ill."

"You have servants, I presume?" the man sneered. He had no opinion of young females in cambric gowns who ran about inns unescorted.

"Yes—oh yes," she answered, chastened, and hurried halfway upstairs before recollecting that the groom was the proper person to go on such an errand. She asked timidly if someone would please fetch the groom—Jenkins was his name.

With a disdainful lift of his eyebrow in her direction, the clerk wrote a few lines before summoning a footboy to help out the young—lady. He didn't quite dare say person; there was just something about Miss Mallow that did not permit the slighting reference. Prudence dashed back to her mama and waited for what seemed an eternity for the physician to come, while her mama retched and moaned and writhed in pain. At length, Prudence could stand it no longer, and ran again to the clerk's desk. Her groom was just returning—alone. The doctor was gone to Bath himself on a holiday.

174

"Oh—what shall I do?" she wailed. "Whatever shall I do? There must be another doctor in Reading."

The door of a private parlour opened, and a tall gentleman dressed in the first fashion came out. Upon seeing Miss Mallow, his first thought was to dart back into the parlour and close the door, but when he observed her agitation, he stepped nobly forward to involve himself in her problem.

"Miss Mallow—my dear Miss Mallow—what is the matter?" Mr. Seville asked in alarm. Returning from Bath to London, he too stopped at "The George" to break his trip.

"Mr. Seville! How glad I am to see you!" she said. He feared she was about to throw herself on his bosom in a fit of tears. The dreadful thought struck him that the hussy was staging a scene to ensnare him, but her agitation soon freed him from that worry.

She told him her story in a distracted manner, breaking into sobs in the middle of it. "You great thundering cloth-head," Seville turned on the clerk in wrath. "You know perfectly well Dr. Knighton is put up at this very inn. Summon him at once!"

The clerk, seeing Miss Mallow was 'connected,' as he politely phrased inferior persons who knew superior ones, became more civil. "He particularly asked not to be disturbed," he said, but with an eye already running over the ledger to discover his room.

"Get him at once, moron," Seville shouted. "Give him my name."

"Yes, sir," the clerk bowed meekly, and ran up the stairs himself to summon the doctor. Seville and Miss Mallow too ascended to the sick lady's room. Within three minutes Knighton had arrived with his black bag, administering magic liquids and reassuring words of hope.

"This is not the first case I've had tonight," he said. "There was bad food served here. Shellfish, I fancy, is the culprit. Did your mother eat oysters, Miss Mallow?"

"Yes, she did."

"That's it. They are the cause. Mrs. Dacres had them, too—thought they tasted odd, and ate only two. She was not nearly so ill as your mother. I have already told the proprietor to take them off the menu. We will pull your mother through, never fear. I think she has rid herself of them all. She was sick to her stomach, you say?"

"Yes—dreadfully," Prudence answered.

"Good. Good, the sicker the better. We want to make sure they are all out. I'll administer a saline draught."

There was a great bustle and commotion. Knighton sent for his valet who came with more chemicals. Miss Mallow hovered about the bed, then went into the adjoining room, her own room, to talk to Mr. Seville, to assure him and be assured by him that all would be well with Dr. Knighton on hand. So very fortunate he had been there.

At length the invalid was settled down, her stomach purged of poison, a draught administered to calm her, but no laudanum. Knighton thought it best that she remain with normal consciousness, lest any severe pain occur later. It was nearing ten before he left, only to be called away to another oyster eater, caught before the warning was out. "I shall look in on your mother again before I retire," Knighton promised Prudence.

"Thank you, Doctor," she said with deep gratitude. "I don't know what we should have done without you. Be sure to send me your bill." She began to write out her address at Bath.

"It is an honour to serve the creator of *The Composition* and such books," he said. "I read all your works and like them immensely. In fact, I shall tell you a little secret. The Prince of Wales likes them, too, and means to have you to visit him. They were recommended to him by his mother, Queen Charlotte. She allows her daughters to read them. It is unusual to find a novel suitable for young ladies that is still entertaining," he laughed. "In fact, I should not be surprised if you are given permission to dedicate your next to the Prince. And in lieu of a bill, I shall request you to autograph my copies when you return to London."

"I shall be very happy to," she said, staring at him with a smile of great delight on her face. The Prince of Wales—Queen Charlotte! To think of the Royal Family reading her stories, and liking them!

After Knighton had bowed himself out, she turned to Seville. "Dear me, what an honour. I did not expect anything like this."

"It is not in excess of your merits," he bowed formally. For a moment he regretted his opera dancer. Miss Mallow, as he had been one of the first to divine, was on her way up in the world.

"Indeed it is! I never looked for such honour. To dedicate a book to the Prince Regent! It is beyond anything great."

"You are too modest. Dr. Ashington had high praise for your works in that fine review he did last month."

She acknowledged this praise with an external smile and an inward sneer. "This is not the time to be wallowing in my own glory," she reminded herself. "I must go to Mama. How can I ever thank you for your kind help, Mr. Seville? I should have been lost without you. Only think, a physician at the inn all the time, and the clerk not telling me. Mama might have died for all he cared."

"I mean to speak to the proprietor about that. Serving tainted food, and then doing nothing to help the victims. Maintain a haughty and injured manner, Miss Mallow, and at the very least you will have your stay without expense."

"I should never have thought of that," she said, but once it was mentioned, it seemed a good idea, and no more than was her due.

"You are not up to snuff at all," Seville told her. Looking at her tired, wan little face, he came at last to believe it. Here she stood in her bedroom alone with a man, seeing no more impropriety in it than if they were at a ball. The fear that she was trying to trick him here at the inn had long since faded. "I shall go down and speak to the proprietor at once. Demand

177

anything you want of the inn—don't fear the cost. You will be staying a few days till your mama is recovered, and shan't pay a cent for it. I'll look in before I retire, after Knighton's visit, to see all is well for the night. Your servant, ma'am." He bowed and left, and put such a bee in the owner's ear that he was all for removing Miss Mallow and her mother that very moment to the best suite in the inn.

With all restored to peace and quiet—Mama sleeping soundly in the next room with the servant standing guard and the most famous doctor in the country coming later to check her—Prudence allowed herself a few moments to consider her latest achievement. She was to be recognized by the ruler of the land. Possibly to dedicate her next book to him. She had arrived! She knew Miss Burney and Wordsworth and Coleridge, Dr. Ashington had reviewed her in *Blackwood's Magazine*, the king's physician admired her and wanted an autograph instead of her money. Her cup was overflowing, or should be. But the contents came all from one side—on the personal side it was empty. The contents of the other side were filling a suite at Finefields, and showing no intention of leaving it. She sighed, and took up a paper to read till Knighton returned.

It got to be eleven o'clock, then eleven-thirty, and still Knighton did not come. Seville tapped at the door and asked if he had been yet. "No, and I am so sleepy. I wonder if he means to come."

"Yes, he said he would come. I'll order you a cup of tea to keep you awake," Seville said, and went to do so. When he returned, Knighton had just arrived. He was with Mrs. Mallow, and found she progressed satisfactorily.

"She will be weak for a few days. I don't advise you to move her before two days. I leave tomorrow, but I'll give you the address of a local physician. Mention my name, and he will be happy to come at a moment's notice."

178

"Thank you. You are so very kind." What a difference it made, being somebody. She was quite struck with it. Being somebody with a potential lawsuit to hold over the inn brought her another surprise. The "cup of tea," when it arrived a little later, proved to be a feast comprising everything in the inn's larder but sea food. There were meats and cheeses, breads, fruits, and a sweet.

"Oh, they have brought a *meal!*" she laughed. "You must stay and join me, gentlemen."

Knighton accepted a cup of tea, and Seville too sat down. When Knighton left a little later to check up on Mrs. Dacres, Seville saw no harm in sitting on a moment while Prudence ate. There is something about a calamity that lowers the barriers ordinarily pertaining in society. And there was her mother right next door, too. He mentioned opening the door, but Prudence objected that the noise might disturb her mother.

When a loud knock was heard without, they neither of them jumped up in guilty alarm. They supposed it to be Knighton, or a menial of the establishment. "Come in," Prudence called, and Lord Dammler stepped through the door, his face haggard and furious.

"How cosy!" he said in a cold tone, and advanced towards them with murder in his eye.

Seville jumped up. "Just leaving," he said, edging towards the door. Dammler blocked his way with his body.

"I will have a word with you first."

"What are *you* doing here, Dammler?" Prudence asked, reeling from the shock of seeing him when she thought him still at Finefields.

"More to the point, what is *he* doing here?" he jerked his head towards Seville.

"He has been helping me. The most dreadful thing has happened . . ."

"I can explain," Seville began, knowing by the cast of

Dammler's countenance that he was more involved with the Miss Mallow than he had ever supposed.

"You had best make it *very good*," he was told through taut lips.

"There's a sick woman in there," Seville began, pointing to the adjoining door.

"You celebrate the event in an unusual manner," Dammler replied, glancing at the laden tray on the table.

"It's Mama," Prudence stated.

"Well?" Dammler asked, his voice rising.

"She had poisoned food and was taken ill," Seville explained.

"That does not account for *your* presence in Miss Mallow's bedroom at midnight!" Dammler snapped, advancing towards Seville.

"He has been helping me," Prudence told him, throwing herself between them.

Thus protected, Seville headed for the door. "Miss Mallow will explain everything," he said.

"I'm not finished with you," Dammler rapped out, pushing Prudence aside and hastening to grab Seville's shoulder before he got the door open.

"How dare you!" Prudence flew to him. "Making a disturbance when Mama is lying ill in the next room. What right have you to come in here, making insinuations. *You!* You, of all people!"

Dammler turned to her, the anger shocked out of him. "Miss Mallow will explain," Seville repeated, and got out the door while he had the opportunity. He took the precaution of bolting his own door, then went to put his ear to the adjoining wall to see what he could overhear.

"I want a full explanation of this, Prudence," Dammler told her.

"Do you indeed?" she turned on him, her blue eyes flashing. "I see *one* explanation has already occurred to you. The very one I might expect to occur to one of *your* moral laxity. The explanation is that Mama very nearly died, and would have died had not Mr. Seville summoned a doctor for her. He has been everything that is good and kind, as he always is. *He* is a perfectly honourable and worthy gentleman."

"How does it come about you two are here together, at this inn, with rooms next door?"

"I don't know what brings him here. Very likely he is returning to the City from Bath, but I am very glad he is here. But for him I should have been distracted."

"I have a very good idea why he is here. You are travelling together."

"Yes, in opposite directions!"

"You are on your way to Bath with him."

"Am I indeed? It is kind of you to tell me so. And what great event managed to tear *you* away from your lover for a moment? It must be something of major importance—a new Phyrne perhaps."

"Lady Malvern is not my lover."

"She is, and all of London knows it. Do you take me for a fool?"

"I take you for a scheming, designing hussy!"

"That's enough. Get out! Out this instant, or I shall call for help."

"Seville never offered to marry you. He offered you a *carte blanche*, didn't he?"

"No."

"Yes, and you regret you didn't accept it, too."

"Is it so incomprehensible to you that a gentleman should want to *marry* me?"

"He no more intended marrying you than he intended flying to the moon. It is known all over town he has offered for Baroness McFay."

"He offered for *me* first."

"Offered to make you his mistress. With his flowers and diamond necklaces. Did he say 'Will you do me the honour to be my wife?' or did he not?"

"Yes. No, I don't know. I don't recall his exact words. How should I?"

"But you recall hailing him on Bond Street? Telling him you should *love* to go to Bath with him. *That* cannot have slipped your very convenient memory."

"My memory is not deficient, Lord Dammler. I remember very well meeting Mr. Seville on Bond Street. I also remember meeting *you* there one night, in your cups, and dragging a redhead along with you. I remember as well seeing you making a fool of yourself at the opera with a blond lightskirt, and though I hadn't the dubious pleasure of seeing you at Finefields, I make no doubt you were equally attentive to your brunette. Certainly you wasted no time on your work."

"I was working like a dog!"

"Ah, well, when lovemaking becomes a *chore*, it is time to move on to the next woman. You will be all out of complexions, and have to turn to grey-haired ladies next, like the Prince of Wales."

"Don't think to get out of it by dragging up my past."

"Past? You are confused in your tenses, milord."

"The fact is, you were alone in your bedroom at midnight with that scoundrel of a Seville."

"It's none of your concern if I was in my bed with him! You have no right to come charging in, demanding explanations. I am alone in my bedroom past midnight with *you*, but I assure you I have no intention of losing my virtue."

"You cannot lose that which you lack to begin with."

"I doubt you have any to lose. *Honi soit qui mal y pense*, Dammler, if I may borrow your phrase. Now perhaps you will be kind enough to leave."

"I will leave, and you may tell your lover I will call on him tomorrow. This is not the end of it."

182

"If you bother Mr. Seville with these absurd accusations, I'll . . ."

"Kill me?" he asked. "You might as well, but first I'll have the exquisite pleasure of putting a bullet through that jackrabbit's liver."

He turned and departed, closing the door quietly behind him. Prudence sat on the chair and cried into her lap, from worry and fatigue and nervousness.

Next door, Seville had heard enough to send him into a state of shock. Dammler was out to kill him, and all because of a misunderstanding. The girl had assured him she was not under Dammler's protection. How the devil was *he* to know? He sat on the edge of his bed, his hand on his brow. He recalled the conversation to himself, looking for a respectable escape. His chief consolation was that the silly chit still thought he had meant marriage. He must convince Dammler of the same thing. Now what had he said to Lady Melvine? Hinted at the truth, but not quite stated it. He'd have to get to her and convince her she had misunderstood him. Dammler couldn't call him to account for making the girl an offer in form. No insult in that. Dashed compliment—and what if the Baroness heard it? Then there was this night's work to straighten out. Knighton—get *him* to tell Dammler how sick the mother was. Wouldn't think he'd been making up to Miss Mallow with the mother dying in the next room. He wasn't that big a gudgeon.

His instinct for self-preservation warned him to flee. To get into his carriage that very night and bolt for London. Give Dammler a chance to cool down. Miss Mallow could soothe his ruffled feathers if she weren't such a goose cap. Crazed about her. Yes, and she could get him to marry her, too, if she were half as smart as everyone said she was. Trying to bam her he wasn't playing parlour games with Lady Malvern. Why the deuce *was* he, if he was so crazed about Miss Mallow? Half an hour later, Seville came to a decision. He would write Knighton a line, mentioning that Dammler was here and concerned about Mrs. Mallow. Thus Dammler would learn the old lady was really sick, then he would pen a note to Miss Mallow couched in such respectful terms as were bound to lead Dammler to know there was never any impropriety in his thoughts. A deft mention of their former association . . . "Though you declined the offer to be my wife, I hope we may always be friends." Something of that sort. She'd be bound to show it to Dammler. By Jove, he couldn't afford a duel with the papers all ready for the Baroness to sign. Slip out the back door at dawn, and be halfway to London before Dammler knew he was gone.

He executed this wily scheme, and saved his liver from perforation.

Chapter Seventeen

When Dammler called on Seville the next morning, he was
gone, and when he went to see if Miss Mallow also was gone,
he found her in conference with Dr. Knighton, receiving in-
structions for the tending of her mother.

"Seville wrote me you were here," Knighton said to him. "He
was a big help to Miss Mallow last evening. Can you believe,
the foolish fellow here at the inn didn't call me, but had Miss
Mallow sending around town for a physician. There is no accounting for such stupidity. I had mentioned I did not wish to
be disturbed, but had no notion he would take me so literally.
An emergency, of course, was quite a different matter. I have
just been telling Miss Mallow her mother must not be moved
for one or two days."

Knighton soon took his leave and Dammler, somewhat
calmer but still furious, said, "Your friend has turned tail and
run. Did you warn him I was coming after him?"

"Don't think he would be afraid of *you*," she answered in a
sneering way. "I had a note from him. You will find him in London, if you are intent on making a fool of yourself and a shambles of my reputation."

"Your reputation needs no help from *me* to be made a shambles of."

"Would you not convince everyone the affair between myself and Mr. Seville was dishonourable by calling him out?"

This aspect of the matter had already occurred to Dammler and he was regretting his rash statement, but having made it, he did not intend to retreat. Nor was he entirely convinced Seville was innocent. "No names need be mentioned. If anyone suspects, it will be a lesson for Seville to be wary in his dealings with you, and to avoid making the sort of offer he made."

"For your information, Lord Dammler, Seville's offer was not as you think. He mentions in his note, you see," she handed it to him, "that though I declined the offer *to be his wife*, he hopes we will remain friends. And so we shall, too."

Dammler took the letter, read it, and felt a great fool. Hettie, the blundering idiot, had misunderstood. "It does not excuse his being here last night," he said, trying to save some small portion of his face.

"As to what passed last night, I should prefer to forget it. I must go to Mama now."

"Your mother, does she prosper? She will be all right?"

"Yes, but loud, acrimonious discussions in the next room are not good for her."

"Well I'm sorry, Prudence, but I misunderstood."

"Yes, misunderstandings are likely to occur when we judge others by our own standards," she replied bitingly. "Having nothing but lechery in your own mind, you naturally impute it to others."

"I had no lechery in mind with regard to yourself."

"I realize *I* am not your type, and thank God for it."

He stood uncertainly, hoping to re-ingratiate himself before leaving, and seeing it would be hard going, with Prudence in the boughs. "You go on to Bath then?"

"In a few days."

"I will be happy to stay and accompany you."

"How very kind, but I should prefer to go without any disreputable companions and see if I can't recover from the shame of having received an offer of marriage from an unexceptionable gentleman."

He swallowed this with difficulty. "I only wanted to help you."

"I find your help a sad hindrance, however," she said airily, and succeeded at last in goading him to anger.

"Then I shall remove my hindering presence. I wish you good day, ma'am."

Prudence nodded her head silently and watched him leave. I never thought to ask him how he came to be here, she remembered after he was gone. And how very badly he behaved, too, accusing me of carrying on with Seville. Behaved like a childish, jealous young hothead. And why should he have been so jealous, if he doesn't care for me more than he knows? And I was the same—showing my jealousy of Lady Malvern and all his other flirts. Prudence hardly knew which of them had been the bigger fool, but she could not be entirely despondent. He seemed to be realizing slowly that he loved her more than as a mere sister.

With all her helps and hindrances gone, the two days before she might proceed to Bath passed slowly, despite the most solicitous concern on behalf of the management of "The George." The three cases of food poisoning caused a slight stir in the local press. The event of the eminent Dr. Knighton's presence made it more newsworthy, and when picked up by a journal in Bath, it was discovered that Lord Dammler, always of prime interest, had also been present, apparently on a visit to another young writer. The other writer was found out, and a brief interview with her added the information that she was on her way to Bath, and that she was working on a new book. When the story was finally published in Bath, it had become a large piece of human interest.

Bath hadn't presently many great persons visiting it, and even a minor somebody assumed importance. A letter from the

Prince of Wales complimenting Prudence and inviting her to Carlton House upon her return to London was soon added to her luster; and after she had been in Bath a few days, Mr. King called in person to invite her to put her name on the register at the Pump Room, and to attend the local assemblies. Within a week, she was a *bona fide* celebrity, whose entry into the Pump Room each morning with her mother caused a stir of no small degree. Her books were displayed in the shop windows, and—glory upon glory—a cartoon of her appeared in the window of the lending library. She was portrayed as signing autographs for her books, with crowds clambering all around her.

Prudence was too busy to write it all down for Uncle Clarence, but she laughed to herself to think how happy he would be. Uncle Clarence had one other correspondent besides herself. Her mother, who as often as not elected to remain home from the "do's" when her chaperonage was not required, was busy with her pen and sent off cuttings from the newspapers vaunting Prudence's new fame in her letters.

When these reached London, Clarence realized he was missing out on a deal of interesting activity, and posted off in his carriage—again hiring an extra pair of horses to arrive in a style befitting his niece's renown. He scarcely took time to dash over to see Mrs. Hering and Sir Alfred and tell them of his trip.

"Well, Prudence, so you are the talk of the town, naughty puss," he beamed in approval when he saw her. He discerned the reflected glory of a letter from Carlton House on her brow, and a cartoon in the shop window in her eye. "You are up to all the rigs. You won't be recognizing your old uncle next thing we know. Hardly a line for me."

"Oh, but Mama wrote. There was no point in both of us writing the same thing."

"Aye, you are too busy. I know just how it is. I am very busy myself. We all are. I painted the Chilterns all done up in style, but had time for only one study of Richmond Hill with so much going on."

"What was going on in London, Uncle?" she asked eagerly. Her own thoughts often flew to London, where she imagined Dammler to be, though she didn't actually know it.

"Why, everyone wanted to hear of your success. I have had a dozen callers a day stopping to congratulate me."

Prudence correctly interpreted this to mean he had been running around telling his friends of her fame, and smiled weakly.

"So, Wilma, you became ill eating oysters," he chided gently.

"I never eat an oyster. They are no fit food for human beings. They are well enough for seagulls, but I never serve them at my table. Nasty looking things. But Knighton came to help you. That was well thought of, Prue, sending to London for Knighton."

"He happened to be at the inn. It was the greatest chance."

It was well done of Knighton to be on hand, but not quite as wonderful as having him dash down from London, and this was soon transformed into the more acceptable story. "He is very good about making a call. I'll say that for him. I will have him over to look at my chest when I return to the City."

"What's the matter with your chest, Clarence?" his sister asked.

"It is giving me a little trouble," he answered vaguely, having just that second thought what consequence it would add for McGee to see Knighton's carriage outside his door. "But the waters might cure me. We will all go to the Pump Room tomorrow. I daresay there is quite a little stir when you walk in. Everyone turning and staring and wanting a book signed."

"Yes, there is quite a commotion," Wilma assured him.

"Very unpleasant for you. Very unpleasant indeed," he smiled his gratification. "We will go early. I want to have a look at your cartoon in the window first. You didn't describe it to me at all, Wilma. Is it well done? Have they given her a good profile? I know those fellows never tackle a front likeness, with foreshortening. As to hoping for an eyelash . . ."

"It is very like," Prudence told him. "I am sitting at my table in the Pump Room, with one person knocking my glass over, and another climbing up on my chair."

"So that's how it is, eh? It is well I am here to fend them off," he smiled.

"It is not really so bad as that. They exaggerate in a cartoon. I am gratified to be asked to sign an autograph."

"You are good-tempered. It sounds dashed encroaching to me," he decreed, pleased as punch.

His next overture was, "Where is Dammler? I thought he would be here with you. I don't see you wearing his ring."

"Ring?" Prudence asked in alarm. She had expected to have to make excuses for Seville's absence, but counted on her cartoon in the window to tide her over. That Clarence thought Dammler to be on the verge of offering for her was a nasty shock.

"He came chasing after you to give you a ring, did he not?"

"No, he is not here. He has never been here at all. You read perhaps that he was at the inn at Reading . . ." His appearance at "The George" at that ill-fated moment had bothered Prudence considerably. She assumed that it was pure bad luck that had brought him.

"Read it? Why, he told me himself the day you left he would be there at Reading if he had to drive all night."

"What—he called on you that day?" Prudence asked, wondering if there was so much as a grain of truth in this.

"In a great pelter he was. Jealous of that Spanish fellow you know—Barcelona is it, or Madrid . . ." Seville was out of it entirely. His name had not once appeared in the papers.

"How could he know Seville had come to Bath? He could not have heard it at Finefields surely."

"I didn't think to ask him how he knew, but he certainly knew of it."

190

"Did *you* tell him?" Prudence asked.

"I don't know." Clarence for once in his life admitted to ignorance, there being no glory attached to any other course. "But certainly he knew—got your address from me and said he would catch you if he had to drive all night. He was very put out at your coming here with Seville."

"I did not come with Seville. He was gone before we arrived."

"Ho, you are a sly puss, playing them all off, one against the other."

Prudence couldn't press her innocence as she had encouraged Clarence to think Seville was her reason for coming, but she desired to hear more of Dammler's visit. "Did Dammler think I came *with* Seville?" she asked.

"No, I told him you came with your mother and four horses." The four horses had a ring of truth to it. Certainly Clarence would have mentioned that startling fact. "He was very jealous. 'I will knock his nose out of joint,' he said. Very angry and jealous, just as he should be."

This statement had too much of the aroma of Clarence's own brand of daydreaming to be taken seriously. "Where is he anyway?" he persisted. "He has gone on to get his abbey ready for after the marriage, I collect?"

Clarence had too often wed her to all her acquaintances for her to place the least faith in his word. "There is no marriage, Uncle," she said.

"You turned him down, did you?" he asked, a little disappointed. "I thought he was a pretty good fellow."

"He didn't make me an offer."

"Ho, prudent as ever. But it is nothing to be ashamed of—a marquis, and a pretty good rhymster from what I hear. Still, there is no saying, with your going to Carlton House, that you couldn't do better than a poor deformed poet. They could bend the Royal Marriage Act a little if they took it into their heads. It is only to keep actresses and Papists out of the palace. The Duke of Clarence was always sweet on you . . ."

Prudence looked at her mother and sighed. There was no getting any sense out of Clarence. She'd leave, before he had her married to one of the royal dukes.

She deduced Dammler had indeed been at Grosvenor Square, but what he might have said would never be known. The fact of his having been there at all gave her a point to ponder. He *had* come to "The George" just to see her then, and if he had been to see Uncle in the afternoon, he must also have driven half the night. And then there was that very satisfying jealous passion. She had expected to see him again soon, but now ten days had passed, and not a sign of him.

The days had passed in an interesting manner. As Prudence was now a celebrity, she was invited everywhere. She had her regular suitors for drives and walks and standing up at the balls—old retired soldiers and widowers and such, but a pleasing number of them. And also—really it was too ridiculous—who should be here but Ronald Springer! For years she had sighed after him, and now when she no longer cared, he seemed to be developing quite a *tendre* in her direction. A day seldom passed that he did not call on some pretext or other. Now accustomed to such interesting men as Dammler and Seville, Prudence was no longer impressed by his country elegance. There was also just a little something of Ashington in Springer—a dropping of a classical quotation, a too-frequent reference to his Cambridge days, an assurance that he was doing her a favour to call. No, she did not look towards him in any romantic way, but it was rather interesting that he was here, and dangling after her. She remembered with a smile that Dammler never liked him.

With all her going about and partying, Prudence had had to enlarge her wardrobe. She had become one of the models followed by the young fashionable Society of Bath. If she wore a green bonnet with her yellow sarsenet gown to church on Sunday, one or the other of the shops on Milsom Street was sure to have a similar ensemble in the window on Monday.

When she pinned a bouquet of posies on her sun parasol one day, she had the satisfaction of seeing a dozen ladies with theirs similarly adorned the next afternoon. Encouraged by these successes, she went a little further. Her gowns, while always remaining within the bounds of propriety, became more sophisticated, decolleté, and Colonel Bereseford told her she had shoulders like the "Venus de Milo." She undertook to repay some of the social favours conferred on her, and set up a small salon, to which select groups were invited to talk about literature. Twice she was so daring as to attend public functions with no chaperone, but only a male escort. She purposely chose elderly gentlemen for this honour to squash any rumour of her being fast, but Springer had not liked it. Still, it had not slowed down his visits.

A few elderly eyebrows were raised at her daring. The Countess of Cleff, known locally as the Pillar of Propriety, was said to have frowned. Twenty years earlier she had been the supreme arbiter of the *ton*, but as she aged and conventions relaxed she had become dated. Still, she wielded considerable power, and one did not intentionally offend her. Prudence curtailed her unchaperoned appearances when she heard of the Countess' displeasure. The "Pillar" had not yet passed judgment on Miss Mallow. She liked to see young notables come to her city, and so long as Miss Mallow could be directed, she might take her up. She watched and waited.

Yes, Bath was a more pleasant change than Prudence had dared to hope, yet she would gladly have been back in her little study, unknown, if only it meant Dammler would come unannounced to her door every few days to entertain her. To think she might have thrown over a chance for even greater familiarity than that bothered her. Ten days had passed, and the silence from her old friend was deafening.

In the morning, Clarence had to view the cartoon and the Pump Room, where his niece was treated with enough curiosity to satisfy him. "I see there is a concert at the Upper

Rooms tonight," he said, reading a poster.

"Yes, but it is only an Italian singer," Mrs. Mallow pointed out. "You will not want to bother with that."

"Why, there is no one who can sing a tune like an Italian. Certainly we will go." He had a new jacket, purchased in honour of his niece's future attendance at Carlton House, that would be previewed on this occasion. He could hardly wait to put it on. He purchased three tickets before they left to ensure getting a good seat. Wilma decided not to go, but Prudence knew there was no getting out of it.

She went to the concert happily enough. It was better than sitting home with Clarence, and the literary salons would be curtailed if her uncle came. She looked forward to daydreaming her way through the concert in peace.

She was not allowed to do so. No sooner had she taken her seat than she saw a tall, dark-haired man enter on the arm of the Dowager Countess of Cleff and take up a seat across the hall from her. It was Dammler, and if he glanced at the stage at all, it was no more than a glance. His head was turned in her direction throughout the first half of the performance, till she was fatigued with pretending not to see him.

Chapter Eighteen

Prudence dreaded intermission, yet thought it would never come. The Italian sang at length to thunderous applause. The only change in posture of her observer was a brief mild clapping of the hands at the end of each selection, without once looking to the stage. Her uncle had reserved a table for tea at the intermission, and with her equilibrium in tatters, Miss Mallow went on his arm to take her place. Dammler would come now. Say something—she hardly knew what. Present them to the Dowager very likely. They had not met, but the Countess was known by sight to Prudence. And what on earth was Dammler doing in the company of such a stickler?

He didn't come. She refused to gape about the room to find him, but as they resumed their places in the hall, he bowed ceremoniously from the waist in her direction. She wondered that he had not come to say a few words at the break; was he still angry over the incident at Reading? It was strangely unlike him to bear a grudge. Flare up and then have done with an argument was his usual manner of proceeding.

During the second act, Dammler looked mainly towards the stage, with only a dozen turns of his head to the left, each seen and counted by Miss Mallow out of the corner of her eye. They did not pass in leaving, and it was with a strange mixture of feelings that Prudence took her way home. Clarence had not seen him at all, which was a blessing. She didn't have to hear that he had come dashing down to Bath, driving all night, to marry her. But why *had* he come?

After leaving Prudence in a high state of resentment at "The George" in Reading, Dammler had driven back to London. First he went to Hettie, to inform her she was mistaken about Seville's intentions towards Prudence.

"I know it well. He has been here already," she told him. "Such a pity about her mama. He told me the whole story, how he happened to be there and got Knighton to help them. Shocking the way these inns behave. Is Mrs. Mallow recovering?"

"Yes, she will be all right. What did Seville say?"

"I must have mistaken him previously. He was quite cut up that Miss Mallow rejected him. He had meant to reform, one supposes. He found her innocence refreshing, he says, which would account for his treating her with respect, as you say he did. I still find it difficult to see how Phrynes . . . but never mind. He was quite sincere, and asked me to let him know if I hear anything, so what have you to tell me?"

"They were to go on to Bath in a few days."

"And?"

"And I have been turned off."

"The fool! She turned *you* down, too? What ails the girl?"

"I never had a chance to offer. Such a trimming as she gave me, Hettie, and well deserved, too, every word of it. My moral laxity, my lightskirts, my drinking . . ."

"Why, you don't drink more than your bottle a day, and as to the other . . ."

"I got her started by lacing into her because Seville happened to be there when I arrived."

"What time did you arrive?"

196

"Midnight."

"She was with Seville at midnight?"

"I thought he told you all that?"

"He didn't tell me it was midnight!"

"Don't start working me up about Seville again. I still have a strong urge to kill him. Nothing would put me more in her black books than that. She has a high opinion of him. A perfectly honourable and worthy gentleman."

"Perfect poppycock."

"We judge him by our own standards."

"I judge him by the new piece of fluff he had picked up on the eve of his nuptials to the Baroness."

Dammler shrugged. "I am determined to say nothing against him."

"And finding it grim going, if I am to judge by the clenching of your jaws."

He smiled ruefully at this, then fell into a brown study, looking at the floor.

"What you need is a new love o' life to cheer you," Hettie said gaily.

"Hettie, damn your eyes, can't you see I'm in love?"

"There is nothing like a new love to shake off the shadow of the old."

"Leave me with at least the shadow."

"Lud, Dammler, what a dead bore you are turned into. What do you mean to do? Wallow in self-pity and remorse? Turn Methodist and give up wine, women and song?"

"You don't have to be a rakehell to have fun. I had more enjoyment sitting with Prudence Mallow talking about books and other things than I have had anywhere else. I mean to reform."

"I wash my hands of you, absolutely."

"And I'll reform you, too, old cat," he said, standing up with a smile. "Though if you go on wearing those damned turbans I shan't have to worry about the men pestering you. You look dreadful."

"I see you don't plan to reform your manners. There might be hope for you yet."

He came to rigid attention, but with a glint of amusement lurking in his eyes. "Your most obedient servant, Lady Melvine," he bowed formally. "May I have your kind permission to call tomorrow?"

"Devil, you couldn't reform if your life depended on it."

"It does, and I can." With a careless wave he was gone.

He proceeded to make good his promise of reforming. He dropped his flightier friends, worked during half the day, dined with dowagers and their dull friends, and was perfectly miserable. He had no illusion it was the loss of his drinking companions and women that had him in the hips. It was the absence of a quiet little lady with eyes of a penetrating blue, that widened when she was shocked or amused, and turned this damned grey world bright again.

For a week he was a model of propriety, but the futility of it was soon borne in on him. Prue was in Bath. She wouldn't know he had changed. It was not reported that Lord Dammler sat at his desk six hours a day trying to work, or dined with his publisher. No, he would have to risk going to Bath and incurring her displeasure to demonstrate how saintly he had become. Not dally and badger her, or bring any of his infamous friends along. Attach himself to some perfectly respectable people and proceed with caution. She might hate him, but he felt sure she loved him, too. She wouldn't have ripped up so about his Phyrnes if she'd been indifferent. She didn't fly into the boughs to hear any other gentleman of her acquaintance had a mistress. Hadn't used to bother her that *he* had either, but it bothered her now. That was a hopeful sign.

He settled on the Dowager Countess of Cleff as the likeliest person to lend him respectability in Bath. A cousin of his late mama, a prude and a crashing bore, but with no shred of disrepute. Harbouring himself would be the closest she had ever come to sin, and she would do it only if she were assured she was saving him from the brink of brimstone. Prue had called him 'morally lax' and he recognized it for a euphemism. She was too nice to call him what she thought him—a rake, a lecher, a libertine. Well, he would change. And in Bath, Prudence regretted she had ever called him anything so strong as 'morally lax.' He was modern, sociable, a little free perhaps, and she was a prude. They each set about changing to be what they were not to please the other, although each was, in fact, very well pleased with the original.

The Dowager took him in, after first subjecting him to an endless lecture on what rumours had reached her ears—and really she seemed to have heard very little. She had a nose like a parrot, the stature of a grenadier, and the voice of a sergeant major. Her sagging cheeks, painted orange, jiggled as she harped on at him. It would be nearly unendurable, he saw, but he would endure it for as long as it took to convince Prudence he was not utterly lost to decency. The evening at the Italian concert was the first entry into the gay whirl of Bath society. It was tolerable because Prue was there to look at, letting on she didn't see him, but turning her head his way every two minutes. That was on Saturday.

The next morning Dammler was rudely surprised to be jostled from a sound sleep by his doughty hostess in person, decked out in the ugliest peignoir he had ever seen—cerise and peacock blue, with black swansdown trim. Now who would have thought the Pillar had such a streak of barbarism buried beneath all those stays? In public she appeared in nothing but black.

"It's ten o'clock, Allan," she said.

"Ten o'clock," he repeated stupidly. "Ten o'clock, eh?" What, he wondered, was the magic significance of the hour.

"Church is at eleven o'clock," she told him.

"Church?!" he asked in alarm.

"Church," she repeated, staring down her parrot nose at him. "I trust you go to church on Sunday."

"Yes. Oh, yes," he told her. Good Lord, what had he gotten into? She'd be enrolling him in Bible classes next.

"I'll send up cocoa and toast. We'll eat an early lunch after."

"Thank you," he said in a small voice, then when she left, put his head beneath the pillow and laughed till his valet came to see if he was ill.

"My best morning coat, Scrimpton. I am going to church."

"Yes, your grace," Scrimpton answered, taking the news like a rock.

At five minutes to eleven, the Marquis of Dammler and the Dowager Countess of Cleff caused a considerable stir when they walked up the aisle of Bath Abbey, not least in the heart of Miss Mallow, who stared after them as though they were a pair of tigers or elephants. Clarence nudged her in the ribs and nodded sagely, as though to say, there he is, chasing after you again. Her mother glanced at her, too, but with an unreadable face that was trying not to smile.

Once again Prudence felt she would be accosted by Dammler after church, but on this occasion he could hardly be accused of dallying. He looked at her several times and smiled the smile that went with his shrug, though in company with the Pillar, one did not shrug. Coming to her was physically impossible for the crowd that hovered around, having heard who was visiting the Countess and wishing to meet him.

"We'll just wait till those few people go along, to say how do you do to Lord Dammler," Clarence suggested. His niece would have none of it. She had him into his carriage and on the way home before anyone got a look at his jacket.

"Well, he knows where you stay. I gave him your address when he called in London. We will be seeing him before the day is out."

When he failed to appear, Clarence decreed that he had been driving all night, and was likely tucked into his bed, not wanting to show Prudence such a harried face. "Those handsome fellows are as vain as ladies about their looks. He will be along tomorrow."

Dammler would have liked to have gone along to the memorized address that same day, but the Pillar had other plans. She had invited the presiding minister at Bath Abbey and a few honoured guests to join her for luncheon, to meet Lord Dammler and set his feet on the path to righteousness. In the afternoon she requested his escort on a drive in the country to commune with nature and a widowed friend seventy years old, and at six o'clock it was back to Bath for a heavy dinner of mutton. The evening saw him taking her to a church discussion group on Dissenters. By eleven o'clock he was more than ready for bed. He felt as if he had swum to America and back.

On Monday a trip to the Pump Room was made by the Countess to set her up for the rigours of the week. It was also necessary for Clarence Elmtree. No one at all had seen them on Sunday, with Prudence hustling them into the carriage and home so fast. He was torn between being there early to make a good long visit, and entering late and causing a fuss. He opted for the former and drank two glasses of the foul sulphur water to keep his chest in shape till he got back to Knighton, who, over the few days, had become established as his physician. His advice was quoted on several complaints to people in Bath. He was just informing a Mrs. Plunkett of the efficacy of a certain paregoric draught when Lady Cleff and Lord Dammler came into the Pump Room.

Scanning the room Dammler's eyes stopped when he saw Clarence's party. He bowed formally and smiled before sitting down with his cousin to partake of the water. Soon some elderly friends of the Countess had joined them and Dammler sat on staidly, conversing with them. Prudence didn't see him smile once the entire time he was there. What a dull time he is having, yet he doesn't bother coming to talk to us, she thought. In half an hour, she convinced her uncle it was time to go and look at her cartoon in the window again. It was necessary for them to pass the Dowager's table to get out, and as they approached, Dammler arose to greet them, bowing to the ladies and shaking Elmtree's hand. He begged the honour of presenting them to his cousin, which honour was granted.

The Dowager raised her lorgnette and examined them one by one, as if they were three indifferent specimens of Lepidoptera pinned on a board, said "Charmed" to Mrs. Mallow and Prudence, and allowed Clarence to shake three fingers briefly. She was in a particularly genial mood that day.

They were just turning to leave—no offer of joining the Pillar's table was extended—when another gentleman seated across the room hastened towards them. He was of Dammler's approximate age and height, but slender and of fair complexion. Lady Cleff's smile broadened as she spotted this addition to the group.

"Ah, Mr. Springer," she said, offering him all four fingers and the thumb. "Dammler, here is someone who knows you, I believe. Just the very friend for you. I think you are dull with no companions but my old crones."

A few stiff and stilted phrases were exchanged between the two old colleagues, giving a foretaste of how agreeable they found each other's company. The Mallows and Mr. Elmtree made their farewells and left.

"I see you are anxious to be off, Mr. Springer," the Dowager said coyly. "We shan't detain you, but you must be sure to call. We will look forward to seeing you at Pulteney Street very soon."

Springer fairly dashed off after the departing company, and Dammler was left with yet another obstacle in his wooing of Miss Mallow. A rival, one who had the advantage of a long acquaintance and an unblemished reputation.

He turned to his cousin. "Springer is Miss Mallow's beau, I take it?"

"Yes, he is often with her. Usually escorts her home from the

Pump Room. Truth to tell, I wish him success with her. She seems a nice enough sort of a girl, now that I have met her. Not forthcoming in the least. I had heard she was just a trifle *fast*—oh, not *loose*. I do not mean to imply she is loose. With a good solid husband like Springer she would be no poor addition to Bath society."

This suggestion of Springer being considered as a husband for Prudence threw Dammler into alarm. "Surely they are not on the point of an engagement. Prudence—Miss Mallow—has not been here above two weeks."

"It is a long-standing attachment. Quite romantic, really. Friends for years in Kent. It often happens that old friends met under different circumstances become *more* than friends. I think she might get him if she plays her cards well."

This idea so appalled Dammler that he abandoned his plans of being circumspect and wearing the costume of a dull, respectable gentleman for a few weeks. He went that very afternoon to Laura Place and asked Prudence to drive out with him. In fact, he arrived just as she was leaving the luncheon table.

Her chagrin was possibly greater than his own. She had already given Springer permission to call that same afternoon. "I am busy this afternoon," she said, in a stricken voice.

"Oh. I see," he answered with sinking heart. "Busy, eh? Well, I had better leave you then."

"Oh, no—that is, I do not go out till four o'clock. It is only a little after two o'clock. We have time for a little visit."

Clarence was smiling and nodding in one corner, and Mrs. Mallow furrowing her brow across the room. There was no private study where they could pretend to be discussing literature, and the situation appeared hopeless.

"Would you like to go for a short drive?" Dammler asked, knowing it sounded absurd, as she had mentioned her outing was to be a drive.

"Yes, that sounds delightful," she answered promptly, and went straight off to get her bonnet.

There was so much to be said between them, yet both were bereft of meaningful words. They mentioned the weather, the sights of Bath, even their respective states of health.

Sensing that his precious bit of time was slipping away, Dammler asked bluntly, "Are you angry with me for coming to Bath?"

"No, why should I be? You are free to roam as you like," was her unencouraging reply. "You have been in London till now, I collect?"

"Yes."

"How is Lady Melvine?"

"Very well. Murray also. I told him I would enquire how your book goes on."

"I have written to Mr. Murray just recently."

"He cannot have had your letter when I saw him last then."

"No."

After a quarter of an hour's uninteresting conversation of this sort, they were on Milsom Street, and Dammler asked her if she would like to get down and walk a little. The outing was going so poorly that he feared he had lost her to Springer, but he didn't want to hear it confirmed, so he did not ask.

As they strolled they passed the circulating library, and Dammler drew up to see her cartoon in the window.

"Your uncle will like this," he said. "You might get that other shelf out of him yet."

"Oh, now, with you borrowing all my books I scarcely have need of the two I have."

"Have I been borrowing your books?" he asked, hoping to get back on the old footing with these joking references to old times.

"Indeed you have, and you with ten thousand of your own. Hog."

A few people were standing beside them looking in the window display, where Miss Mallow's three novels were on view. One lady, her attention caught by the prepossessing appearance of Dammler, noticed that the lady with him was none other than Miss Mallow. She had just bought *The Cat in the Garden* and, with an apology for disturbing them, asked if the author would sign it.

"I read all your books, Miss Mallow. I like them very much."

"Thank you; you are very kind," Prudence said, signing her name.

"I am surprised you come to Bath to work," the woman went on. "You must find it dull after London."

"No, I like it very much."

"I have heard a rumour Lord Dammler is here, too, but I shouldn't think it's true."

"Oh," Prudence turned to Dammler, thinking to present him, but he shook his head discreetly.

"No, there would be nothing here to interest *him*," the lady continued in a disparaging tone. "No harems or Indian princesses." She thanked Miss Mallow and went on her way.

"Lo, how the mighty have fallen," Dammler said sadly.

"It is your not having on your patch that prevented her recognizing you," Prudence consoled him.

"You try to put a good face on it to recover my disgrace, but it is clear you have outpaced me."

"How nonsensical you are."

"She has my number. Harems and Indian princesses. But you see she is wrong. I *am* here in dull old Bath."

"Why *are* you here, if you find it dull?"

"Why do you think?" he asked with a long look that caused Prudence to take a great interest in her cartoon. He said no more, but offered her his arm to continue their walk.

"You are staying with Lady Cleff, aren't you?" Prudence asked.

"Yes, she is a cousin. A very *respectable* cousin."

"She is quite the terror of Bath. You will not care much for her set, I think."

"I like them excessively. I hardly know whether I am more interested with the Right Reverend Thomas Tisdale or the gentleman—the name eludes me but he resembles a sheep—who is doing a study on the Dissenters. I was shocked to see you missed the lecture on Dissenters, Miss Mallow. Very informative. The Scottish Anglicans, you know, are not included in the group, nor are the Recusants. They dissent, but for some reason they are not officially included in the group."

"You are become highly religious."

"Our company is not comprised solely of Divines. We also include a brace of octogenarians interested in finding a cure for gout and a man, or possibly a lady with a moustache, who means to revolutionize the calendar and give us a whole month of summer. The three days in June we presently enjoy do seem insufficient to me after my sojourn in the tropics. I mean to take up membership in the moustache's group."

"You haven't changed a bit," Prudence laughed, shaking her head, and happy to see him behaving more like himself.

"Yes I have. Truly I have, Prudence, but I must just let off a little steam after being under such pressure with my cousin." He sounded so intense that Prudence stared at him.

They resumed their seats in the carriage, and Prudence decided to discuss what must be in both their minds, the evening at Reading. "Did you see anything of Mr. Seville in London?" she asked, to initiate the subject.

"No, but he was to call on Hettie—told her about having offered for you. I did him an injustice," he admitted stiffly.

"But you didn't *tell* him so?"

"I am telling *you* so, that is more to the point. I behaved very badly and have been wanting to apologize."

"Yes, you did behave abominably," she agreed. He said nothing, but firmed his resolve to reform.

Prudence thought he might now give some reason for his atrocious behaviour. Surely the reason had been jealousy, and jealousy just as surely must have been rooted in his love for her, but though she allowed him a full minute to say so, he said nothing.

"Oh, there is Sir Henry Millar," she said, nodding and smiling to a passing acquaintance. "He is down here to rent and furnish a house for his mistress, an actress from Covent Garden. No doubt you know her—she goes by the name Yvonne duPuis, though she is actually from Cornwall. She is not here at the moment."

This coming on top of his own efforts at respectability angered Dammler. "I dislike to hear you speak so openly of these matters, Prudence. They are not things a young lady ought to discuss with a gentleman."

She was first dumbfounded, then scornful. "I have always heard a leopard does not change his spots, Dammler. Tell me now, as a world traveller, is not that true, or are you an exception to the general rule? You were not used to be so nice in your ideas of subjects suitable for discussion with a lady."

"You don't have to remind me of my past. I am trying to change . . ."

"Your *behaviour* or your conversation?"

"Both."

"But we writers, you know, are up to anything, as your old friend 'Silence' Jersey says. Come, you claim to detest hypocrisy. Confess the truth. You are bored to flinders in dull Bath, and languishing to get back to the City an your Phyrne."

"I have got rid of my Phyrne."

"Wilted on you, did she?"

She could see he was reining in his temper and about ready to burst with the effort, but was in no way dismayed. "No, she was flourishing under the protection of a certain baron when I left."

"I should like to know, in case I ever have to write about it, how one goes about getting rid of a Phyrne. Is she given an annuity, or just sold outright to the highest bidder?"

"Prudence!" he said in a warning voice.

"Or was she on straight wages—so much a day, or night."

"You are not likely to require such information for anything you write, unless you have changed your style of writing a good deal."

"Ah well, who knows? Seville only offered marriage, but I may end up with a *carte blanche* in my pocket yet."

"That is *not* amusing, Prudence," he said, a flash of anger leaping in his eyes.

Satisfied at the effect of her goading, she answered quite sweetly, "It was supposed to be."

"Well, it wasn't. Don't talk like that."

"I was under the misapprehension you held a high opinion of the world's oldest profession. Much better than wives who carry on intrigues, you said."

"You are not a wife yet."

"And not likely to be in the near future," she returned airily. She was vastly annoyed that he did not follow up this excellent lead, but he looked quite relieved. He didn't know what degree of intimacy she had achieved with Springer, but apparently marriage was not in her mind.

"My aunt tells me you see a good deal of Ronald Springer," he said, making it sound careless.

Piqued at his lack of saying anything more to the point than this, she answered, "Yes, we are quite back on the old footing. There is hardly a day I don't see him. In fact, we ought to be getting back. What time is it?"

"About half past chapter ten," he replied, without looking at his watch.

She looked at him with the blankest incomprehension. "What would that be, Greenwich time?" she asked.

"Three thirty. I'll take you home."

He asked if he might bring his aunt to call the next day, and Prudence agreed. When she went into the house, she was displeased with the outing. He had intimated he was here only because of her, but made no move towards an offer. What was he up to? And there was a new stiffness, almost amounting to priggishness, in his manner, that irked her excessively. But she would take care of that!

Chapter Nineteen

The next day Dammler brought his cousin to visit, and after reminding them of each others' names, he took a seat beside the Pillar. The Pillar then began her catechism, to see whether or not she had erred in coming to visit persons in rented lodgings.

"Dammler tells me you *write*," she said to Prudence in an accusing tone, lifting the lorgnette.

"Yes ma'am, I write a little—novels."

"I suppose they are *Gothic* novels."

"No, they are realistic modern novels."

"I do not read novels," she said, and turned to Mrs. Mallow. "You have been ill, I hear."

Illness proved more acceptable than writing novels. The nature of the malady was explained, and the Countess shook her head sadly. "It is an error to eat at inns. One should not eat when travelling."

"Lord Dammler would have found that inconvenient on his tour around the world," Prudence remarked, becoming annoyed at this haughty tone.

"He should not have gone travelling," she was told, as

though such a corollary should have been self-evident.

"Knighton took good care of my sister," Clarence mentioned, always wanting to be mentioning a famous name. "He is very good about making a call."

"You had Knighton," the Countess said, nodding her head in approval. About one tenth of her chill dissipated, though nothing approaching a smile appeared on her orange cheeks.

"I always have Knighton when I am out of sorts," Clarence told her.

"I will give you my doctor's address, here in Bath," she offered. "Remind me, Dammler. You are fond of art, I believe, Mr. Elmtree," she said next, having apparently had a résumé of each before coming.

"Yes, I am always painting. I did the whole Chiltern family just before coming. Seven of them. I hope to get a little time in on some landscapes while I am here."

"You will want to paint Beecher Hill," she said. "There are some nice scenes there."

Clarence stored up the name, to write in his first note to Sir Alfred that the Countess of Cleff had recommended it. "I usually do portraits, but each spring I find myself drawn outdoors to try my hand at Nature."

Lady Cleff approved of Nature. "That is wise," she allowed. "What sort of portraits do you do?"

"Oh pretty good ones, I think, if I don't flatter myself too much. I think Dammler will tell you I paint a pretty good picture."

"Very good," Dammler confirmed readily. "In the style of *Mona Lisa*, Cousin."

"I like that," she declared. "There is too much of dressing people in outlandish outfits like Grecians or nymphs and sitting them in strange poses. Phillips and Romney, for instance—always rigging their people out in ridiculous costumes."

"Ho, Romney, he knew nothing of painting," Clarence said

with enthusiasm. "He is dead, you know. One ought not to speak ill of the dead, but he knew nothing of painting."

"Romney painted *me*," the Countess informed him, her parrot's nose achieving a sharp point in disapproval.

"You shouldn't have let him near you. I daresay he gave you a sharp nose and too wide a form."

Prudence drew in a sharp breath at this telling description of their caller, and looked at the Countess in fear. She found a smile of gratification on that white and orange face. Glancing at Dammler, she thought he was unmoved, till she noticed the laughter lurking in his eyes.

"You should have Mr. Elmtree do a proper likeness of you, Cousin," he suggested to the Dowager.

"I am past all that," she demurred, but in no very conclusive manner.

"Nonsense," Clarence stated firmly. "I could make you look very nice. I know just how to get that bright orange for the cheeks, and the nose would be no problem. I am quite good at a nose."

These blatant insults were accepted with a smirk, and a preening hand went to the turban on the Countess' head. "Well, I may have another portrait done. I never thought Romney did me justice."

"Mr. Elmtree is the very one to do you justice," Dammler said, flickering a look at Prudence, who shook her head ever so slightly in disapproval.

"I have my paints with me," Clarence urged on the scheme. "I should be very happy to try my hand at such a challenging model."

The Countess read even this slur into a compliment, not knowing the challenge lay in her ugliness. "I shall consider it," she decreed.

She accepted a cup of tea, and when she arose to take her leave she said, "You will call and take Miss Mallow out for a ride one day, Dammler." She had found the persons satisfactory.

No one present, even including Clarence, saw fit to tell her he had already done so. "She will be happy to go," was his only comment. "She works too hard." Prudence had hardly set pen to paper since coming to Bath, and never when he was present to see it.

Dammler made no protest whatsoever, and the Countess said when leaving, "It is settled then," very well pleased with this highhanded manner of arranging young peoples' lives.

As the two drove home, the Countess said to Dammler, "I am happy to see you have some worthwhile friends in London. Mrs. Mallow has nothing to say, but Mr. Elmtree is quite unexceptionable, and the girl is well enough. She does just as she is bid by her uncle, and it is reassuring to see *that* in a young lady nowadays. No doubt she will settle down now that her uncle is here. She was racketing about not chaperoned as she should be, but that will come to an end."

"Yes, she has a great respect for her uncle," the deceitful creature corroborated, without a blush.

The Countess had bid him drive out with Miss Mallow, and he intended doing so the next day, but alas his cousin had other plans for him. She was ordering new draperies for her Purple Saloon, and required his escort to the drapery shop. There was only one bolt of purple in the shop, but this by no means meant she only looked at it. She also had to consider red and blue and a dozen patterned ells before agreeing to the purple, while Dammler walked back and forth, drawing out his watch and calculating how quickly he could get her home if they left immediately. He knew he had missed his chance when they had been there an hour and a quarter. It was graphically illustrated when they at last went out into the street in time to see Prudence atop Ronald Springer's curricle. She waved to them in a friendly manner.

"Ah, it is Springer, with that Mallow girl," the Countess said. "Perhaps you shouldn't take her out after all. Springer might take it amiss."

This was the very phrase to ensure that Dammler would be at her door early the next morning and so he was, only to hear that she had gone off for the day to see Blaize Castle with Springer and a group of young people.

Help came from an unexpected quarter. To pay homage to her caller, and to show off her new purple drapes, the Countess would throw a party. Dammler was permitted to ask a few people under seventy, and he was not tardy in sending a note to the Mallows and Clarence. Unfortunately, the Dowager had the inspiration of including Springer, as well, but it could not be helped. The party was scheduled for three days hence, and the only sight Dammler had of Miss Mallow in the interim was to bow to her twice across the Pump Room in the mornings; the rest of the time he was kept busy.

The party, which the Dowager called a drum, was a major event in her life, and much discussed. "It is what the rackety crew nowadays call a rout," she explained to Dammler. "Cards and conversation for the civilized members of the party, with a small parlour given over to dancing for the savages. I shall hire a fiddle."

"And perhaps someone to play the pianoforte," he suggested.

"No, no, Allan. It will be only a few country dances. A fiddle is what Papa always had."

"Yes, but nowadays, Cousin . . ."

"Fiddle!" she said with a hard stare, and a fiddle it was.

The refreshments were to be equally antiquated and austere. Orgeat, lemonade and punch were to be the beverages. Not a mention of champagne, and the food was to be a frugal luncheon with no lobster or oysters or even roasted fowl. Dammler began to perceive the drum was an appalling idea, but the invitations were out and accepted before the full

214

meagerness of the evening's entertainment dawned on him. Decorations consisted of one palm tree rented from the floral shop, and an extra brace of candles lit in the main saloon, to show off the purple drapes.

The austerity of the whole was made more ludicrous by the degree of formality to be observed. Formal dress was called for, and she spoke of "a reception line," to consist of the pair of them, to greet the guests as they arrived, thence to be handed over to the butler for announcing. She kept notes to help the *Bath Journal* write it up for the social column, and sent her distracted cousin on a dozen useless errands to arrange various details of the "orgy." The only consolation Dammler could see in the scheme was that Prudence would see him in a new light—respectable, above reproach. She would see there was a serious, worthwhile side to his nature.

The great evening of the drum finally arrived. Lady Cleff decked herself out in a severe black gown, enlivened with a gray fall of Mechlin lace and a cameo for the night's frolic. Dammler took up his post beside her in the doorway of the main saloon, wearing satin breeches, a black coat, and his most dazed expression. The majority of the guests, relicts like the Dowager herself, saw nothing absurd in the proceedings, but both Springer and later Miss Mallow were stunned. Prudence gazed in wonder to see Dammler playing his part in this charade, standing at attention with his aged relative, shaking hands with doddering old crones. She remembered him smiling and debonair at the opera, at Hettie's ball, and at a hundred other gay places which existed for her only in imagination from his having mentioned them. She could hardly credit he was the same person. Formal wear being called for, she had worn a new gown of pale lilac, cut low in front, with lilacs at the bodice. Lady Cleff glared at her shoulders and lifted her lorgnette to Dammler as though to say, "What have we here?"

Prudence observed, and she too looked at Dammler with a question in her eyes. The first opportunity she had after the reception line broke up she said to him, "You should have warned me it was to be a mourning party and I would have worn black like everyone else. I feel a very peacock among the crows."

"My cousin is old-fashioned, but even *she*, I am sure, does not expect a young lady to wear black to a drum."

"Except perhaps to a "hum drum," she replied, looking about the room, where everyone sat in silence. No one had yet gone to dance or play cards.

"You look lovely, Prudence," he said, taking in every detail of her toilette.

"Oh thank you. My shoulders are much admired here in Bath, but I *do* wish I had brought a shawl, preferably black."

Dammler felt a pulse of anger at this remark. "Who in Bath particularly admires them?"

"The gentlemen," she answered pertly. "I can't recall that I ever received a compliment on my shoulders from a lady."

"I suppose ladies who wear immodest gowns lay themselves open to that sort of impertinence," he said angrily.

She was too shocked to answer. Her gown she knew was beautiful and not immodest—certainly not to a person accustomed to London styles, as Dammler was. "You are hard to please, milord," she said when she had her speech back. "You have upbraided me before for wearing grandmother's gowns, but I hadn't thought you would object to this."

"I object to gentlemen making impertinent speeches to you, and I object to your inviting them."

"I cannot think I invited this particular impertinence," she said, and turned angrily away.

Luck was not with Dammler that evening. The first person to come up to Prudence was Springer, and the first words to leave his mouth were, "How stunning you look this evening, Miss Mallow. What a marvelous gown."

Dammler did not hear the rest of the speech, but he heard that, and he knew that Prudence knew it, too, which irked him.

216

He hurried after them, and by a dexterous bit of maneuvering toward two chairs, he got Prudence to himself. "I'm sorry about that," he said, quite humbly. "My nerves are a bit on edge."

"It's no wonder, if this is the way you've been spending your time." She looked around the room at this spectacle that was called a party and suddenly laughed at the incongruity of Dammler's being here. "Are we permitted to speak aloud, or should I be whispering?" she asked.

"You may speak, but don't laugh—just smile."

"A pity Uncle hadn't brought his paints. It looks as if he would have a roomful of models, not moving a muscle the whole night long."

"It may not be a gay party, but you must own it is eminently respectable," he pointed out.

"Must the two be mutually exclusive?"

"At one of my cousin's drums, I'm afraid so. Shall we dance?"

"By all means, if it gives us an excuse to leave this wake. But we daren't go *alone*. How do we get permission, and five or six chaperones?"

"I'll speak to Lady Cleff."

The Countess duly announced dancing for the youngsters, and Prudence went with Dammler to the tiniest dancing parlour she had ever been in. The marquis took her arm, with a jealous glance at Springer, who followed close behind them.

"If there are to be more than six couples in here, we will enjoy an indecent degree of intimacy," Prudence said.

"Certainly *I* plan to enjoy it," Dammler answered, before he set a guard on his tongue.

"Oh, ho, your celibacy is getting to you. You will be in pinching the dowagers before the night is over, and breaking your thumbs on their stays."

This talk bordered on the edge of what Dammler had decided to avoid. He knew his own propensity to talk too freely and feared from the permissible levity he would sink into indecency. "I don't think so, Miss Mallow," he said rather stiffly. "We are to lead off."

Little conversation was possible during the country dance, and at its end they changed partners. Mr. Springer was waiting for Prudence. She fared better than Dammler, who was obliged to partner a Miss Milligan who taught at a local lady's seminary. She regaled him with an often-repeated tale of woe regarding a vicious girl who had spread lies that she was beat at school. They then changed partners again, and at the end of three dances the fiddler required a rest, and a glass of beverage that looked depressingly like pure lemonade.

Dammler found his way across the room to Prudence's side. "Enjoying yourself?" he asked.

"About as much as you were with Miss Milligan. I gathered from your consoling expression she was telling you 'the lie'."

"An unfortunate incident," he allowed, still on his best behaviour. Prudence had hoped for a little frivolity from him to dilute the tedium of the evening, and raked her mind for something to get him started.

"This is quite a change from your regular evenings out in London," she essayed.

It was not a successful gambit, being the very topic he wished to avoid. "A less mixed company," he admitted cautiously.

"I should say so. What possessed you to go along with this? You are like a fish out of water."

"I hope I know how to behave in any company."

"I hope so, too, but I doubt your staying power. You must confess a rolling drunkard or a nice vulgar Cit would liven us up no end."

"I don't know why you think I *dislike* being in respectable company."

"Oh, Dammler, what *are* you up to?" she asked in honest bewilderment. "Next you will be saying you never had such a fine time."

"I can honestly say there is nowhere I would rather be," he told her with a glowing eye that somewhat mitigated his strange behaviour earlier. From his look there seemed little doubt why he enjoyed the party.

"And nothing you would rather be drinking than a glass of orgeat, I suppose?" she parried, accepting a fluted glass of the almond-flavoured drink. Springer and Miss Milligan joined them, and ruined the promising chat.

"Delicious punch," Miss Milligan complimented the host. "I do believe your aunt has put a drop of wine in it."

"Possibly a drop," Dammler agreed.

"Delicious. How lovely to be out in such charming company. Very lively we are become in Bath these days. I really should not stay late. I must be in the class room tomorrow at eight-thirty as usual. No rest for the wicked. But I shall leave early."

"Do you have a drive home, ma'am?" Springer asked, thinking to make an early exit himself from the dull drum.

"Lady Cleff sent her carriage for me, and it will take me home. So very kind of her."

"I will be happy to take you, and I must leave early myself," Springer continued.

After more talk, the fiddler scraped his bow and the dancing resumed. No party ever extended beyond midnight at Lady Cleff's home. When Miss Milligan spoke of leaving early, she meant eleven o'clock, but as the sparse food was served at that hour, she stayed to partake of it, and got her wrap at eleven-thirty.

"May I give you a lift home, Miss Mallow?" Springer asked.

"Miss Mallow will be returning with her mother," Dammler told him.

"Thank you, Ronald. I shall wait for Mama," Prudence added in a kinder tone.

He was charged to deliver two other ladies home, and the party was in a fair way to breaking up.

"Your friend has some peculiar notions—offering to take you

home," Dammler said aside to Prudence.

"You would have done the same—about two hours earlier—had your situations been reversed," she replied. "And I should have gone with you, too."

Her last phrase pleased him, and he thawed sufficiently to say, "It was bad, wasn't it?"

"No, Dammler. It was *horrid*. And horrid of me to say so, too, but then I hope I don't have to keep up a good face to *you*."

"At least I was in your company for one evening. That made it worthwhile to *me*."

Yes, pretty fine speeches, Prudence thought. "But what is to prevent you from being in my company as much as you wish? And so well chaperoned, too, that I could not pester you with my unsuitable conversation, or lure you with my immodest gown. Next time don't feel you require your cousin plus a bishop and two judges. Lady Cleff will always be sufficient to keep me in line."

He longed to answer her in kind, or better to sweep her into his arms and kiss that saucy smile. When had Prudence become such an accomplished flirt? "My cousin may be enough to hold you in check; I require the full weight of clergy and the law."

"You have set yourself a new standard, I gather?"

"Yes."

"And are quite determined to stick to it?"

"I am."

"*Tant pis*," she said with a toss of her head, and turned to join Clarence and her mother.

Provoking girl, he thought, watching her go. No, provocative girl. She is doing it on purpose to bait me, but she won't succeed.

Across the room, Prudence was similarly occupied in considering Dammler's behaviour. He had become as stiff and proper as a martinet. The old lightness and fun had gone from him, and she couldn't understand it. In off-guard moments, she noticed his eyes looking at her longingly, so why was he being distant? If he had come to offer for her, why didn't he do it?

While the youngsters and savages had been dancing, Elmtree and the Countess had made great advances in their friendship. They were two chunks cut from the same bolt, and hadn't a flaw to find in each other. Elmtree had received gracious permission to paint her, and the very next morning was agreed upon as the first of the three sittings. Prudence felt a great fear she would be called upon to chaperone them, and to make it more inconvenient, the picture was to be painted here, at the Countess' home.

"I will want a corner of the room in the background," she was saying. "The Purple Saloon, I think, with Papa's picture in the background."

"We can do better than that for a symbol," Clarence informed her. "Some heraldic emblem or crest. We won't want any room in the background. Your colouring calls for a solid curtain of blue, to bring out your bright cheeks, with the family crest for a symbol."

The Countess considered this, and found it not wanting in taste. It was agreed, but when Clarence mentioned that he would go to Beecher Hill one day and paint some Nature, the Countess was visited by inspiration. "Gainsborough," she said.

"Eh?"

"You will paint me surrounded by Nature, as Gainsborough painted my mother."

"A green curtain would do as well as a blue, with the orange cheeks," Clarence said. Certainly trees, grass and shrubs would merge into a curtain of undifferentiated green in his rendition. It was settled that the green curtain of Beecher Hill would provide the backdrop for tomorrow's painting session.

"You will come with me, Dammler," she decreed.

"Why do we not all go and make a picnic of it?" he

suggested, to secure Prudence's company.

Mrs. Mallow hastily excused herself, but Prudence agreed to go, and the next morning under a lead grey sky they went to Beecher Hill to paint sunny Nature.

Chapter Twenty

The Countess proved an admirable model. She asked what Clarence was doing with every moment of the brush, and was appreciative of ochre shadows and the impossibility of foreshortening. Her hands seemed to fall naturally into the correct pose without a word being said. The two went on so merrily that Dammler ventured to mention that he and Miss Mallow might go for a stroll till it was time to eat.

"Yes, run along," the Countess said. "You disturb Mr. Elmtree with your fidgetting and prattle. An artist needs peace and quiet to work."

"How very well they rub along," Dammler said as they began to walk away. "My cousin spoke last night of going up to London next Season. I think Elmtree has been getting to her."

"Hussy. I should stay behind to protect my uncle. I was never before allowed to abandon him to such peril as a titled widow. But she may find herself at point nonplus. *He* speaks of buying up a little cottage in Bath."

"Do you suppose we've unwittingly brought about a match?"

"Let us wait and see if the magnum opus pleases. She may not like having a button nose and a sylph-like figure."

"She can console herself with the family crest."

"I don't know that it will be a consolation. Uncle has never painted a lion rampant before. He will likely turn it into a pussy cat, and don't think for a moment he will disfigure the unicorn by including the horn. That will be removed entirely." She strayed behind a bunch of thorn bushes as she talked, and her companion pointed out that it might be better if they stayed in sight of their relations.

"Why?" she asked.

"My cousin is a Trojan for propriety," he said, but his only reason for mentioning it was to let her see his own new awareness of decorum.

It seemed so foolish to Prudence, after the degree of latitude pertaining to their former intercourse, that she laughed outright. "I believe the Divines have got to you, Dammler. I fully expect to see you standing up to take the reading at the Abbey next Sunday." She scampered out of the protection of her uncle, and Dammler followed at no dragging pace, but intent on being punctilious to every minutia of respect.

"You will be a sad disappointment to your friends if you carry on so in London," Prudence warned him with a teasing smile. She did not like this new Dammler nearly so well as the old, and was determined to change him back.

"I mean to discontinue association with such friends as would be disappointed," he answered carefully.

"Do you indeed? So I am to be cut, am I?"

He stopped walking and turned to face her. "I am *trying* to be a perfectly honourable and respectable gentleman, Prudence, and you are not of much help."

She pouted. "You did not treat me so formally before. Why must you change?"

"To please you. Why do you think I languish in that barracks of a place my cousin has, with no agreeable company, going to lectures and discussions on the Reformed calendar, but to please you?"

"Please *me*? I wouldn't do such things myself. Why should I expect it of you?"

"*I* have a past to expiate."

"You will have a worse future to expiate as well if you carry on in this way much longer. I see you chafing at the bit to laugh and joke and so on."

"Especially so on." The temptation was too much for him. He grabbed her, first by the hands, but soon had both arms around her in a strong grip and was trying to kiss her.

At twenty-four years of age, Prudence had never been in a man's arms before. Never had been kissed. She had wanted to turn Dammler back to his old funning self; she had never expected this violent result, and pushed him off in surprise.

"That was not called for," she said, gasping for breath.

"Don't tease me if you don't want me to reciprocate. I'm too new at respectability to withstand this repeated temptation. You're flaunting yourself at me, Prudence. With those low-cut gowns and fast talk. If you really want me to be worthy, don't do it."

"I am not flaunting myself," she replied in indignation.

"You've been egging me on to misbehave since the moment I came here. I came determined to be good, respectable, to please you. I would not have borne what I have these past two weeks but for you, and you repay me by trying at every chance to make me break my resolve, so you can throw in my face what a rake I am."

"I did not."

"You did, my girl, and you wouldn't be so angry if it weren't true."

"How was *I* to know why you were acting so unlike yourself? You never said a word to me."

"And you, who know me better than I know myself, couldn't imagine why? Why did you think I went flying off to Reading to make an ass of myself in front of you and Seville, green with jealousy, if not because I loved you."

She opened her mouth to answer, closed it again, and finally said, "Well, why didn't you stay then?"

"You made it perfectly clear you had no use for me. I asked you if I could come on with you to Bath, but you didn't want any *disreputable* companions accompanying you, so I tried to change myself, to become whatever it is you think you want. Well I'm finished with it. I'm not a saint, and I can't become one with you cutting me at every effort I make. You didn't like my old self, and you don't seem to like the new one any better. You delight in torturing me. If you've turned into a flirt, be one full-time. I like it very well, but don't slip back into being an outraged spinster the minute I respond."

"I am not a flirt!"

"You're giving a fair imitation of one. There is a name for girls who lead men on, only to swat them down at the last minute. I shan't sully your virginal ears with it, but you'll hear it from someone soon enough if you go on in this way."

"Why stick at telling me then, since I am so clearly lost to all sense of propriety?"

"You'd like to have something else to beat me over the head with, but I'm on to you now, Miss Mallow. You knew all along what I was. I may have been a damned fool, but I was never a hypocrite."

"No, not before you came here with a poker up your spine and this pompous air of self-righteousness. You—*you* of all people, to be reading *me* a lecture in morals!"

"The tables are turned, are they not?"

"I never lectured you, much as you deserved it."

"Indeed you did not! You enjoyed leading me on to reveal every last shred of my shame, while you sat with your mouth pursed and to ask me another leading question. But you've led me on for the last time. This is the end of it."

A clap of thunder pealed, and a flash of lightning rent the sky. These ominous signs were followed by a sprinkling of rain, and the argument had to be discontinued while they ran back to the carriage. No further squabbling was possible with the Dowager and Clarence present. They elected to continue the painting session at the Countess' home, and Prudence in a tight voice said that she would like to be left at Laura Place.

She was sure she had lost Dammler. She considered his lecture, and while it angered her, she had to admit there was some justice in it. He had been behaving very properly since coming to Bath, and she had been chaffing him. In fact, the more proper he had become, the harder she had tried to make him stop. And he loved her, he had even said that, and she hadn't known how to turn it to her advantage. She may have been trying to flirt, but she realized she had a long way to go. How could she have stood there and heard him tell her he loved her and managed to send him away angry? "This is the end of it."

Dammler went home to Pulteney Street even more perturbed. As usual, he had said too much, too violently, been too quick—made a fool of himself. There was perhaps some justification in what he had said, but it was no way to go about conciliating an angry lady. He hadn't the patience to hang on in this shilly-shallying manner. Wise Prudence had seen through him, knew he was no stodgy worthy, and didn't care for his pretense. She had liked him best as himself, so he would be himself. He couldn't go on pretending to be what he was not for the rest of his life.

Dammler went into town, ordered six dozen red roses to be delivered to her that day, and a dozen dozen the next, and sent off to the Abbey for the family engagement ring. He then went to his cousin's home and sat in the Purple Saloon, watching the rain glide down the windows.

The first six dozen red roses were delivered to Laura Place, where they caused a pleasant stir.

"He means to do it up proper this time," Clarence said. "He will be here today if he has to drive all night."

"He is only staying at Pulteney Street," Prudence reminded him.

"Aye, so he is. He should be here any minute."

Looking out at the sodden earth, Prudence didn't expect he would come that day, nor did he. This is a little reminder to me, she smiled to herself. When a gentleman takes to sending an excess of flowers and diamonds, he means no good. She looked carefully among the flowers for a diamond, but there was none. He is telling me that what I *deserve* after my flirtation is a *carte blanche,* but still it was not what she expected. She had no dread on that score. The only question in her mind was when he would arrive in person. When the dozen dozen roses arrived the next morning, Mrs. Mallow was thrown into quite a tizzy.

"What can he mean by this?" she asked her daughter. "It seems so very odd, but no doubt it is some sort of a joke."

"Yes, it is a joke, Mama," Prudence told her.

Mrs. Mallow looked at her daughter's satisfied smile, and though she did not see the humour of the situation, but only the foolish extravagance of more flowers than they had vases for, she was happy.

At three o'clock Clarence returned from the second sitting, bringing the canvas with him, two-thirds finished. Already a snub-nosed Mona Lisa was taking shape, her orange cheeks standing out against the background of unvariegated green. There was only the family crest to be done, and a few finishing touches. Dammler came along with him.

Prudence, half-hidden behind a tub of roses, asked how the Countess liked her painting.

"She is well pleased with it," Clarence asserted. "I saw that poor shabby thing Romney did. Pitiful. Made her look like a parrot. Well, well, I see we are bathed in roses. Madrid in town?"

"Seville do you mean?" Mrs. Mallow asked.

"The Spanish fellow who is always dashing after Prudence."

"No, Dammler sent these flowers, Uncle," Prudence told

him. "Such an abundance—almost an *excess*," she peered at the Marquis as she said this. He was trying to look nonchalant, but there was a question in his eyes, and an unsteadiness about the lips.

"I guess we know by now what *this* means, eh?" Clarence announced with a smile of approval.

From Prudence's blushes and Dammler's self-conscious expression, Mrs. Mallow assumed her brother was right for once, and thought of a way to allow them privacy in these tight quarters. "Oh, Clarence, you'll never guess who is here," she lied brightly. "Mrs. Hering."

"Eh? No such a thing. I had a note from her only this morning and she is in bed with flu, poor soul. I shall tell her to have Knighton drop round to see her. He is always happy to make a call. He will go anywhere."

"Not *that* Mrs. Hering. Her sister-in-law—the elder Mrs. Hering. She has taken the rooms right below us. We must go to see her."

"Yes, we'll drop down this evening and make them welcome."

"Let us go *now*, Clarence," Wilma persisted with a rueful glance at Prudence, who bit her lip and nodded her head vigorously. "There is no study here for Prudence and Lord Dammler to chat about books in private. Writers want a little privacy. We'll run along to see Mrs. Hering now, shall we?"

"I am always happy to listen to talk of books. They need not avoid the subject on *my* account."

"Yes, but she is waiting for us *now*, Clarence," she persisted, then took him by the arm and suggested he bring Lady Cleff's portrait for Mrs. Hering to admire.

Clarence, Wilma and Lady Cleff's picture hastened into the corridor, and Wilma carefully closed the door behind them.

"An unlooked-for piece of tact on your mama's part," Dammler said with a tentative smile.

"What delayed my uncle's catching the hint even longer than usual might be that the elder Mr. Hering is a bachelor, you see."

"In that case, they won't be long talking to Mrs. Hering."

"No." Prudence glanced to the door nervously, afraid her mother might not manage to keep Clarence out of the way. He would want to be in on the proposal, though he wasn't properly dressed for it. Her impatience transmitted itself to Dammler. He arose and crossed the small room to where Prudence sat.

"Thank you for the rose garden, Dammler. I have been ferreting in all the boxes this past hour looking for a stray diamond. Did you forget?"

"The diamond, I trust, is by now on its way to you from Longbourne."

"Just *one?*" she asked with a pout.

"Just one. I don't mean to spoil you. If you prove satisfactory, I may give you another on our fiftieth anniversary."

"Hmm. It seems to me a certain platinum-haired woman was wearing a great deal more than *one* at the opera . . ."

"She wasn't wearing one on her finger."

"To be sure, I didn't notice her finger. With so many other interesting parts of her anatomy on view I overlooked that."

"Darling, I've missed you terribly," Dammler said, drawing Prudence to her feet.

In joyful confusion, she peeped at him a brief moment, then stared out the window. "It looks like rain again," she said.

"Yes. Darling, my time at Finefields was utterly wasted. London was a desert without you. As to Bath, it has been the worst of the lot, with my trying to reform."

"I daresay it *will* rain before evening," she answered, examining the sky with a keen interest.

"Prudence, why do you keep staring out the window, pretending you don't notice I'm calling you darling. I expect you to tell me how improper it is, that I might reassure you as to my intentions."

Her heart took to capering on her, and the tumult welled up into her face, revealing itself in a mild form in a shy smile. "I noticed," she said.

He placed his hands around her neck; they felt warm and pleasantly stimulating. "Well, Prude, no lecture to read me?" he said in a soft, caressing tone, his eyes glowing.

"Prude! Just bring on your Ottoman and see how wantonly I can disport myself."

"Stop batting your amorous blue eyes at me, Prudence, or I'll kiss you to death."

"What a novel way to die," she answered, batting her eyelashes in a blatant bid for murder.

His head made a lunge towards her, but she pulled back.

"I am a trifle worried by all these flowers. And I haven't heard the magic formula either. 'Miss Mallow, will you do me the honour,' it begins," she reminded him.

"Prudent to the last gasp. I don't mean to give you and Shilla any leeway in future. It's back to the harem for her, and Longbourne Abbey for you."

"I expect an abbey has been the scene of a love nest before. Especially Longbourne Abbey."

"Shrew."

"If there is a single mention of matched bays and a fancy set-up for the park, I shall certainly decline."

"You shall marry me, Prudence Mallow, with or without the fancy set-up." He pulled her into his arms without further bantering, and kissed her with the experience of a man versed in six tongues, plus a smattering of Hindustani and Chinese, and the passion of a poet in love for the first time. She responded as best she could in English, and a few phrases of French, with which language Dammler seemed well pleased. He did not despair of making her fluent. The first lesson went remarkably well and he was an enthusiastic instructor.

Some moments later they sat together on the sofa, with

Dammler's arm around her shoulder and Mrs. Hering and the relatives totally forgotten. "When did you fall in love with me?" he asked.

"When I read your *Cantos from Abroad*. Why should I be different from all the other ladies?"

"Before you met me? Then it wasn't the fine teeth and the tumbling lock that did it? I was certain I was Hero Number One, who palled around chapter ten."

"What conceit! As though I would put you into a book. And when did you discover I was neither a man nor your sister, and that your life was barren without my shrewish presence?"

"Not till I left you. I thought of you constantly in London, and was never happy but when I was with you, but I didn't know it was love. I was quite happy with Shilla at Finefields. She was very good at first. Turned her damned hypocrite holy man out, just as I told her to, as soon as he asked her to copy out his sermon."

"A bit of an Ashington, was he?"

"Of course he was. I loathed him. That should have tipped me the clue that you were Shilla, but till I got looking about to find an acceptable lover for her, it didn't dawn on me. I realized it was no other than myself meant to have her, say what she would. It was during a heart-to-heart talk in which I was telling her that an English lord—Lord Marvelman, in fact—would dash to her rescue that her eyes widened, turned blue, and I knew. What a damned fool I've been all these months, Prue. Why didn't you tell me I loved you? I wager you knew."

"No, no, when you urged Seville on me I had no notion you were interested in a *ménage à trois*."

"Oh, Seville—I knew you didn't love him. He would not have had anything but your body."

"You have no objection to that?" she asked in a voice containing incipient pique.

"I have *now*! And who was the fellow who was admiring your

shoulders? If it was that snake of a Springer . . ."

"Do you have your duelling pistols with you?"

"No, I'll pull him apart with my bare hands and anyone else who looks at you too closely."

"Oh, but most of my Bath beaux have to look closely—becoming short-sighted in their dotage, you know."

"Don't try to wiggle your way out of it; you've been flaunting yourself, Prudence. Those old dotards are the worst ones. I didn't even notice at first that you were beautiful. It was such an unusual experience for me to fall in love with a lady from the *inside* out that I didn't recognize it for love. Well you know my former views on that. I was always susceptible to ripe, luscious . . ."

"Yes, I don't think it will be necessary for you to remind me again, Dammler. Ever. I suppose you are still susceptible to them."

"No, only you. I've sown enough wild oats for ten men, from one end of the world to the other, and regret each, but at least they are all sown. How should I have time to think of such things, when every man you meet falls in love with you. I won't have time for any passion but jealousy. Well, maybe a *few* minutes a day to love you."

There was a warning rattle at the door, and Clarence and Mrs. Mallow entered. "It was all a hum," Clarence said angrily. "Mrs. Hering is not here at all. Wilma has been taking me upstairs and down looking for her, and there was never an empty apartment in the building at all." Something in the air told him events had transpired in his absence; perhaps the proximity in which his niece and Dammler sat, or their intertwined hands. "What have we here?" he asked suspiciously.

"Lord Dammler has asked me to marry him, Uncle," Prudence said.

"I told you he only wanted a little encouragement," he advised her, smiling fondly at his niece.

"She never gave me the least encouragement," Dammler accused severely.

"She was always backward. I daresay she might have had a royal . . . well, well. Never mind that. So you are to become Prudence Merriman, eh? The Marchioness of Dammler," he rolled the title on his tongue, savouring its heady flavour. "Aye, and you will still be well-named, too. Doesn't she look merry, Wilma?"

Wilma smiled happily, and embraced first her daughter, then, rather shyly, Dammler. Noticing her reserve, Dammler put both arms around his new mother, and hugged her. "I love you, too," he said.

"He is strangely susceptible to mature women," Prudence warned her mother. "You will want to stay out of his way when I am not about to protect you." Mrs. Mallow laughed self-consciously, still wondering how her little daughter had managed to make herself so free with this lord, of whom she remained in awe.

"Prudence Merriman," Clarence repeated. "Well named on both accounts."

"Another name to live up to," Prudence said with a sigh.

"And a title," her uncle said. "A *real* title, not like Seville's old foreign handle, eh, Nevvie?" he added to Dammler, whose eyes enlarged visibly at this familiarity. "You don't mind my practicing up the term? It will take a little getting used to."

The frequency with which it was soon repeated led the Marquis to believe his new uncle would have less difficulty mastering it than he feared.

"I shall do a wedding portrait of the pair of you," Clarence promised. "I have been wanting to get you on canvas a long while, Nevvie. But I am very busy. We all are. It is a good time for us. Lawrence, I read, is doing the Prince of Wales and his brothers and I have had the whole Chiltern family to do, five girls and two boys, each with a squint to be got rid of; but I

234

have no trouble with that sort of thing. No trouble at all. Lawrence, I daresay, will give the whole Royal Family a broader form than he ought. But I will do you and my niece up nicely. You needn't worry; I will put that quirk in your eyebrow. I will just lower it a fraction of an inch and you will not look deformed at all."

Prudence opened her mouth to protest, but Dammler silenced her with a glance. "Can you do anything at all to make my wife look less hagged, Uncle?" he asked in a playful spirit.

"Ho, you are practicing, too, I see. My wife—very good, Nevvie. And Uncle—you will get on to it in no time. Yes, I will make my niece look as good as new or better. Well, well. I am not much of a one for writing letters, but I think this calls for a note to Mrs. Hering and Sir Alfred. They will want to hear that it is settled." He arose and said to his sister, "Come with me, Wilma. We may leave these two alone a minute. Prudence, you know, always lives up to her name."

They left, and Dammler turned to his bride. "Uncle is an original, isn't he?"

"When we cease to live up to our jolly name, we can always have him to Longbourne Abbey to tease us. He has been good to me, Dammler, I hope you have not taken him in dislike . . ."

"Dislike? I adore him. He is half the reason I am marrying you. Come now, Prue, don't laugh at me. If you were a natural girl at all you would be demanding to know what is the other half."

"I'm afraid you'd tell me."

"I will anyway. I never know when to hold my tongue. I shall need an amanuensis when I do some serious work. In fact, I'll break you in on my play for Drury Lane. No, seriously . . ."

"Now Allan *Merriman*, you too must live up to your name. Don't turn serious on me."

"But I want to tell you the other half a reason. I love you, Prudence."

"If you ever stop, I'll spill ink all over your manuscripts. You see how conniving and managing I mean to be. I'll keep you under cat's paw."

"The very way to deal with me. Prudent. You are well-named."

YOU CAN RENEW
BY PHONE!
623-3300